Blue Of Blood

Wil Ogden

Copyright © 2017,2023 William Ogden

All rights reserved.

ISBN: 9798864869840

ALSO BY WIL OGDEN:

FANTASY GENRE:
Sheillene: Choosing Fate and Other Stories
The Nightstone
Of Maia's Mist

VAMPIRE ADVENTURE/URBAN FANTASY
The Blooddaughter Trilogy
(Available in one combined tome or individual books)
Second Blood
Blood Huntress
Blood Reprisal

Vance Silver, Vampire, Hunter
Nine Princes of Blood
Law of the Blood Queen
Blue of Blood
Blood of the Heartstone
Bound Blood Eternal
Blood of the Elementals
Silver Blood

HISTORICAL VAMPIRE ADVENTURE
True Tales of Elizabeth Bathory, Vampire
Blood Atonement
Blood Armistice

Elena the Hunted

To the Last Drop

URBAN FANTASY
The Fury: Vengeance Book I

PARANORMAL ROMANCE
Evelyn: Love Fiend in Training
Lite Nite Bites
Lite Nite Bites: San Francisco

DEDICATION

Dedicated to good people everywhere.

CONTENTS

DEDICATION iv
CONTENTS vi
ACKNOWLEDGMENTS i
I 3
II 15
III 22
IV 29
V 38
VI 57
VII 61
VIII 63
IX 68
X 74
XI 78
XII 85
XIII 92
XIV 96
XV 102
XVI 108
XVII 113
XVIII 121
XIX 129
XX 131
XXI 141
XXII 148
XXIII 158
XXIV 165
ABOUT THE AUTHOR 167

ACKNOWLEDGMENTS

Eternal thanks to my wife, my proofreader, my fans and everyone else who keeps me writing.

I

"Vance! What the hell?"

When Vance realized the woman's voice he had heard wasn't that of the woman cuddling with him under the sheets, he woke up.

"Lanie?" Vance asked. Dreams he couldn't remember hadn't relinquished their grasp on his mind. He didn't know if he'd spoken her name aloud. He asked again, "Lanie, is that you?"

"Since when do you sleep at Three a.m.?" Lanie asked. "When Dai texted you at Nine, I expected you'd be gone a couple hours. Your phone hasn't stopped ringing or blaring out text notifications since midnight."

"Huh?" Vance opened his eyes, trying to adjust to very bright lights. Lanie must have turned on every light in the room.

"That 'J' guy is contacting you frantically. He's got a shipping container belonging to that criminal mastermind you're trying to bust. Dougal, is it? He seems to think you need to be there now, and that was three hours ago."

"Where is my phone?" Vance searched the bedside table. It vibrated as he found it. He didn't have to ask Lanie how she knew when his phone got calls. She acted as his talent agent, and in that capacity, she screened his calls to keep his fans a safe distance. Only Lanie, Dai, and maybe two or three other people knew his personal number, the number Lanie didn't screen. Should someone try to contact Vance, they'd call his professional contact number, and their call would hit Lanie's phone first before being forwarded, if Lanie approved. Sheriff's business hit his phone on a separate number; all those calls and texts were screened by Lanie's phone as well.

"Dai, what did you do to my boyfriend to tire him out?" Lanie asked. "Seriously, I want every detail."

"I'll tell you when Vance leaves," Dai said. "Since I kept him for so long, I'll let you watch me shower while I tell the tale. Well, tales."

"You've got a deal," Lanie said. "Can I wash your back?"

"No," Dai said.

"Can I take pictures?" Lanie asked.

"No." Dai climbed out of bed. She had on Vance's old sheriff shirt—one from his TV costume, not one of his real Los Angeles County ones.

"Oh well, still a deal," Lanie said. "Vance, get your cute butt out of here and on the job."

"I am never going to understand this relationship," Vance said.

"You don't have to understand," Dai said. "Like everything else in life, you have duties, and you reap rewards when you perform your duties well. Tonight was more about my reaping rewards for performing your duties well."

"Ooh, ouch," Lanie said.

Dai's words had been the first in months to suggest Vance had been slacking on his duties as the sheriff of Dai's kingdom. The Kingdom of Heaven seemed to be fine, though Vance had been doing his best not to know for sure. Since the burning of Hallows and Zylpha murdering all his cast-mates from Midnite Starr, he hadn't been anywhere near where Hallows used to be. Dai's theatre, The Nocturne, stood only half a block from Hallows. Unable to get there without risking too painful a reminder of what he couldn't have prevented, Vance hadn't attended court at all since the massacre.

He expected that Dai would have given him instructions if she needed him to do something. She might have been respecting the distance he'd been keeping, and not demanding anything of him until he was ready. He wasn't sure when that would be.

"I have human sheriff duties, too," Vance said. "Dai insisted I legitimize the badge I wear, so it's her fault I'm so busy. This Dougal guy falls right into the area I'm using as a cover for working nights all the time. It's my job to track down crime lords like the Nine Princes, and Dougal, from what I've seen so far, certainly qualifies." Dougal focused primarily on human trafficking, but dabbled in other forms of smuggling, such as weapons and drugs. In three weeks on the case, Vance knew he'd nearly missed getting a glimpse of Dougal four times and stopped exactly zero of Dougal's crimes. "If 'J' is right, I need this break."

"Is this a real case?" Dai asked. "If this 'J' is another booty call, I will have issues. Lanie isn't the jealous type, but…"

"You are," Vance said. "I've been stabbed by you. I do my best to not anger so I don't get stabbed again." Dai's reasons for stabbing him had nothing to do with her jealousy. He wasn't sure she wouldn't stab him should he invoke it. Vance didn't know enough about J to describe even their gender. He assumed J was a guy, because the person worked as a henchman for a crime lord. "I wish I could tell you more about J, but I don't even have a name, just the initial."

"It's a real case." Lanie held up her phone and read the latest text. "Sheriff Silver, I hope you're on your way. I'm risking my ass texting you and there are women chained in this crate. If you don't get here before Dougal does, the crate may get loaded onto a ship and no one will see these women alive again."

"Well, fuck!" Dai said. "Long Beach or L.A. docks?"

"Port of Los Angeles," Lanie said. "He included a map in a few of his texts."

"Vance, you have my permission to fly," Dai said. "You won't make it back downtown by sunrise. I'll tell Katina and Azure you'll be staying with them at their place."

Vance grabbed his pants and pulled them on. He pulled his shoes closer with his mind as he strapped on his Kevlar. "The house in the cove?" He pulled a black sweater over the bulletproof vest.

"Their hotel room was undergoing renovations, last I heard," Lanie said. "This is good timing; they want to see you. I keep meaning to tell you. It's been in the works for a few weeks, but you must see them today." She grabbed his foot and slid a sock over it, then started wiggling on a shoe.

"I guess fate is pulling me south this morning," Vance said. "Lanie, will you be meeting me at Katina and Azure's?"

"I have business to handle for most of the day," Lanie said. "I'll be down in the afternoon."

"Lanie, send Cynthia that map," Dai said. "Vance shouldn't handle that kind of thing alone."

"I guess you've got business to handle, too?" Vance asked Dai.

"I really didn't have time to cuddle afterwards," Dai said. "I have so much crap to do, it's not funny. Lanie, you're working for me this morning, right?"

"Yeah," Lanie said. "My Six a.m. appointment is you. Eight is that security contractor for the real estate deal. Nine-Thirty and Ten-Thirty are inspections. Until four o'clock this morning, I have time to watch you wash your hair, and whatever else you need to wash. Did you get sweaty?"

Vampires didn't sweat as much as humans did. Their physiology didn't let them waste moisture that way. Vance did remember a little sweat, though.

That Dai had cuddled, and if Vance recalled correctly, she'd been lying on his chest since sometime before one a.m., surprised Vance. Dai didn't normally cuddle; she never had before. He'd have to get his mind straightened out and put the Hallows massacre behind him. Dai may not have needed him recently, but she would soon. He needed to be all-there when she did, even if it meant passing by the empty hulk of the building that once housed Hallows and his and Lanie's apartment.

"Details after Vance leaves," Dai said.

Lanie handed Vance his badge. "Sweetie, as much as I'd like to keep you here, too, I can't. So, you need to hurry up and get out."

"Vance, here!" Dai handed Vance his shoulder holster with his county issued firearm snapped in. His badge was affixed to the strap. "Fly!" she commanded.

Vance ran out of Dai's apartment to the stairwell then went up one floor to the roof. He took out his phone and activated the map, then pushed off with his mind, flying off to the south. He knew how to fly in a city without being seen. Staying just below the rooftops and east of the taller buildings, he wouldn't be on the scope of the airport's radar. He had to avoid the buildings with balconies by at least a block. Outside of downtown, he stayed between seventy and a hundred feet from the ground over the brightly lit streets, and he flew fast. Streetlights face down and blind people to whatever's above them.

With all the guidelines of how to do it without being noticed, Queen Dai had one law concerning flying in her city: Don't.

Minutes after leaving Dai's apartment in downtown Los Angeles, Vance landed near the container 'J' had mentioned, just beyond the edge of the light from the nearby building. He watched and waited. If 'J' was right, he might finally meet Los Angeles' newest crime lord. No one he'd questioned had seen or spoken directly with Dougal. For someone with a reputation for being involved and heavy-handed, the only evidence of Dougal's existence were texts on his lackey's burner phones. He considered calling his FBI contact, Special Agent Hannah Dwyer, and letting her know he had a solid lead, but if Vance had to fight to free the women, there would be blood. With blood, Vance's curse of the bloodeyes could take over and every human he could smell might die.

He waited for Cynthia because she had the tool to stop him. Vance didn't like having a sword thrust through his chest, but he'd rather suffer that pain than endure the guilt of killing blindly.

By the look of things, he could probably save the women without hurting anyone. A single man leaned by the cab of a truck, smoking, and watching a movie on his phone. He could hear six distinct women's voices in the container on the back of the truck, but he couldn't understand what they said. Four men inside the building were talking about their fantasy football teams. Vance couldn't pick out many words through a wall from as far away as he was hiding behind stacks of plastic barrels. He sent a text to 'J', "I'm in place, just waiting." He heard an alert from a phone in the building. That night, in addition to rescuing the women in the truck, he'd meet his inside man.

He then got comfortable and waited. If Dougal showed before Cynthia arrived, Vance hoped the steel of the container would keep the women inside safe from him. He considered rushing the driver and coercing him to walk home, but even a small chance the driver could make it messy was too much risk.

Half an hour passed with nothing happening except the driver went inside once to use a toilet. He didn't stay inside. When he returned, he checked the container, making sure the lock had been opened. Dougal wouldn't want any unnecessary delays in inspecting the women before shipping them off.

"Hey!" Cynthia said, jogging up to him. "Ready to be heroes?"

"We're waiting on Dougal," Vance said.

"You know he's coming?" Cynthia asked.

"My contact is expecting him. The driver unlocked the back," Vance said. "Dougal should be here to inspect his goods before they ship."

"Women," Cynthia said. "They're people, not goods."

"I know. I'm thinking like Dougal must," Vance said. "My contact is expecting him."

"Has your contact met Dougal?" Cynthia asked.

"Not yet," Vance said.

"Dougal won't show," Cynthia said. "At least the odds are against it. That truck is running, though that might not be a sign they're ready to go. It's a diesel, they don't shut those down if they don't have to. But they could be getting prepared to move soon."

Vance didn't know trucks were left running on purpose. "But the back is unlocked. Wouldn't they lock it while preparing to move?"

"Do I hear henchmen in the building?" Cynthia asked. She had far more acute hearing than a human, but she was a dhampyre, not a vampire. As a dhampyre, Cynthia had all the benefits of being a vampire, to a much lesser extent, but none of the drawbacks.

"Yes, four of them," Vance said.

"They're getting ready to get in the truck," Cynthia said. "That truck holds three people in the cab, which means two of those guys are riding in the back."

"Less than a year ago, you were a struggling actress getting ready to head home to Utah, and now you're an expert on trucks and criminal tactics?" Vance asked. The question wasn't looking for an answer. Vance meant to express his amazement.

"Unlike you, an Assistant Sheriff with a cushy job and no expectations to actually get directly involved in law enforcement beyond giving orders, I'm a deputy. I have to study four hours of training every week. I work fifty hours a week for the county and twenty hours a week for Dai."

"I didn't mean to…" Whatever he'd triggered, Vance wished he hadn't. Cynthia wasn't wrong to feel overworked.

"Hey, don't get me wrong, I love the life of the queen's personal bodyguard," Cynthia said. "The money's great. Never aging is awesome and you can't beat being able to heal from any illness or injury. I'm just saying I worked for my knowledge. You deserve everything you have. You've earned it with effort, pain, and blood. You're just not really a cop. You're a vampire king who plays at being a cop."

"Vamp sheriff, not king. I don't play at anything. I'm not on TV anymore," Vance said.

"Season two of Midnite Starr premieres in November, less than a month from now," Cynthia said. "You may never film another episode, but to the rest of us, you still play a part more than enforce the law. I'm sorry. I respect you for the hero you are, but this is serious law enforcement, and we need to go in while we have a chance to save the girls. The sooner we go, the easier it will be. That driver could jump in the cab and drive off. Then, any rescue involving a moving truck is a thousand times more dangerous than us going in now."

"If we were doing this by the Sheriff's Department protocols, we'd have called in backup," Vance said.

"Well, we know why we can't do that," Cynthia said. "You're still my boss, both as a sheriff and in the vampire world. You just need to tell me the plan."

Vance's tactical training involved going after one vampire at a time with a team of two or more hunters. He thought about asking Cynthia for her trained tactical ideas, but she needed him to be a worthy leader. Since every law enforcement tactic started with superior numbers, they wouldn't be using Cynthia's training. "You're right," Vance said, letting her know he valued her opinion. "We need to act now. Like they say, a bird in the hand, right?"

"Thanks," Cynthia said. "So, we going in shooting or are you going to try to talk them into early retirement?"

"They work for Dougal," Vance said. "They'll fear him more than they fear the law. I'm going to go try to talk our way out of this, but there will be shots fired. Let's hope there isn't much blood."

"Damn!" Cynthia said. "I left my sword in the car. Dai usually handles your risky nights. I haven't taken the sword out of the sheath since we arrested Mikhail for killing Lady Brandy."

"Brandy's dead?" Vance asked. "Mikhail killed his own bloodmother?" Vance didn't know either vampire well, but he remembered meeting them a few times. They both seemed close.

"Brandy kept Mikhail on a short leash and a shoestring allowance," Cynthia said. "Dai didn't take pity, she sent Mikhail to the roof. That was three months ago, back in July. Are you seriously that out of the loop?"

"I guess I am," Vance said. "You're going to go over to the left of the door. I'm going to go tell the driver to walk away and then I'm going to honk the horn of the truck. When the guys come out, I'll try to talk them down. If I can't, you shoot them. Kill shots. I can't promise to deal well with living blood. If I go berserk, make sure I stay clear of that container. You know how to shoot past a vest, right? If I'm berserk I won't be in the right stance to cover the gaps."

"Armpits and through the neck," Cynthia said. "I might just go for kneecaps."

"Please don't. Bones take hours to heal right and hurt like hell while they do."

"I know you want me to do whatever I have to," Cynthia said. "The important thing is the lives of the women in the shipping container. Go get 'em! I'll be in position when the goons come out to play."

Vance unsnapped his holster but didn't draw his pistol. He stood and walked calmly towards the driver. The driver saw Vance as soon as he entered the light and drew a pistol from his belt. "You need to leave, bro!"

Still too far to assure enough eye contact for his coercion to hold, Vance tried anyway. While walking slowly forward, he said, "Go home. Take what money you have and move…"

The driver fired, missing Vance. Vance drew his gun and rushed close before the man could fire again. Vance grabbed the man's wrist and aimed the man's pistol toward the harbor. The man kept pulling the trigger, hitting only water. "Let me try this again. Drop the gun. Take your wife and kids if you have them, and move somewhere far away, far inland. Go, now. Run until you can't, then walk."

The driver ran off. Vance didn't have to get that specific. The man would not kill himself running. Coercion couldn't override natural instincts. It couldn't even make someone do what they wouldn't do. It straightened the thought process, creating a shortcut to whatever decision the vampire suggested, if such a decision could be reasonable for the person to make.

Vance didn't even get the chance to bend over to pick up the driver's gun when the door to the warehouse burst open and a man ran out shooting. Vance stepped farther from the truck and shot back, hitting the man in the thigh and shoulder, just as he'd aimed. His training taught him to shoot for the center of the chest, but he needed to make sure he had someone to question. The next three might come out as a group and Vance might not have the time to aim for non-lethal areas.

The next man came out and fell to his knees, throwing his gun.

The last two emerged together and one yelled at the man on the ground. "Get the hell up and shoot back!"

"Don't be stupid," the man on his knees said. "That's Vance Silver. You're not prepared to kill him."

"Is he a vamp?" the yelling man asked. "Dougal wasn't just being insane? Bas, run back inside and grab the machete. We'll need it after I drop this guy with a couple of brain shots." The yelling man's head then sprayed forward, as did the other man who still stood.

Cynthia stepped up behind the man on his knees and said, "You better pray you're the one Vance doesn't want to kill. Are you his informant?"

"I am Julian, Petra's human," he said.

Cynthia fired again. Her shot tore into the chest of the man Vance had shot in the knee and shoulder. Julian winced. "Don't feel the need to shoot me in the leg to make me seem less complicit. I'm a pet, it'll heal too fast."

Vance walked over and picked up Julian's gun and then handed it to Cynthia. He had a brief realization that at least one of the men they'd shot hadn't yet died. Vance smelled living blood. The world turned red.

§

When Vance came to his senses nothing around him had changed. He expected to wake as he usually did, among a messy pile of carnage. He only smelled vampire blood. His nose hurt like hell and blood ran over his lips—

his own blood.

"You broke my nose?" Vance asked Cynthia.

"I've warned you not to stare at my chest," Cynthia said, nodding slightly toward Julian. No one could know of his bloodeyes or even vampires would want him dead. Cynthia's nods told him to go along with her ruse.

"I'm sorry?" Vance tried not to make it seem like a guess. He failed at making it sound like an apology. Vance's informant wouldn't be in a state of mind, with the recent gunplay, to notice.

"If I'd had my sword, I'd have stabbed you. But I had to improvise." Cynthia shook her hand. "If it makes you feel better, I broke at least two knuckle bones on your face."

"You're Dai's dhampyre, aren't you?" Julian asked. "I've seen you at court, but I've never been this close. I always assumed you were just a pet, but you don't move like a pet. I didn't believe she had the gall to keep a dhampyre. Most vamps and pets in L.A. think it's just a rumor to make us afraid to cross Dai, like we need more inspiration than not wanting to suffer the wrath of Asmodeus or Vance Silver. But you're not a vamp and you're not a pet. Seeing you this close, I can tell. You are what they say. The devil among us, a dhampyre."

"That's me!" Cynthia said. "Sunbathing and vampire killing."

"You're fucking ruthless," Julian said. "You just murdered these guys because they had five minutes of training in how to kill vamps."

"To be trained, they had to know about vamps," Cynthia said.

Julian shrugged. "They had been given tools to kill vamps. I bet until they saw Vance, they didn't believe those odd orders were anything other than another of Dougal's insanities. One time he sent twelve of us to guard Shamu's tank in sea world."

"Twelve of you for one tank? I guess the tanks are big," Vance said.

"Well, it's all confusing because when we got there, there wasn't a killer whale named Shamu and there were about a dozen of them. So, we each guarded one. I guess we did a decent job of whatever it is we were supposed to do. The next day we each got a thousand-dollar bonus."

"So, what you're saying is that we didn't need to kill anyone," Vance said.

"Don't go there, Vance," Cynthia said. "Let's not forget they were armed with machine guns and getting ready to shoot you. If we were to write this up with the sheriff's office, we'd spend two weeks at a desk with daily counseling to help us get past taking a life, and then we'd get a medal."

"I try to be better than being the guy who kills because I can," Vance said.

"I'm Dai's proxy here, not yours," Cynthia said. "Dai would have killed them. And don't try to back off the responsibility, here. You literally, just two minutes ago, told me to take kill shots."

"Let's face it, if you hadn't killed them, I would have, just less elegantly," Vance said. "I'm sorry, I take killing seriously, but there are times when it's unavoidable without exposing us to far more risk than we should."

"Don't worry about it," Cynthia said. "I'm no monster. I just know what needs to be done and I'm trusted to do it. Maybe that makes me a monster, but I don't kill lightly."

"I've got to run," Vance said, noticing the sky seemed several shades lighter.

"Leaving me to the grunt work while you go off to play with your girlfriends?" Cynthia asked.

"The sun's coming up," Vance said. "I have an appointment with Katina and Azure."

"I know, Vance," Cynthia said. "I'm teasing you. You do know I'm your friend, right? I couldn't give you this hard of a time if I didn't like you."

"It's been so long since we've worked together," Vance said. "I didn't really get a chance to know you before Hallows burned and I haven't seen much of you since."

"You know where I am and when I'm there," Cynthia said. "You really should be those places, too. This time I'm not messing with you. Dai won't say it, but I will. You have a lot of grief over losing Hallows and all your friends, but you also have duties to Dai and your kingdom. Dai hasn't needed you for anything I couldn't handle, but she might, soon. I'm not as strong as you and I don't have your powers."

"I'll be back into things soon," Vance said. "Take the truck to Nocturne and make sure the girls are safe and get them whatever they need to be healthy. Do you drive this kind of truck?"

"No," Cynthia said. "I mean, I have the CDL, but no time at all in a big rig diesel."

"I'll drive," Julian said. "You busted me. It's not like you were just going to let me go home. I don't know where vamp jail is, but I bet I'm heading there. Do I get a phone call?"

"Yes, there's a couple cells," Cynthia said. "Yes, one of them has your name on it, tonight. Of course, you get a phone call. It's the best way to get Petra into the other cell. You should probably just tell her to meet us at Nocturne."

"She'll sacrifice me, and herself," Julian said. "Dougal knows where Petra's grandkids live and has been using Petra as his inside vamp. Dougal thinks the Nine Princes still run things in Los Angeles and, when he's ready, he plans to go to war against them. Petra's been feeding him lies about which prince oversees which part of town. Dougal is oblivious, I assure you. I spend two nights a week at Concentric, reporting on Satan and Asmodeus' drug imports.

"Dai wasn't into the drug trade," Vance said.

Julian tilted his head and smiled at Vance. "She's not into anything illegal, except that she kills anyone who interferes with her power over the city."

"Careful," Vance said.

"Her body count is way down, but she did lay waste to like a hundred guys from that civil war biker gang. Not everyone believes when Dirk's bar burned that it was Zylpha. Why would a council member care about a bar in Los Angeles?" Julian asked.

There had been sixteen bikers, and Vance had killed them all while berserk from his bloodeyes. He didn't feel it necessary to correct Julian's details about the biker gang. Zylpha was a sore subject, however. Vance had to watch her execute three innocent people in cold blood. They'd been the last three survivors of her massacre of every single member of the cast and crew of his show, Midnite Starr. "I guess Petra doesn't have any inside connections to the council," Vance said. "Zylpha lost her own kingdom and…"

"Vance!" Cynthia said. "I'll explain it all to Julian on the way to the theatre. You have to get to the cove, and you probably have just enough time to run there without having to run faster than an early morning jogger. Two more minutes of jabbering with this pet and you'll either be arriving smoking and steaming and stinky, or you'll have to run faster than a human can. It's already too light out to fly.

To Vance, it felt like over a hundred degrees, though the actual temperature was closer to seventy. "I'm going. Thanks for taking care of this." He jogged off. As he approached the exit gates from the harbor, he slowed and walked past the security station. He pointed at his badge hanging from his shirt pocket, only because he carried his shoulder holster in the open and didn't want to alarm the guards. They barely looked his way. As he almost got out of sight of the guardhouse, someone getting out of a car in the parking lot yelled his name.

"Sheriff Silver?" Vance hadn't heard the voice except through the phone or over a video conference.

"Special Agent Dwyer?" Vance called back and jogged over to a woman in a suit. She had a physically imposing presence, standing as tall as Vance and nearly as muscular. She kept her blonde hair pulled into a short ponytail, which seemed far more severe and tighter, in person than it had over the video conferences she sometimes used to plan their investigation. Unlike most of the people Vance knew, at around Six a.m. Special Agent Dwyer would be just starting her day. Her ponytail hadn't had time to loosen,

"It's good to finally meet you in person," agent Dwyer said. "You found something of Dougal's in there?"

"I did," Vance said. "My deputy is taking care of some human trafficking victims we found. No concrete links to Dougal, but I suspect he's involved."

"Good thing you didn't follow the lead I sent you, then," Dwyer said. "Though, a response would have been nice."

Vance checked his phone. He had two messages from Agent Dwyer from just after midnight. Both gave the address of a parking garage in Hollywood and told Vance to be there between three and six. The second message also asked if he got the first message. "I totally didn't see these," Vance said. "It was a busy night and it's not done yet. I really have to go!"

"You're running off?" Agent Dwyer asked. "Surely, there is a crime scene to investigate and henchmen to question. By the bloody nose, I can see they didn't go down without a fight. But they did go down, right?"

"One got away. I don't know what became of the other henchmen." Vance hoped Cynthia found a way to dispose of the bodies and cover up any pools of blood. "I do have somewhere I need to be. I'm sorry I can't discuss this right now. Call me, we'll video chat after lunch. I'll have more details then."

"Need a lift?" Special Agent Dwyer asked.

Looking down the street, Vance knew he wouldn't have time to make it to Azure and Katina's home before the sun rose. He checked his watch. He had ten minutes until sunrise. "I'm headed to the third hotel down along the beach," he said, remembering which hotels had the Night Watchman's Suites. "A ride would be nice."

"Hop in!" She got back in the car and pushed the passenger door open.

Vance climbed in.

"You know Vance, for someone who's supposed to be my partner, I don't have any missed calls this morning," Agent Dwyer said as they pulled from the parking lot.

"That explains why we didn't get any FBI backup," Vance said. "I'll have a chat with my deputy about why she didn't call for assistance."

Agent Dwyer asked, "Are you one of those old-fashioned sheriffs who doesn't like to use your cell phone?"

"I was too close, physically, to make a phone call without risking detection," Vance said.

"Sounds like a tactical error," Agent Dwyer said.

"If you've heard I'm perfect or that I'm a savant at law enforcement, you've been talking to my girlfriend." Vance looked toward the eastern sky. The bright colors seemed to make him sweat, or maybe he sweat from Agent Dwyer's light interrogation. She drove slowly, under the speed limit, slower than traffic, and far slower than Lanie drove. They had plenty of time to make it to the hotel, but Vance couldn't help but worry he wouldn't make it on time.

"You're a good man, Sheriff Silver," Agent Dwyer said. "You're not a great cop. I'm having trouble believing you earned your position the normal way. Assistant sheriffs are usually in their fifties. I thought it was the webcam making you look young, but, seeing you in person, you're half the age I'd expect of an assistant sheriff."

"I don't know how to explain it," Vance said. "Maybe the sheriff is a fan of Midnite Starr."

"What's Midnite Starr?" Agent Dwyer asked.

"For an FBI agent, I'd have expected you would have done a full check of my past," Vance said.

"You can bet I'm going to be spending my day doing just that," Agent Dwyer said. She pulled under the overhang of the hotel. "Don't get me wrong; I like you. You have a lot to learn about how to be a lawman. The first lesson is to call for backup before assaulting even just a handful of bad guys."

"Even if it wakes you up, I'll call you before I shoot anyone," Vance said. "Thanks for the lift." He gave her an unsure smile. He'd meant it to be friendly, but he felt his lips tighten, betraying his uncertainty with how he felt about her. He walked quickly into the hotel; the pre-sunrise light felt like steam.

II

Vance rested on the bed of the Night Watchman's Suite. Even when he didn't spend much time enraged by the bloodeyes, just entering the berserk state exhausted him. Usually, he'd feed while under the control of the bloodeyes, but Cynthia had stopped that from happening. He'd already texted Lanie to explain where to find him. Then he'd texted Azure and Katina to explain why he wouldn't make it. They texted back by asking which hotel he stayed in. An hour after his response, his phone vibrated with a text from Katina inviting him up to the penthouse.

If a vampire could invite him up, she must've secured it from sunlight. He stopped outside Katina and Azure's door when his phone buzzed.

Agent Dwyer had texted him. "You're a fucking actor whose only experience in law enforcement is playing a sheriff on TV? You're not the first totally unqualified lawman I've worked with and you're not the worst, but you'd better not get in the way of my investigation. I know I'm supposed to treat you like a partner, but I'm going to be treating you like an apprentice. Get used to it or stay out of it altogether."

The door opened. Karlo, Katina's pet, held it and gestured for Vance to enter. "Would you like something to drink?" Karlo asked. "Karlo can get wine, beer, water. Not blood though. Karlo thinks it is weird to let men drink from him."

Katina's pet talking in third person always threw Vance off. "I'm fine, Karlo. I'm here for Katina and Azure."

"Karlo will take you to them," the pet said. He led Vance into a hallway leading into the suite.

"Vance!" Azure came from a kitchen area holding two glasses of white wine. Every time he saw her, he could only think how jealous Lanie was of Azure's electric blue hair. Lanie wore wigs to give her hair color because, to remain respectable as an agent and lawyer, she had to have normal hair. Azure had the freedom to dye her own exceptionally long hair and had the money to make sure the color stayed vibrant, and her roots never showed.

"I told Karlo I didn't need anything," Vance said.

"These?" Azure held up the glasses. "If you want one, I'll give you one and go make another. But I made these for Katina and me."

"Should I have responded to the text to say I'd be right up?" Vance asked, following Azure and Karlo into the suite's living room. Vance had been in the room before, he realized. Katina and Azure had stayed there when they'd first arrived in Los Angeles. The room had been remodeled since then. Someone had decorated with a strong Greco-Roman classic motif. Bronze statuettes of gods and heroes stood on pedestals spread around the room. Half a dozen floor-to-ceiling columns stood in a semicircle around two couches in the middle of the room. Katina sat on a couch, reading something on a tablet computer. Vance sat down on another couch across from Katina's.

"The room looks nice," Vance said. "Lanie thought you'd moved out of the hotel, but this looks like you're moving in on a more permanent basis. Did the hotel change the decor or did you?"

"We suggested the changes." Katina put her tablet on a table between them. "You've never been here during the day before, have you? You should be warned: this room won't be comfortable for you. The roof is just a tad thin, not enough to keep a vampire safe up here."

The sun could kill a vampire in seconds. The form of radiation that burned vampires wasn't any that could be measured by science. Visible light helped vampires be aware of the threat of the sun, but the radiation that burned vampires took several inches of material to absorb it. A couple inches of wood and tin, like a hotel roof, wouldn't always be enough. "This hotel has vamp friendly rooms," Vance said. "Why are you up here if this is not one of them?"

"I'm very pure," Katina said. "I'm probably twice your purity of Venae. My sister did the math. I can pull up a spreadsheet if you want to know exactly. I'm showing off a bit. This isn't uncomfortable for me. Elsa didn't ever experiment with sunlight on herself, but I have. She lived in penthouses, sure, but they were very over-engineered with two feet of reinforced concrete walls and rooves. When Elsa conducts experiments, she always uses proper scientific methods with controls and multiple cases, just to be sure. It's terrifying and disturbing. I'm not so conservative. I'm willing to be my own guinea pig. But I now know things she didn't. I can be in direct sunlight for thirty seconds before catching fire. It hurts like hell, but I can do it. Five seconds will give me a tan that will last for a couple hours. I can ride in a windowless vehicle, which means, aside from being able to hit all the best shops in town, I can be happy in a penthouse. Should we go down to your room to talk?"

"It's warm, it's not stifling or bothersome," Vance said. "We can talk. Are you ready to call in that favor I owe you?"

"We are," Katina said. "Karlo, why don't you go fetch the food. Be sure to pick up Marisol, so Vance can eat, too. She is still a virgin, right? That is what keeps you from going all bloodeyes berserker, isn't it?"

"It's been too long," Vance said. "I keep trying to stretch it out another day or two. I feel bad using Marisol like I do."

"You're not using her," Katina said. "She's being paid. She'll never have to work once she finishes the contract with you. You do know Elsa is paying her, right?"

"I do," Vance said.

"Accept it and use her as needed," Katina said. "It's just a bite twice a week, and not a lot of blood loss for her. You're not going to build up a tolerance for the bloodeyes. This isn't an addiction or a drug. This is your body chemistry as it's designed. It's a bad design and it takes one hell of a workaround, but it's not going to change. You're hardwired to fight like a rabid badger when you smell blood. But you know all this. Stop trying to be a hero about it. Be responsible, that's more heroic."

"It's not as easy as just doing it," Vance said. "Biting someone always feels wrong."

"Not biting her is making her feel like she's unable to do her duties," Katina said. "She's a virgin so you cannot make her a pet, but she's coerced by Elsa to keep our secret, so it's almost the same thing. Whether or not she's coerced to feel the pain of the bite doesn't matter. To her, feeding you is her job. She expects to do her job on a regular schedule. When you don't adhere to that schedule out of pride, you're damaging her ego."

"Pride?" Vance asked. "Is respect the same as pride?"

"When you do it to uphold your own ego, it's pride. Don't confuse it with honor. Honor is respect. Pride is selfish. The trick is that if you do make choices based on how it will affect your honor, it's pride and not honor. Treat Marisol as she expects. That may or may not be honorable, but it's not dishonorable, it just is. Avoid feeding because it doesn't fit with morality as you define it, and that's selfish. You put everyone at risk when you skip your virgin blood dose. That's selfish pride."

"I didn't come here for lessons in being a vampire," Vance said. "I appreciate your advice; we both know you're right. You called me here for some other reason besides my irresponsible feeding habits. Why, exactly, am I here?"

"You're not going to like it," Azure said, sitting beside Vance, folding her legs under her on the couch with her back to the couch's arm. "Dai says you're super religious and what we're doing might be bad in your eyes."

"If you want me to murder someone, I'm not your guy." Vance looked around the room for the usual open bottle of wine Katina would have. "Is this going to be something you should get me drunk before asking?"

"I insist you be fully lucid," Katina said. "We're not going to kill anyone. This is exactly the opposite."

"You want to give birth?" Vance asked. "If you want me to father a child, that would be difficult. Vampires are sterile, without exception."

"I'm sorry," Katina said. "I didn't mean to be vague. I was thinking a different direction when I said the opposite of killing. I mean bringing someone back from death. And not like making someone a vampire. I mean to bring my sister back."

"Huh?" Vance couldn't help but vocalize his confusion. "Resurrection?

"Like Jesus Christ? Karina, if I recall your stories, died as a vampire. You don't have anything to resurrect. I don't mean to be mean; I'm just beyond confused."

"Magic can do it," Katina said.

"It's been done before," Azure said. "The spell is very forbidden, but it's been done twice in recorded history. Once it succeeded. Once it failed. Cleopatra came back fine, though all the details of the spell were lost when Alexandria burned. No, she didn't live on forever. Her second and final death is the one in the history books with the asps. The last time the spell was tried was 1955, but the healers—mundane surgeons, nothing magical—couldn't fix the body fast enough to support life. I tracked down film of that ritual; that's a long, but boring, story. The report from that failure indicated it would have been better to duplicate the body anew than to try to fix the damaged one."

"Rebuilding a body just takes one bone." Katina set a small box on the table and opened it. It contained a small bone, most likely a finger bone.

"How do you have the bone of a dead vampire?" Vance asked.

"We were twins," Katina said. "This is one of mine, but it's genetically identical to Karina's."

Azure said, "We just need Karina's soul and when we bond it to that bone, it will, with a little help, regrow."

"You do know I can't help but see all this as heresy," Vance said. "I can't support this."

"We're not asking for help with the magic or the ritual," Katina said. "We just want protection when we find the necromancer. There's one somewhere in Southern California. We think we're close to finding him."

"We may find him tonight," Azure said. "He has a reputation for being a murderer; anyone who might a danger to him disappears. At least, so the rumors go. The fact is, we need a necromancer to perform the ritual and he's the only one we know of. There's one in India and another somewhere else in Asia, but this is the only one we can find. We haven't found him yet, but we have a good lead, I think."

"Do you know what a coven is, Vance?" Katina asked.

"Some writers call a collection of vampires a coven," Vance said. "Anne Rice, for example. But lore more often refers to a group of witches as a coven. When it comes to magic, I don't know anything I haven't learned from Azure."

"Covens are banned in the mage world," Azure said. "We allow half-covens, but any group with more than three is forbidden. A coven is a small group of mages, one from each element. It's not a rule we need to enforce, really. The overwhelming majority of mages belong to one of three elements: earth, water, or air. Fire mages tend to burn themselves away before gaining control over their magic. Necromancers are rare. Like I said, I think there are three known in the whole world. And you already know there aren't any healers—or life mages—since the creation of vampires."

"Earth mages can heal a little, right?" Katina asked.

"No," Azure said. "Earth mages have control of inorganic materials. Rocks, metals, even ice. They're shapers. Air is really more about electromagnetic radiation than air. They can relate and manipulate light, create illusions, control electric devices. I even know a girl who can broadcast her thoughts in FM radio. Water is divination and some of us can control liquids, but most can just detect them. Fire is rawer energy, heat, and vibration. Healers, if they still existed, could grow or nurture organic material. Necromancers deal with the energy that actually gives life: the spirit, or soul, if you will."

"So, who grows Karina's body?" Katina asked.

"I wish I were any good with ritual magic, but I've never managed to make a ritual work, unless it directly related to creation or control of water. My friend Stephanie is very adept. She can channel your Venae, performing a ritual of regrowth, but we need the necromancer to hold Karina's soul in the body until the brain and heart are regrown. We need an earth mage to combine the elements into material Stephanie can then use to build a body. Technically, the body knows how to build itself, we just have to make sure the materials it needs are there. In ancient times, this would involve a human sacrifice, but vampires are not made of the same flesh and blood as people. Vampires are physicalized Venae."

"I can't tell the difference, other than feeding, between a vampire and human in terms of flesh and bone," Vance said.

"It's why you disintegrate when you die," Azure said. "You're not really made of the stuff of this earth. Made from, but not of, if that makes sense."

"Not really," Vance said.

"Would it make it simpler if I explained that there isn't a difference between energy and matter?" Azure asked. "Mages have known for thousands of years what physicists are just starting to understand. Everything is energy, it's just in a different state, a different energy. There are dozens of forms of energy out there. This plane, what we perceive as our universe which includes our Earth, is a confluence of several forms of energy. Not all of them interact in this plane. They're all here. They're all everywhere, but they are imperceptible to us and don't affect the materials and energies we know."

"Now you're making magic seem like science, which appeals to me," Vance said. Magic, outside of the miracles of the Lord, shouldn't exist. He didn't say that out loud.

"I got an invite to meet with a coven yesterday," Azure said. "They're meeting tonight."

"And this includes a necromancer?" Vance asked. "Which you think I can protect you from?"

"I have a thirty-aught-six in a case under this couch," Azure said. "Extended barrel, range adjusting scope. Of everyone I know in Los Angeles, you're the most likely person to know how to use that. You can see the parking lot where we're gathering from our balcony. It's a little more than a mile north of here."

"I can use that rifle," Vance said. "I wouldn't trust my aim beyond a thousand yards. Top-notch scope or not, I've never met anyone who could make a shot more than a mile. I hear stories of military snipers, but I don't even know how that's possible."

"I've seen the results of a sniper from almost three miles," Katina said. "I didn't see the shot, just the brains and blood left on the wall. I know Julia of Artemis' line, can make that shot. She's stuck in Paris, though. I've spoken with Thalia and Artemis, and both insist you're the guy for this task."

Why Artemis and Thalia would point to him as a sniper confounded Vance. They had to have ulterior motives. Surely other sisters were better shots and better fighters. They would all be more potent vampires. Of all the sisters, the one thing Vance stood out as, other than his gender, was that he might be the most expendable. "Where are you meeting?" he asked. "I'll find a spot that's in my range."

Katina pulled a map up on her tablet and handed it to Vance.

"You have the app that shows 3D views of cities?" Vance asked.

"I can get it," Katina said. Vance handed her back her tablet.

"You're meeting in a parking lot," Vance said. "What if you go into a building?"

"It's an industrial area," Katina said. "We think it's unlikely. Azure says the coven leader is meeting in a parking lot because it's easy to draw symbols on the asphalt."

Azure said, "I didn't explain what's special about this coven—why we decided now was the time to get your help. Stephanie says this will be a six-member coven. As I explained, four member covens are both banned and rare. Five member covens, well, there might be three. A six-member coven is impossible."

"Who is Stephanie?" Vance asked. "And could they use a vampire as the healer?"

"No mage would ever work with a vampire," Azure said. "We are required to avoid vampires. Have I mentioned that I haven't told my parents about my new lovers? They think I took a job as a personal assistant to some spoiled heiress."

"You have vampire friends," Vance said. "These mages of this coven have already established that they are willing to violate the rules of the mages. They must have a vampire if they truly want all six types of magic represented."

"I hadn't made that connection," Azure said. "We know vamps can't cast spells, but other mages can channel their Venae and use its magic. A vampire could fill a spot in a coven."

"A full coven will make bringing back my sister far more likely to succeed!" Katina nearly bounced off the couch from her excitement.

"Did it occur to you that she might be happy where she is?" Vance asked. "If she's in heaven, which is what I believe, she is happy." Vance didn't believe in hell. Everyone who died went to heaven, so he believed—he wanted to believe.

"She calls to me in my dreams," Katina said. "She's here, with me. I can't see her; I can't hear her. I can't sense her at all, except when I dream. She tells me how she's watching me, wishing she could be with me. When I wake, I still hear her voice echoing in my ears. 'I miss you. I love you.' And then I cry. Every time I wake, I cry."

"I'm going to help," Vance said. "I won't be part of your ritual. I will help keep you safe while you prepare."

"Remember not to kill the necromancer unless he's a true threat," Azure said. "Even if we must use him and let him use us, as long as our lives are not at risk, he lives. Once you see what he does, you'll know he's evil, but we need a necromancer. We believe we're doing good in saving Karina from whatever purgatory she's in just beyond our wakeful perceptions."

Vance had heard enough. He held up his hands to halt the conversation. "As I said, I'm not part of your heresy. I'm just a bodyguard standing at the door."

III

Karlo returned with Marisol and two other women shortly after noon.

When he brought them into the room, Marisol immediately went to Vance and offered her wrist. "Lanie says I'm not to let you go a day without drinking. I told her you skip or postpone meals when they are on Sundays and Wednesdays. So, now you drink every day."

"Wait!" Katrina said. She stood and took each of the other women by the hand. "You won't notice or remember anyone biting anyone else. If you are bitten, it will feel like a suckling kiss." She looked back at Vance and said, "Go ahead, Vance. Do you have a preference of these two?"

Both women had blonde hair, dyed, judging by the roots. Their hair wasn't as pale as Katina's. They only had makeup around their eyes, and both had tans. They dressed skimpily for October and wore high heeled shoes.

Marisol pressed her forearm to Vance's lips. Vance bit. He took only two gulps of blood then licked the wounds closed. "Thanks, Marisol," Vance said. He couldn't really see a difference between the two women. "I'm hesitant enough to drink from women I know. I'm not a fan of drinking from women of the night."

"Don't be rude," Katina said. "These are models, no air-quotes. Karlo doesn't pick up women off the street or at the mall."

"Karlo calls model agencies looking for women who will pose nude, but won't do penetration sex shoots," Karlo said. "Karlo always asks for them to dress sexy, but he always has to change their clothes and Katina does their make-up."

"What's wrong with my make-up?" one of the girls asked.

"Nothing is wrong," Karlo said. "For what I need, it's not right. The shower is in there. There are some roman gowns on the bed. Wash everything. Katina will be in to fix your hair and start fresh with your make-up. The armor and sword are for Vance. They're real, so be careful."

"What?" asked Vance.

"You don't need to shower or change your hair," Karlo said. "Karlo will bring the armor out. The women should have their privacy to get ready."

"I'm not a model," Vance said.

"You are today." Karlo pulled a folded piece of paper from his pocket. "You're bought and paid for. Six hours of shooting, clothing at the discretion of the photographer. Did Karlo not mention the agent he spoke with was Elaine Larsen?"

"Lanie put me up to this?" Vance asked.

"She commissioned the shoot and supplied the models," Karlo said.

"She's selling a series with you as a Roman commander of a Gaelic camp. Karlo will be the director of photography. Azure will be the Gaelic sorceress who is your main adversary and main love interest."

"I couldn't be in L.A. for so long without taking acting lessons," Azure said.

"Lanie didn't tell me," Vance said.

"Not Karlo's problem," Karlo said. "The make-up will take about an hour. Maybe get comfortable and get dressed when we are ten minutes out."

"I've got nothing better to do until sunset," Vance said.

"I do," Marisol said. "I'm raiding tonight and have about a hundred potions to make." She waved a quick goodbye and left.

"She plays a lot of video games," Vance said. "It keeps her off the street."

"Vance, you should never allude to a woman that she might be a woman of the night," Karlo said. "L.A. is full of people who will have sex for money, but never say it. Karlo does not get prostitutes for food."

"We're immune to disease," Vance said.

"You want food that gets excited by sex," Katina said. "When it's a job, it's not always exciting."

"Oh," Vance said. "I pretty much only feed from Lanie and sometimes Dai has someone with her to provide blood."

"You know that won't keep you full strength," Katina said. "You can live on a pint a week, but Lanie can't keep up with even that. You need two pints per week to stay at full strength. You can get the same effect from one pint per week if it's energized with sex or fear, which I'm sure Lanie's is. But she can only feed you twice a month and it really should be only one pint per month."

"Less," Azure said. "Venae refills slower than blood regrows. If you've only fed from Lanie for the past few months, not only are you not getting much Venae to make you strong, she's not running at full strength either. Shauna tried to exclusively feed from me. I can keep her hunger at bay, but she'd never be more than a fraction of her potential power. Now that she's Elsa's sole constant companion, Shauna feeds every night because Elsa feeds every night."

"Shauna?" Vance asked.

"Yes, I'm a council member's pet," Azure said. "And we do see each other once a week to exchange blood. We pick a city, and both fly there and have a day together. Occasionally Elsa and Jackie—I mean Katina—join us. That's weird. I haven't slipped like that in months."

"Mistress!" Karlo called from the bedroom. "Your girls are ready to have their hair done."

"Excuse me," Katina said. She hopped over the back of the couch and glided into the bedroom.

"If you want your blood sex charged, you should go in there in about five minutes," Azure said.

"You know that's not me," Vance said.

"We figured," Azure said. "We have a backup plan. Shauna hasn't taken more than an ounce from me in months. You should feed from me."

"Are you sure?" Vance asked.

"I'm very sure," Azure said. "I'll warn you, though, after ten to fifteen seconds, I'm going to start shaking. It's good for you, though. My blood will be very charged after that."

"You were coerced to get too much pleasure from a bite?" Vance asked.

"Reilla has a sick sense of humor," Azure said. "Shauna couldn't coerce me herself, so she had Reilla do it. Normally a pet is told to feel a bite as pleasant, maybe pleasurable. Reilla used a different word, one that starts with an 'O'."

"I get it," Vance said. "I won't drink much. Three, maybe four ounces sound okay?"

"No," Azure said. "Get your fill, a full pint. This is going to feel odd for you, but I've had Lanie and Dai's permission to feed you, knowing what it does to me, since we first met. It's not just permission to feed you, you know what I mean? Lanie has an odd price. She wants pictures of me, awfully specific poses, very specific absence of clothing."

"Lanie is funny that way," Vance said. "I think you're just her type."

"Exotic and bisexual?" Azure asked.

"Yeah," Vance said.

"And that's not your type?" Azure asked.

"I'm never sure what to do when Dai and Lanie are both in bed with me," Vance said. "I prefer one-on-one time and as pretty and interesting as you are, I don't stray from the two women I have."

"Lanie told me I could have you if I could convince you," Azure said. "She seemed sure I couldn't."

"She's right," Vance said.

"Feed first, pictures after?" Azure said.

Vance nodded. Despite expecting what would come when he fed, he underestimated Azure's response.

§

Vance had finished his part of the photoshoot an hour before sunset. He sat at the bar of the kitchenette, out of sight of the living room, and sipped occasionally from a glass of wine. When Lanie showed up, Vance was about to pour himself a third glass.

"Azure's naked in the living room," he said. "I think everyone is naked by now. We finished our shoot an hour ago and the girls had been booked for three more hours. Since they contracted to shoot nude, I'm sure they are.

Their clothes were already falling off, no longer covering anything above the belt, by the time my part of the shoot ended."

"My poor boy!" Lanie said. "Seriously, I feel bad for you. I know it made you uncomfortable."

"I can handle it when I'm on camera," Vance said. "Then I can focus on playing my part. When I'm not on camera, it feels..." Vance looked for a better way to way it, but Lanie had nailed it. "Yeah, uncomfortable is the right word."

Lanie faced Vance, but her eyes kept darting toward the hall leading to the living room.

"Go on," Vance said. "Go be your voyeuristic self."

"Do you mind if I take pictures with my phone?" Lanie asked.

"Why ask me?" Vance asked. "You need their permission, not mine."

"They signed a contract," Lanie said. "You might not like me having naked pictures of random women on my phone."

"Just go," Vance said. "I'm not going to judge. I already know you like to look at naked women."

From his education as a preacher, he saw pornography as an evil. In counseling, if it came up, he'd been taught to treat it like an addictive substance. It's something to coach against and, if it caused problems in someone's life, he'd arrange an intervention. Like most of the vices, he'd been trained to speak loudly against it before the masses and be quiet and compassionate when encountering it on a personal level.

Lanie returned after ten minutes. "It's not as intense as it could be. Karlo is shooting fully artistic now. So, it's rated R stuff, nothing X-rated."

"Bored you so quickly?" Vance asked.

"Filled the memory on my phone," Lanie said. "Without a legit purpose to be in the room, like taking pictures, I just felt weird."

"If you offered to join in the photos, I'm sure Karlo would find a way to include you," Vance said.

"I don't have the self-control to be so close to a beautiful body and not touch it," Lanie said. "At least, I think I don't. I've never tried it. Doesn't matter, really. Everything Karlo shoots, today, I get a copy."

"Katina invited me here to help her resurrect her sister," Vance said.

"That would be awesome," Lanie said. "All religious and philosophical implications aside, Katina really is half a person without her sister. Of the twins, Katina was the romantic, the fun one. Karina was the business-before-pleasure type, and she ran the most complex financial entity in the world."

"Katina seems like I expect most uber-vamps to be—bored with life," Vance said.

Lanie said. "She's lost a lot of her passion. So much so, that Katina doesn't even go with Azure when she travels to get blood from her vamp and that vampire is Katina's lover."

"I know," Vance said. "I've seen them together more than a dozen times."

"Recently?" Lanie asked.

"Four or five months ago would be the last time," Vance said. "I see through Katina's eyes less and less. I guess that is a sign of depression."

"That's why she needs her sister back," Lanie said. "That's why you're helping."

"I've agreed to protect them, but not to take part in their magic," Vance said.

"That's obviously how they meant for you to help," Lanie said. "I half expected you to turn them down outright."

"I don't judge. People lose siblings, even twins," Vance said. "I think there are better ways to grieve and treat depression. I don't think raising the dead is the right thing to do. I'm helping because I promised to repay a favor."

"You need to care about the cause, or you won't help enough," Lanie said. Karina and Katina are closer than most twins. And I'm not talking about their incestuous sexual relationship. They've been together for two centuries, never spending more than a few hours away from each other, and those hours were rare. That whole time, they were bonded as pets with Elsa. They didn't just share the pet bond with Elsa, they shared it with each other."

"So, you're saying if ever there was a case where someone needed to be brought back, this is it?" Vance asked.

"Yes," Lanie said. "And just to know such power can be held in the hands of mortals is awesome."

"I think it's heresy," Vance said. "All magic is, I guess. I don't really know what to do with heresy. Magic is supposed to be the power of the devil, but I don't believe in the devil. Certainly, practicing magic is a sin. Is it a sin to someone who doesn't believe what I believe?"

"It's big of you to recognize what other people do isn't always your concern," Lanie said.

"If this involves any form of human sacrifice, I'm going to stop it," Vance said. "I hope they know that."

"They know that," Lanie said. "If I understand, the necromancer is exactly the kind of person to use magic that requires a human sacrifice."

"How much do you know about what they asked me?" Vance asked. "Did they ask you before they asked me?"

"They got it all checked out with Dai and Thalia before they came to you," Lanie said. "I happened to be at that meeting. It was before Thalia and Dai had their falling-out."

"Yeah, you seem to be working for Dai. You haven't mentioned that," Vance said.

"Lawyer work. She has me on retainer for a couple projects," Lanie said. "It's not full time by any means, but it's enough to give me capital to cover the demo recordings of some of my acts. Anyone can record on a home computer but having a studio to record in makes a difference. A professional producer can make the difference between booking two-hundred-dollar gigs and two thousand dollar gigs. I have Dire Monotony on a West Coast tour. They like making enough money to cover food and gas and still have enough left to stay in a hotel with clean sheets."

"I haven't heard much of them," Vance said. "Then again, music isn't my business anymore, just yours. All you've really discussed with me is the Fiona Malady tribute record. How's that coming?"

"We're done," Lanie said. "We have her last album coming out next week. It's a collection of records she made in her heyday that were never released and some B-sides. We're giving that three months before we put out the tribute album. I wanted to put them both out together, but it turns out I'm only getting a manager's cut since her old studio still owns all the recordings. I don't have any say when the album gets released."

"Hey!" Katina came into the kitchen wearing a bathrobe. She carried a duffle bag and a long case. "Dai dropped this off for you last night. It's a change of clothes. She included both a sheriff uniform and some casual wear. She wasn't sure what we'd need you for. There's a tux hanging in the closet, too. We need a sheriff, I think."

"If I'm carrying a gun, I want to be wearing a badge," Vance said. "I assume the rifle is in that case. The badge won't go far to explain a sniper rifle, but it might help."

"Get dressed," Katina said. "Spend a minute to get to know the gun. It's laser sighted and as dead-on as it can be. You have twelve bullets, all laser-cut to a precise, perfect, shape, so at seven-hundred yards, you should see less than an inch variance. Thalia vouches for the gun. House Artemis, your house, is an authority on weapons, especially rifles and other hunting weapons. You have a reputation to live up to, but being only twenty-some years old, you need more time to gain wisdom. Lucky for you, almost no one knows you're one of Artemis' descendants."

"The people that care to keep track of bloodlines think I'm descended from Zylpha," Vance said. "Now that I know what that means, and knowing Zylpha, I resent not being able to tell people my true lineage."

"I know what Zylpha did to you was evil," Katina said. "I'm not a fan or a friend of hers. When dealing with elders, always remember they have values from another era. You cannot judge them by modern morality. I'm absolutely certain Artemis has left a larger body count in her wake than Zylpha."

"Artemis hunts," Vance said. "Zylpha murders. I try not to judge because I have to rationalize who I am, who Artemis is. But I know Artemis does not kill innocent people. Everyone she kills has done something to deserve it, at least from her perspective. Zylpha slaughtered a hundred people whose only sin was being associated with me."

"You have a valid grudge against her. She hates me almost as much as she hates you, maybe more," Katina said. "We stole some of her slaves, a few million dollars' worth. Most of that was Marisol. It's hard to give a girl extensive sexual training and have her remain virginal. Zylpha charges a lot for them. Well, she used to. Zylpha is out of business thanks to Shauna and Laura."

"I haven't heard that full story," Vance said.

"I'll tell you later," Katina said. "For now, get dressed. Get to know the gun. Did you find a spot?"

"I did," Vance said. "One of the buildings adjacent to that parking lot is abandoned. The three-year-old street view shows the same 'For Lease' sign that's on the building now. It's closer than I'd like, but I should be able to set up behind an open window. The whole north side, the side facing the parking lot, has windows and many are already broken."

"That rifle will work at such a close range?" Katina asked.

"The scope dials in," Vance said.

"Good," Katina said. "Azure would say that you should double tap the necromancer if he even looks like he's going to ensorcel us. I would say we can't afford to kill him. Ultimately, it's going to be your call to make. No one really knows how much power a necro will have over a vampire. Mages know less about necromancers than they know about vampires. Azure's mage knowledge is whatever her parents taught her and what she's learned from a local air mage she'd met. Stephanie seems more knowledgeable than most. She's the local quartermaster, which means she runs the kind of back-alley occult bookstore you only see in movies."

"Really?" Lanie asked. "Does she sell stuff like 'eye of newt and frog tails?"

Katina laughed. "Maybe. It's a ten-foot by ten-foot space in her basement in Beverly Hills," Katina said. "It's crammed full of pickling jars and books. It's not the kind of store you just walk into and browse. Did I mention it's in Beverly Hills? It's not the kind of neighborhood you hang a shingle over your back door in." She nodded back to the living room. "I've got to put on clothes. If you need to shower, use the one in the left bedroom. Karlo has the models in the other shower."

"Still taking pictures?" Lanie asked.

"If he is, he's not using his cameras. They're still in the living room." Katina winked and went back into the suite.

"Let's take that shower," Lanie said. "You smell like those models and I like you best when you smell like you. I like when you smell like Dai, but mostly I like you to smell like you."

IV

Los Angeles did not treat abandoned buildings well. The electricity in the building didn't work. Anywhere Vance expected to find a light switch, he found a gaping hole. All the wiring had been stripped. The drywall had been torn out anywhere wiring may have been. Vance walked through the office section of the building, trying to find a window that offered a wide view of the parking lot and had already been broken. As bad as the walls were, the bathrooms were worse. Someone had cleaned any debris from the floor, but left the damage. The windows provided all the light Vance needed. As a vampire, he could see fine in very low light. Outside, in the moonlight, the world seemed as bright as it had seemed during the day when Vance had been human.

The offices had modern, double-paned, insulated windows. Many were cracked but none broken through. Not wanting to cause unnecessary damage, he kept looking for a window that had already been broken. He left the office section and entered onto a catwalk above the production floor. Unlike the rest of the building, the floor was covered in red plastic cups, glittery confetti and long-dead glow sticks. The building had hosted a massive party.

An area of the floor had been swept clear. A large white circle adorned the floor. Inscribed within the circle was a six-pointed star. Where the points of the star touched the circle, other, smaller circles were drawn outside the large circle. The smaller circles were maybe a yard across, big enough for a person to stand in. The larger circle had a diameter of several yards. Vance took a picture of the diagram and sent it to Azure. "This is on the floor of the building I'm in. I suspect you'll be invited to come in after you meet in the parking lot."

"We won't be needing you tonight," Azure replied. "Probably not, anyway. That is not a valid pentagram."

"Obviously not. It has six points." Vance texted.

"Pentagram is generic for any inscribed circle. The problem is the central star is a Star of David. While I won't say the Star of David isn't a potent symbol, it's inappropriate for use as a floor pentagram. A true pentagram must be inscribed by a single, continuous line."

Vance tried but couldn't imagine anything but a squiggly line working out that way. "How do you do that with six points?"

Azure responded with two pictures. The first had a hexagon inscribed in a circle. The second had what looked like a flower with six petals. "Either we're dealing with amateurs or someone pretending to be an amateur." The text followed the picture.

"I'll stick around, just to be sure." Vance hit send then looked for a place to conceal himself but let him remain in sight of the circle. The office section had been built as a building within a building. It had a roof that didn't quite reach the ceiling of the outer building. Vance flew up and cleared a space to lay down. He checked to ensure he could support the rifle at the edge of the roof and still see the whole circle through the scope. After adjusting the scope to the right distance, he pulled the rifle back. It would be visible while he shot or prepared to. When they entered, he would need to stay hidden.

After arranging the spot inside and ensuring the rifle had a round chambered, he went back down to the catwalk and watched the parking lot.

Azure and Katina arrived first and waited inside their car. Shortly thereafter, a woman arrived and parked her car near Azure's. She got out and went over to talk to Azure, who'd opened her window. Two more cars and a panel van arrived. Three people emerged from the car and two from the panel van. The people from the van wore black hooded robes. The woman who'd been talking to Azure went to her car, pulled a robe from her passenger seat and began pulling it on. The other three gathered robes from their car's trunk and likewise donned them. Around the waist, each of the robes had a different color sash. Vance saw red, blue, yellow, green, purple and orange. The six headed toward the building with the woman who'd been talking to Azure, waving for her to follow. Azure and Katina got out of their car and entered the building behind the robed people.

The first man in the building, the one wearing the robe with the purple sash, set a thick three-ring binder on a counter then headed to the symbol. The six, three men and three women, pulled their robes over their heads as they went to the circle. Each stood in one of the smaller circles. They raised their hands to their shoulders, palms out, facing forward.

Azure and Katina stopped about twenty feet from the circle. Katina looked up at Vance and said, "Yeah, I don't think you'll need the gun." She had a way to speak so that only the person she spoke to would hear her. She wouldn't have said that so that anyone else could hear.

The robed people barely glanced towards Azure and Katina. They each stared straight ahead. The man wearing the purple sash spoke. "Let us begin the ritual of bindings." He pulled a whiskey flask from his robe and unscrewed the cap. "We share this drink to bind us as one." He took a swig and then walked around the circle to the next robed figure and handed them the flask. He then returned to his spot.

The next person, a woman, said, "We share this drink to bind us." She then drank from the flask and walked it to the next person.

The ritual continued around the circle until the originator took the flask and tucked it back inside his robe.

"Now, let us call the six winds," the purple-sashed man said. "Stephanie, you may lead this one."

Vance didn't understand the words. They sounded musical, nothing like a chant, more like a birdsong. Stephanie intoned her spell and the others tried to repeat it.

"North wind!" the man in purple called.

Though Vance didn't feel the wind from where he lay, he saw the robes of the six rustle. Three more times the lead mage called, "South wind!", "East wind!", "West wind!". Each time the robes rustled with the breeze.

"Cold winds!" The robes barely moved, but Vance felt the air chill just a little, though he considered the effect of that one could have been psychosomatic.

"Winds of change!" the man called. A breeze strong enough for Vance to feel rolled across the room, blowing each of the robed figures' hoods off.

The mages seemed real enough to Vance. He peered over the edge toward Azure, who was whispering to Katina.

"Stephanie is an air mage," Katina said to Vance's ear. "That was all her doing."

"Does anyone have any rituals they need tonight?" the man with the purple sash asked.

The woman in the orange sash said, "I'm heading to Vegas this weekend. Do you know a ritual for luck?"

"I know the ritual," the man with the purple sash said. "With hands clasped over our heads, repeat after me, in unison, seven times: Mercurius invocabo! Dona no is fortuna!"

The six held their hands together over their heads and intoned the words, as a group, seven times.

"That seemed selfish," the woman in the blue sash said.

"Step away from the circle for debate," the purple-sashed man said. The six each took a step straight back.

Immediately, the woman in the blue sash said, "I don't think we should ask for help with gambling."

"It's not like this is real," the man in the green sash said, pulling his hood back. "I can see how the air vents are aimed toward the circle. It's a fun game, but it's just for fun."

The woman in orange chuckled. "Hey, anything helps!"

Vance looked for air vents. He didn't see anything to indicate they aimed anywhere near the circle. The man in green deluded himself to explain what he didn't comprehend. The phenomenon of human rationalization was one of the chief reasons vampires managed to keep their existence a secret.

"Just because we are untrained, which makes our powers weak, doesn't mean it's not real," the man with the red sash said. "Alexander knows what he's doing. The wind is real. There isn't even power in this building to operate a fan. When we're ready for the great ritual, this won't seem so fake anymore." He turned to the man in the purple sash. "Right, Alexander?"

"My translations are nearly complete," Alexander said. He went to the counter and picked up the binder. "This has everything we need to gain near-infinite power in each of our elements."

"May I see?" Azure asked.

"I haven't shown anyone," Alexander said. "Until I publish my findings, I'm keeping this a secret."

"This is Stephanie's friend, Azure," Katina said. "I'm Katina. You can trust us. Show us. We're experts." Vance had no way to perceive that Katina used her vampiric coercion on the man with the purple sash, but Vance would have in her shoes, so he assumed she had.

"Some expert advice would be welcome but, don't tell anyone about this," Alexander said. He slowly handed the book to Azure. "No taking pictures with your phone, please."

She opened the book. It contained dozens, maybe hundreds, of plastic sleeves, each with a photograph. Vance couldn't see the pictures from where he watched.

"You hardly have any language notes," Azure said.

"Don't tell them." Alexander nodded behind him toward the other people wearing robes. "I'm writing a paper focusing simply on the existence of this language. It predates any known written language by twenty thousand years, at least. "We may never translate it. You know, if we hadn't found the Rosetta Stone, we never would have deciphered hiero…"

Katina put her finger up close to Alexander's face, interrupting him. "I can read this," she said.

"Some kind of Russian?" Azure asked.

"No," Katina said. "This is a language Vance, Shauna and Reilla would know. Do you get me?"

"What do you mean? You know this language?" Alexander asked. "I image searched every one of those pictographs and nothing came up on the net except one of the pictographs came up on some vampire fan site. Most likely a coincidence. This language doesn't exist today. You're lying to me."

"I wish I were," Katina said. "The writing is backwards. Was this an etching? Do you have the stone?"

"An etching?" Alexander pondered. "I hadn't thought of that. It's possibly a relief of clay writing or some softer stone. The stone is solid volcanic basalt twenty meters long and three meters high. It's in a cave in Southern Syria. Only I and two assistants know where. I trust you two, but I won't tell you where the cave is. Seeing it as a mold of a softer rock makes so much sense. People at that time didn't have tools to carve basalt, but maybe clay or softer stone."

"You go ahead and think on that and I'll be right back." Katina pulled her phone out and set it to her ear. Vance heard her speaking directly to him again. "We don't have to kill them all. We may have to kill the archeologist. I'm going to show you what he has so you understand why."

Katina put her phone away then went back to where Azure and Alexander stood. Azure held the book, closed, under one arm. Stephanie had joined them and asked Azure if she was impressed.

"Sure was," Azure said. "But it's nothing compared to what I can do. Let me show you what you might be able to do, someday. Gather your friends for a demonstration."

"Hey guys!" Stephanie yelled. "My friend, Azure, wants to show us some actual magic."

"What's she gonna do?" one of the men asked.

"I love your hair," the woman with the orange sash said. "You've got to give me the name of your stylist."

"Thanks," Azure said.

Katina made grand gestures with her hands, ending with both hands pointing at Azure. "Keep your eyes on the girl with the blue hair. Keep your eyes on the girl with the blue hair."

She'd said it twice. If Katina just coerced all six of them, Vance was impressed.

"I'm going to summon a celebrity," Azure said. Vance realized she meant him. Azure proceeded to start chanting and doing some writhing form of dancing. As she did, while all eyes were on her, Vance hopped off the office building and landed in the circle.

"Behold!" Katina shouted and pointed at the circle. "We've summoned Sheriff Vance Starr!"

Several of the robed people gasped. Stephanie asked, "How the fuck did you do that?" Of the six members of the circle, only she knew what to expect from actual magic. Summoning actors didn't seem to fit her expectation of possible.

"I'll teach my secrets in a few minutes. Until then, I actually have legal business with the sheriff." Azure said.

"He's an actor," the woman with the orange sash said.

"Mr. Silver is a Los Angeles County sheriff, too," Katina said. "That badge on his shirt is real."

Vance played it up, walking over with his hands on his belt to join Azure and Katina. "Yes," he said. "I'm many things; actor and sheriff are among those things."

Most of the robed people moved away from them, giving them space to talk. Stephanie stayed. "Seriously, how did you do that?"

"I didn't do anything," Azure said. "Katina is an expert stage illusionist's assistant."

"We'll explain in a minute," Katina said. "For now, we need to figure out what our next step is. This sham of a coven is not what we were hoping for."

"I think it's entirely amusing," Stephanie said. "Alexander actually found something of archeological value. I have no idea if it has any value to the mage community. I've never managed to peek inside his book for more than a split second."

Katina paged through it. "I can confirm the book, and the stone in the pictures, are important. They're far too important to be left in the hands of this ilk."

"You're going to steal it?" Stephanie asked. "That's not the only copy, you know. He has it all on his computer at his office at UCLA. You could certainly run off with that copy and no one would be put out. It's not like you're out to publish his findings under your name, is it?"

"If The Pentacle knew of this, they'd wipe Alexander's mind, or maybe have him killed," Azure said. "It's not terribly hard to find someone who can translate this. This isn't a dead language, just a secret one."

"It's a secret I have to keep," Katina said. "For what it's worth, I'm sorry for what's about to happen."

"Should I be scared?" Stephanie asked.

"No," Vance said. "No one's in any danger."

Katina looked at him, tilted her head, and sighed. "I suppose I can think of something that isn't fatal. They are ignorant as to what they have. I'll be back." She went to where three of the mages were talking and had a brief conversation with them. When they parted ways, the three headed out of the building, laughing. She returned to join Vance, Azure and Stephanie.

"Call those two over," Katina said. "It's time to reveal the secret of our spell."

"Hey, Kim, Alexander!" Stephanie called. "Azure is ready to tell us how she summoned Vance Starr."

"What are we going to tell them?" Vance asked.

"The truth," Azure said.

Alexander and Kim, the woman in the robes with the blue sash, joined them.

"Are you done with my book?" Alexander asked.

"Let's talk magic first," Azure said. "This is going to disappoint you, but it was a simple misdirect illusion. Vance simply came out from where he was hiding while your back was turned. Katina did her job and made sure your eyes stayed on me."

"It's all in the gesture," Katina said. "Keep the hands waving, like jazz hands, and people don't look away. You think you're watching the magician, but you're really focused on me pointing to the magician. In this case, since Vance emerged from hiding behind you, it worked easily."

"Damn," Alexander said. "Now I feel like a fool for believing you actually did something magical. How did we do the wind?"

"Battery-powered fans," Stephanie said. "I have the remote in my pocket."

"Yep," Alexander said. "I'm a fool."

"Kim," Katina said. "You feel like a fool, too. It's time to put this foolishness behind you and laugh it off and find another hobby, another social group. When you think back on this, you'll chuckle and then think of something else. Now, go home."

Kimberly laughed, doubling over. When she could breathe without gasping, she said, "I can't believe I thought this might actually be something mystical. I'm going back to real life. Enjoy your live action role-playing." She kept chuckling as she left.

"Who's next," Katina asked. "Stephanie?"

"What the heck?" Stephanie asked. "I didn't realize you were one of us." She stepped away from Katina. "Holy crap! You aren't using magic. You're…"

"Don't go anywhere," Katina said, interrupting Stephanie. "Say nothing until Alexander leaves."

Stephanie clenched her fists and glared at Azure.

"Hypnotic suggestion?" Alexander ventured,

"Kind of," Katina said. 'That, actually, was a kind of magic. Real magic. Katina bit her thumb and then stuck it past Alexander's lips. She grabbed his cheeks and forced him to look at her eyes. "The stone, it turns out, was a 19th century hoax. Nothing more than some Syrian village trying to gain international fame. You're going to file this whole project away as a bad lead and move on to something else you are interested in. This whole magic business is nothing more than an amusing mistake. Laugh it off and go home."

Alexander tore his robe off and threw it on the ground. "How silly is it that I actually believe in this crap?" He seemed more frustrated than amused as he left. His chuckles seemed forced.

"Azure, you told me Katina was a muggle." Stephanie glared at Katina then stepped away from her and hid behind Vance.

"Muggle?" Vance asked. "You actually use that Harry Potter terminology?"

"Some do," Azure said. "At least, since the movies came out. The word didn't exist before J.K. Rowling invented it. It's common enough slang in many subcultures to describe people who aren't part of their subculture."

"Azure didn't really lie," Katina said. "I'm not a mage. I'm a vampire."

"Well this sucks," Stephanie said. "We're not supposed to interact with vampires, Azure. Are you a traitor to our kind or is she a traitor to hers?"

"I guess I'm the one defying the rules," Azure said. "I'm no traitor, however."

"Except, she's going to eat me, isn't she?" Stephanie said. "I'm going to fight back. I don't know if Azure told you, but I'm among the three most potent air mages on the West Coast. You wouldn't even know we're fighting. You'd be in your happiest dream world and I'd be doing whatever I wanted to. And then you might wake up or you might starve before your mind lets go of your fantasy. We could just skip the fight and all agree to go our separate ways."

"You're safe," Azure said. "Vamps have to keep their secret, but mages already know of them, so killing you to keep the secret is like trying to plug the hole in the titanic with a Band-Aid."

"Vance wouldn't let me kill you anyway," Katina said. "For now, I'm just telling you to not discuss, in any way, with anyone but the three of us, what you learned here tonight. And trust Azure, she's still a good friend."

"I guess this is where I go home," Stephanie said.

"You're clear," Vance said. "As far as I'm concerned, mages and vampires can continue to pretend the other doesn't exist."

Stephanie backed away and then sprinted out the door.

"Would Dai have killed them all?" Vance asked.

"I don't know Dai as well as you, Vance," Katina said. "I don't know any vampires, royals or otherwise, who would kill six people just for seeing some of our written language. The word 'vampire' never came up for most of them. I know a few that wouldn't have let Stephanie leave alive, but Dai isn't known for killing humans. She's known for killing more vampires than any living vampire."

"Top of that list?" Vance asked. "I know she's killed maybe two hundred vamps."

"Particularly bloodthirsty royals may have body counts around fifty," Katina said. "Few vamps who aren't royals get to kill more than one vampire before spending the day in sunlight. Even John Bertellus, between he and his minions, very notoriously decimated Europe, killing around a hundred and twenty vampires. Human killing, Vlad Dracula wins hands down. He might even give Dai a run for money in terms of vampire body count. Though, in the vampire culling, he took more of a leadership role and didn't personally bloody his hands."

"Now you're making me feel like a notorious vampire killer," Vance said.

"Vance Silver, vampire hunter," Katina said. "People who know you think of you as a killer. People who don't know you fear you because you're a vampire killer. Ninety-nine percent of vampires live their entire existence, from creation until their death which, for most vampires is suicide by dawn, without dealing with life-threatening violence."

"Dai tells me, the most common cause of death for vampires is at the hands of another vampire," Vance said.

Katina gave Vance a little nod and shrug. "I guess, from her personal experience, that's true. Every vampire I've known who has died, has died from a sword or by getting strapped to a royal's roof. Well, I did see one get drained dry, which will also kill a vamp."

"We should go," Azure said. "Vance, keep the gun. When we find the real necromancer, bring it with you."

Vance flew up and grabbed the rifle. He removed the magazine and cleared the chambered round before putting it in the case. He then texted Lanie, "I'm ready for pickup."

"I'm parked outside," Lanie replied.

When Vance emerged from the building he found Lanie leaning against her motorcycle. The gun case was over four feet long and a foot wide. Vance immediately saw a problem.

"That's not going to fit in my trunk," Lanie said.

"I can fly," Vance said. "I'm one of two people who can give me permission to do that in the city, right?"

"Just hold it in your lap, tight against my back," Lanie said. "I'll deal with the additional drag. We're going to Nocturne, and I know you don't want to fly near there. You might accidentally see Hallows."

"I think I could see it again," Vance said. "I mean, we didn't leave the burned hulk of a building there, right?"

"Yeah," Lanie said. "We didn't leave the ruins. Too much liability."

Vance got on the bike and, as Lanie suggested, held the rifle case between them. The ride to Dai's theatre normally took them past Hallows, but Lanie got off the highway an exit early and meandered through the city until she parked the bike in the alley behind the Nocturne.

V

Vance tried not to look, but two buildings down, where Hallows used to stand, someone had built a new building already. "Wow," Vance said. "Whoever you sold the lot to got an apartment complex up already."

"I know," Lanie said. "Remind me to introduce you to the new owner. He's a pretty decent guy."

"I don't know that I could deal with seeing something that's not Hallows in Hallows spot any easier than I could deal with Hallows as a pile of black burned brick."

"For as much as it affects you, you don't talk about it much," Lanie said.

"I don't know why it affects me so much," Vance said. "I don't know how to talk about it. I just know I don't want to talk about it." He got to the back door of Dai's theatre and realized he couldn't get in. The locks were new, and his key wouldn't work. The new system seemed to be a small scanner. "Is this an eye scanner?"

Lanie put her thumb over the scanner. The door clicked. "Retinal scanners are terribly expensive. Fingerprints are just as secure and far cheaper." Once she opened the door, she pulled out her phone. "Wait a sec," she said as she navigated through her apps. She pointed to the scanner and said, "Okay, put your thumb on until the light turns green. Pull it off and, when the light turns red, do it again. Five times."

When Vance finished, Lanie said, "That'll work for the trapdoor on the roof as well. Come on."

Pushing past a red velvet curtain, they emerged from backstage onto the stage. Two thrones sat overlooking the audience seats. Other than Lanie and Vance, the room was empty.

"Dai's downstairs," Vance said. He had a bond with her, and being so close, he could feel exactly where she stood as clearly as he could tell where Lanie was. He also could see a bright pinpoint of light in his mind where he sensed her. Another light stood next to Dai. Thalia or Katina could be with her. Vance leaned the rifle case against the back of his chair. He could think of Dai's as a throne, and collectively they were thrones, but singly, his was just a chair.

"How does Dai explain my absence to the vamps of the kingdom?" Vance asked.

"The events at Hallows hit you pretty hard and you needed time to come to terms with what happened," Lanie said. "This is the twenty-first century. We don't need to pussyfoot around the fact that people have emotions."

"Do you know who's downstairs with Dai?" Vance asked.

38

"You're the one with all the extra senses," Lanie said. "I just expect Dai, Cynthia and six Russian women."

"The women in the cargo container are Russian?" Vance asked. "If I'd known that, I'd have invited Katina to come talk to them."

"If you can see another vamp down there, knowing that Dai also has Katina's phone number, I would bet we'll find Katina and Azure down there too." Lanie said. "You know how to solve this mystery?"

Vance smiled and kissed Lanie. He then went downstairs. Cynthia stood by the door of the green room. Inside. Vance heard several frantic voices in a language he assumed was Russian. "Is that Katina? Is she arguing with the women?" Vance asked Cynthia.

"I have no idea," Cynthia said. "Despite what you may think, all Russians don't speak English if you talk loud and slow. One of them studied English for a year in school. The rest don't. Katina got here five minutes before you. She's only been in there for one or two minutes. I have no idea if that's arguing, frantic storytelling, or singing."

"Funny," Lanie said. "That's mostly complaining with some arguing. I don't speak Russian, but no one in there is happy."

"If none of them speak English and Dai isn't letting them leave, they still think they're prisoners," Vance said.

"Which is probably why Dai called in Katina," Cynthia said.

The voices in the room got louder. Among the cacophony of several voices, Vance could make out Katina's.

Dai came out into the hall. "What are you doing out here?" She grabbed Vance by the arm and pulled him into the room. The room got quieter for a moment, but not entirely. Two women were still nose-to-nose with Katina, screaming at her. Katina spoke calmly but didn't seem to be getting anywhere.

Two of the other four women came over to Vance and started screaming at him, punctuating sentences with hits to his shoulders. They were gesturing for him to leave.

"Dance," Katina said. Her voice rang clearly in his mind, overriding all the cacophony.

Vance stared at Katina. She didn't know him well if she thought he knew how to dance. He knew one waltz, but this didn't seem the right stage for that.

"Pose your arms like a bodybuilder, flex your biceps and gyrate your hips," Katina said to him. "Think male stripper."

"I don't know what that is," Vance said.

"Think belly dancer," Katina said. "You don't have to be good, though it'd help. You just have to be suggestive."

Vance took a deep breath and flexed his arms. He spread his feet apart and gyrated. He felt very awkward, but he tried to keep a confident smile. He didn't have to fake the confidence long. Within a few seconds, two of the women were dancing with him and the other four gazed on silently.

"What's happening?" Vance asked.

"No one ever told you that vampire dances fascinate in a very profound way?" Katina asked, again speaking just to him.

"I think your dancing is entrancing them," Dai said.

"Neither of you know about this?" Katina asked aloud.

"I'm not the dancing type," Dai said. "I learned three waltzes as a teenager but haven't danced since. By the time I met anyone to be a mentor, they assumed I knew most of the basics. Thalia taught me a few new tricks, but this isn't one of them."

"Now I can get enough focus from them to calm them." Katina went to each woman and said something in Russian. Most didn't keep her gaze beyond the words, choosing instead to look at Vance. The two that were dancing with him wouldn't look at Katina at all.

Relieved to have a reason to stop, Vance slowed his dancing until he just stood there staring one of the women in the eyes. Katina managed to squeeze between them and repeat the words Vance didn't understand.

The women talked with Katina for a few minutes, but they frequently came to points where Katina would struggle for words, often falling back on English, but that didn't seem to work any better. Just as often, she'd make the Russian women say things in other ways.

"Is Karlo back with the coffee?" Katina asked.

"He's no…" Dai started to say.

"Karlo is here!" he yelled as if he were saving the day by his presence. He squeezed past Dai into the room, deftly carrying two fast-food coffee holders, each with four large cups. Karlo had only gone a few blocks to a burger place, and not one that had aspirations as a bistro. "All black," Karlo said. "I have sugar packets in my pockets."

"They don't speak English," Vance said.

Karlo then said something in Russian. From the reactions of the girls, he was telling them about the coffee.

"You speak Russian?" Katina asked.

"Lovely Katina spends so little time with Karlo, he gets bored. Karlo's been taking classes, online at first and with a private tutor, a grad student. She teaches Karlo Russian and Karlo teaches the tutor what he knows best." He wiggled his hips suggestively.

"You're teaching her photography?" Katina asked.

Karlo shrugged. "Of course. What did you think Karlo was talking about?"

The women said something in Russian to Karlo and he responded with a lengthy explanation, also in Russian. He still frequently used his own name.

"I didn't realize Russian had changed so much," Katina said. "I thought when I grew up, Russian, as a language, was becoming concrete, nearly finished developing with the advent of Peter's alphabet. I haven't really kept up, apparently. I made it through Anna Karenina in the first Russian edition. This is not that language."

"Your words are mostly right," Karlo said. "You have many archaic words. Soviet Union standardized it more than anything. Modern communications, like it did with English, erased many local accents, though your accent had probably been dead for far longer. Karlo learned everything he could about it. Karlo can speak modern Russian and Karlo can speak the Russian you speak in your sleep."

"These women don't seem to realize they were kidnapped and about to be shipped off into the world of sex traffickers," Katina said. "They keep denying they were going anywhere. They say they are from here. The binder of documents we found in the truck would seem to back that claim. They're excellent forgeries."

Karlo spoke with the women for only a minute or two and then spoke with Katina again. "The women aren't going anywhere," he said. "They arrived from Russia yesterday. They didn't travel in the container. They travelled on an old yacht, one with sails. They were treated very well and promised good jobs as private dancers when they arrived. They seem to think this will lead them to marrying rich American men or at least, becoming the kept mistress of rich American men."

One of the women started talking again, getting more excited and raising her voice as she talked. Katina managed to calm her, but she didn't stop with her long tirade.

"She says they're not stupid. They know they're whores. It's better to be a whore to one rich man than to be a whore to three or four men every night," Karlo said. "They have a hard case of Pretty Woman syndrome."

"I don't know what to say to that," Vance said. "If they wanted to be prostitutes, maybe we didn't actually save them."

"God, Vance!" Dai yelled. "I know Lanie thinks that some prostitutes have the right to choose that life. These women clearly would get Lanie's approval."

"Umm…" Lanie said from the hall. "I didn't…"

"I'm not finished," Dai said. "This isn't my business. I have Petra and her pet to deal with, and these women are here because you brought them here. I respect your need to fix this, and I'll help, but only if you actually fix this. These are not women who know they have choices. They're all young, not one over twenty?" Dai asked, looking at Karlo.

Karlo asked something in Russian. After each woman gave a short response, most of them saying the same thing, he nodded to Dai.

"See, too young to know what they could be," Dai said. "Karlo, could you use some full-time models, perhaps create a modeling team or whatever they call it?"

"Karlo will do this," he said. He explained to the women.

"Tell them it won't involve any sex," Katina said.

"What did you think Karlo started with?" Karlo said. "This will not involve sex, but you will all have good jobs. That's what Karlo said. Dai, are you paying for this?"

"Hell, no," Dai said. "I'm a financial consultant. I don't actually invest my own money in this kind of thing."

"I'll cover it," Katina said. "Well, Elsa will cover it. We share accounts, but it's all her money. I just get to use it."

Vance nodded. He lived in a similar situation with a debit card from the John Harker Trust. He didn't know whose money it was. Lanie called it his, but he had no idea where it came from beyond it being a trust from the hunter organization that had recruited him out of college.

"Cynthia!" Dai called. When Cynthia popped up at the door, Dai said, "Work with Karlo and see if these women know anything about Douglas."

"Dougal," Vance said.

"Human matters," Dai said derisively. "Not that I'm one to talk. I have to go deal with a room of idiot humans to finalize some real estate problems I've been having. I hate zoning petitions. You'd be amazed how often coercion won't work in business meetings. It's like it's against these bureaucrats' nature to do their jobs instead of seeking personal gain. Greedy fucks. Lanie, you're with me. Vance, you might not recall, but tonight is a court night. It starts in an hour."

"And you want me to sit by your side for the first time in months?" Vance asked.

"Did I mention zoning?" Dai asked. "Zoning is a bitch and will take most of the night, maybe longer if I don't handle the bribery right. Have I ever mentioned how much I hate real estate? You're in the hot seat tonight. Court's all you, tonight."

"You want me to go sit in your chair for the night?" Vance asked.

"Your chair is just as good," Dai said. "But if it makes you feel more powerful, go ahead and sit in mine."

"Sit in yours, Vance," Lanie said. "To sit in hers would tell people your chair is inferior, which admits to your being inferior when you're not in her chair. Dai is really pushing you as her equal in power."

"Mostly equal," Vance admitted. He knew Dai's explanations came just short of calling him either a king or her consort. He'd never even heard her use either of those terms.

"Vance, dear," Dai said. "You have my full support in whatever you do tonight. You speak with my voice and spank with my hand. The vamps of L.A. are to see you as they see me. Katina, since Cynthia needs to be down here with Karlo to help him ask the right questions, could you stand in as Vance's bodyguard?"

"Sure," Katina said. "Do I get a sword?"

"I have the sword and armor from that photo shoot in my car," Lanie said.

"It's a gift for Vance," Katina said. "The form-fitting chest plate is not formed for my chest. Vance's about twice as big as I am. What do you weigh, Vance? Two-twenty?"

"One-ninety," Vance said.

"Well, you look big to me. I'm a good six inches shorter and a size three. Looking threatening isn't going to work for me," Katina said. "Not next to him."

"Just keep him safe," Dai said.

"So, my job is just to sit and watch for something too strong for Vance to handle?" Katina asked.

"Mostly, you get to hold the chain to the collars around Petra and Julian's necks," Dai said. "The first order of business will be to try and sentence them."

"Petra and Julian are going to come to court just to be sentenced?" Vance asked.

"They're in the oubliettes in my office," Dai said.

"You have oubliettes?" Katina asked. "Oubliettes are cool. Literally and conceptually. Can I see?"

"My office door isn't locked. Go take a look anytime you want. Oubliettes were the only way to go. I didn't want to give up any of my rooms and I couldn't build out or up, so I dug some holes. It takes a vamp who can fly and phase to get through the grate. I didn't design it to open. Each oubliette is just a six-foot round room with a toilet, a shower head, and a drain in the floor. They're ten feet under my office with just two-foot-wide tubes leading up to steel grates in my office floor."

"I can't even get them out," Vance said. He'd known Dai made cells. He didn't understand what she'd meant before she just described them.

"You should be able to phase, someday," Dai said. "See if Katina can teach you. I can't be late to meet with the city zoning officer. He gets moody if I make him wait. Moody will probably cost me a Rolex."

Lanie and Dai worked their way out of the crowded room.

"Wanna stay and help with the interrogation, or go talk with whoever Petra and Julian are?" Katina asked. "I'd love to stay and watch, but a friendly interrogation, like the one about to happen here, is awfully slow and boring. Perhaps you need to torture Petra a little?" Katina seemed hopeful. Knowing her background and knowing she'd spent two centuries with Elizabeth Bathory, Vance forgave her enthusiasm for torture.

"I'm grabbing a six-pack of beer from the fridge over there," Vance said, nodding to the kitchenette of the green room. "Then I'm going up to sit backstage and see who I remember of the vamps that come to court. You know I won't condone torture, right?"

"You are very gullible, Vance Silver," Katina said. "I've seen Elsa torture exactly one person. Since that person is your friend, Henry the Inquisitor, I won't go into detail. I didn't watch much, but it bothered me quite a bit and it wasn't just the pain, the screaming, or the blood. I was just a pet at the time, so blood wasn't as much of a good thing back then. Mostly it bothered me to see how much Elsa knew about what she was doing. She didn't seem to express as much glee as I expected while she interrogated him. But it bothered me just to see how well she knew what to do."

"Ironically, Henry taught me several ways to torture a vampire," Vance said. "If it weren't for Henry, I wouldn't know anything about causing pain or fear. It's odd, I didn't notice at the time, but in the light, I remember him, it makes more sense and seems more wrong now than it did at the time. He taught me that fear is more important than pain when it comes to torture, but he seemed to repeatedly tell us to make sure the vampire suffered because of some bullcrap about balancing the scales. I've never had a reason to try anything I learned from him about interrogation. We never captured a vampire to interrogate." He found the fridge full of beer and took three in each hand. He wouldn't drink them all. He expected to share half with Katina.

They worked their way back upstairs and sat with their backs to a wall backstage. "I'm not as good at any of this as I thought I was," Vance said. "My FBI partner pointed out how terrible I am as a sheriff. My only real success as a vampire hunter came after I became a vampire. Now I'm a vampire sheriff who can't even make it into work once a week."

"Dai and Lanie are telling you it's time to pull yourself together?" Katina asked. "It's been too long since Hallows burned and you've had time to mourn and now it's time to man up?"

"I never should have let myself slide so far down," Vance said. "I should have just used my duties to distract myself from my failures with Zylpha."

"All three of you are right," Katina said. "You have my sympathies for what happened. As strong as becoming a vampire has made your body, your mind is still basically the same, just a little smarter. Your emotions aren't driven by hormones anymore, at least not the same hormones. You still feel emotional pain. Yes, we all would be happier if you'd've let Father Guillermo end Zylpha. But would avenging the deaths of all your friends have made you react differently? They're all still dead. Hallows is still gone, and if you'd killed Zylpha, that wouldn't have changed. You'd be sitting here, drinking beer with me right now questioning whether you acted with morality in letting Guillermo kill her. It was a big thing you did, backing Dai's honor. She sees you as the greatest man who ever lived because of what you did. You stood up to a vampire as strong as I am, knowing you couldn't win, just to let Zylpha live so Dai wouldn't be in violation of another Royal's borders."

"You're right," Vance said. "From every morale standpoint, letting her live was the right thing to do. But she's evil and if anyone deserves to die, it's her."

"Yes, absolutely." Katina popped the lid off a beer and guzzled half of it. "But you know, you did the right thing. If for no other reason than making Dai love you."

"Love?" Vance asked. "Dai doesn't love me; at least, not like that."

"You think the sex is just sex?" Katina asked.

"I know she loves me, but that love isn't romantic. Its fraternal, like soldiers who've fought in many battles together."

"Now, you're just stupid," Katina said. "Is that how you feel about her?"

"I love Lanie romantically," Vance said.

"I didn't ask about Lanie," Katina said. "I asked about Dai. Do you love her like a brother?"

"I," Vance stopped himself. "I wouldn't sleep with her if I didn't lust for her. In time that lust developed into love. I won't tell her because she wants me to be a booty call and not an entanglement. I don't want her to feel pressured to love me differently than she does. Plus, most importantly, I love Lanie."

"I don't think I can explain this to you," Katina said. "You're that backwards in the head. I can't have an intelligent discussion of romance with you."

"I don't understand what you're saying," Vance said.

Katina sighed. She drank the rest of her beer, looked Vance in the eye for a moment, then sighed again.

He realized he'd just made her point for her.

"I've been in a polyamorous relationship for pretty much my entire life," Katina said. "Can I assume you don't recognize that you're in one as well because of your religious background?"

"You're accusing me of being in denial?" Vance asked.

"I think you and Dai are both in denial," Katina said. "I'm less sure about her, but certain about you. If I could coerce you to see the light of day, I would. I find it hard to override deep faith. I think you're okay with being in a pre-marital and sexual relationship with Lanie and having casual sex with Dai. Both are common sins in your eyes, so they're not so bad. Polygamy is too big of a sin, so you won't see that you're already doing it."

"I don't have the faith I should," Vance said. "Are you sure you cannot coerce me to understand?"

"You said 'should'," Katina said. "You're still a religious man. I wasn't raised religious. I think my parents were old Norse pagan. We never went to church. My father sold my sister and I when we were teenagers. The man who bought us was a mage, and they are almost always animists or pagan. This guy never tried to teach us religion. I did live in nineteenth century America. People don't realize how fucking religious this country was back then. That's when I learned I couldn't coerce deeply held religious tenants out of people. Well, not me, Elsa. I couldn't coerce anyone since I was just a pet. The gist is that you can coerce people of a lot of things but changing their core beliefs cannot be done."

It dawned on Vance that the Russian women in the green room might have already been coerced to be compliant with the move to America. "Katina, you may need to go uncoerce those women. We know Dougal has at least one vampire working for him. Would it take much to get a Russian stripper to want to come to America and make ten times the money for a fraction of the work? Could you coerce a stripper to become a personal prostitute?"

"Easily, with the right lean-in and some thought-provoking conversation. I wouldn't be able to convince every stripper. Some know where the line is between stripping and prostitution. Others see both as various shades of selling their bodies. The latter could be coerced easily, I'd think. People are actually easier to coerce when they're contemplating." She looked down at the floor. "Didn't you say you have a vampire named Petra locked up downstairs? Are her crimes related to this case?"

"Yes," Vance said. "Her pet worked as one of the henchmen guarding the container with the women."

"Petra is a Russian name," Katina said. "Of course, those girls had been coerced to not only go along with this scheme but want it. I doubt she went to one club and coerced all six girls working that night. She could have prowled through a few clubs, finding women her coercion would take hold. I'll meet you back in the green room." Katina phased, fading to semi-transparency, and sank through the floor.

By the time Vance navigated the stairs and the hallway, Katina met him, dragging Petra behind her. Katina picked Petra up by the neck and set her on her feet. "Run and I'll kill you."

"Don't kill me," Petra pleaded. "I had no choice."

"This isn't your trial," Vance said. He opened the door to the green room and Katina shoved Petra in. She and Vance followed.

"Petra!" One of the women greeted her.

"So, yeah," Katina said. "This will help."

Several of the women started talking to Petra. For a moment, the room seemed about to fall back into chaos.

Karlo shouted, "They're all asking Petra to explain their great job opportunities to us. I know she promised them birth certificates and American social security numbers, but we found those. They fall back often on the mantra: It's better to work for one man as a private entertainer than work in a club for many groping hands. They're still convinced they'll make way more money selling their bodies than working for me as models."

Katina said something in Russian. Karlo repeated mostly the same words back. Katina nodded, then grabbed each woman one at a time and forcibly said her words to each of them. Then the room broke into chaos as the women started clawing for Petra, smacking her, punching her, and grabbing for her hair. Vance pulled Petra from the room and closed the door.

"You need to tell me what you did to them," Vance said. "What did you make them believe?"

"I told them I would introduce each of them to their own rich American man. These men needed women who could provide daily sex, if not more. The men would treasure any women who could do this for them, probably even marry them. In any event, they'd be rewarded with millions of dollars. That blonde-haired vamp friend of yours ruined it all."

"What did Katina say?" Vance asked.

"She told them to rethink everything I ever said and consider if I could have been telling the truth. Apparently, they all decided I told nothing but lies."

"Was everything you told them a lie?" Vance asked.

"Pretty much," Petra said. "They would be having sex with rich men. At least I think they would. Dougal doesn't deal in street whores. Those women would have to sell for twenty grand each just to cover the expenses of getting them here. Dougal will likely want a lot more. I just recruit; I don't know for sure what Dougal ultimately does with them."

"Tell me about Dougal," Vance said.

"He's ruthless," Petra said. "No one meets him in person. No one. It's said if you meet him, it's because he personally tortures anyone who betrays him."

"I don't get it," Vance said. "Why would you work for him?"

"It's not for the money or the benefits," Petra said. "Dougal pays okay money; enough to keep his henchmen in decent homes, anyway. But he holds it over you. He knows where you live. If you betray him, he burns the house down, making sure any family you have is inside."

"And quitting is a betrayal, so you can't quit?" Vance asked. "You should have come to Dai or me. We can keep you safe. We can move you far from here. You must know a dozen ways to get a new identity. All vamps have to, right? If you don't, we can help you find the right people for that as well."

"I have sixteen grandchildren and great-grandchildren living in Los Angeles," Petra said. "I brought all of my descendants with me when I moved to Los Angeles twenty-five years ago. Dougal knows where all of them are. He sends me new photos of them every month. When Dougal finds out Julian survived the gunfight at the docks, everyone I love is dead."

"I don't have the resources to save sixteen people simultaneously," Vance said. "If we start relocating them, is there a chance Dougal will notice and react?"

"Certainly," Petra said. "He's done it before, or so the stories go. One guy stole five grand and realized he'd be caught, so he called his whole family, every cousin, and told them to get out of the country. According to that story, Dougal wouldn't have cared about five grand, but that the guy decided to go on the run offended him. When they started moving en-masse is what alerted Dougal. Three of thirty-four family members survived, including the guy who stole the money. That's how Dougal works, he doesn't kill you, he kills everyone you love but lets you live."

"Then don't do anything," Vance said. "I'll have to consult Dai, but we'll figure something out."

"Like strap me to the roof?" Petra asked.

"We haven't executed anyone in that way," Vance said. They hadn't as of the time Vance stopped showing up to court, but he'd heard of one since. "There was one recently, I guess, but that was for murder of his bloodmother."

"Where the fuck have you been?" Petra asked. "Queen Dai strapped two vamps to the roof three weeks ago. They were dealing meth or trading meth for blood. I don't know all the details, but I do know the two vamps and their pets died."

"I didn't know about that," Vance said. "I've been busy."

"Then it's a good thing you're the one holding court tonight," Petra said. "At least you won't send me to the roof."

"I'm going to do something," Vance said. "Don't think you're getting off free. I have to do something. It just won't be a death sentence. Come to court, bring Julian. I'll get Katina to bring him out." By the yelling, it would be some time before Vance could tell Katina anything. "If Katina comes out, ask her to bring you and Julian up. If she doesn't, come alone. Excuse me, I need to go upstairs and greet people."

"Dai doesn't do that," Petra said.

"Neither do I, but I'm done with you until I have some kind of solution to your problem and an appropriate punishment for your crimes," Vance said.

"I see," Petra said. "Can I make suggestions, or should I leave the thinking to you?"

"I'll think on it myself," Vance said. "If I don't like what I think of, I might ask about your ideas. Excuse me." He walked quickly to the stairs and took a deep breath before climbing them. This would be the first time in months many of the vampires had seen Vance. He wouldn't remember many of them.

He didn't think he'd been downstairs long. He'd left an empty auditorium moments before. When he returned, the theatre had hundreds of vampires working their way into the seats. He checked his phone and saw that he still had ten minutes before the regular starting time for court.

"I'll be holding court tonight," Vance announced. "I'll take concerns involving multiple vampires before court. I'll see those who need individual assistance after court."

Vance thought of standing for the whole time but decided to sit in his chair. The first vampire to bow before him looked young. Vampires didn't age, so most looked young, but this one dressed like a skater punk, which led Vance to think he was new to vampire life.

"Your Majesty, I am Ken Walberg," the young vampire said. He bowed and then knelt before Vance. "My crew and I have been preying on the kids who hit the beach down by Venice at night. It's been our hunting grounds since The Beach Boys grew their first beards. Recently, there's a vampire named Yvette—I think she's new from San Diego—and she's been taking kids off into the dunes every night. I mean, every freaking night. She's not just taking boys. Sometimes she takes couples, sometimes girls, sometimes boys. We've asked her to move up a ways, out of our territory, but she laughs and tells us if we can make her move, she'll move."

"And you tried and failed!" A woman stood from a seat near the back.

"If you're Yvette, please come here," Vance said.

She bounced up and then hopped and ran across the seat backs of the empty seats. She then leapt onto the stage. She took a bow towards the audience then bowed to Vance. She also knelt when she approached. "Kenny here isn't telling the whole story. First, he invited me to hang out with him. Since he extended this invite while we were both down in Rio de Janeiro, it's not something I let him rescind just because I didn't come up here to be his lover. Not that we didn't. We did. I'm just not the 'settle for one guy' type. He took it personally and tried to kick me off the beach. I like the beach. I have a nice basement apartment just a hop, skip and jump from the beach. I see no reason to leave the prime hunting of young, drunk, sexually vibrant humans to him and his loser friends."

"Be nice," Vance said. "There are probably hundreds of kids along that beach every night. If you're feeding every night, you're not draining more than a couple ounces, right?"

"If that," Yvette said.

"Ken," Vance said. "I respect your hunting grounds, but that's not really a thing. It's a tradition. It's respectful to acknowledge another vampires' hunting territory. It's not forbidden to violate those boundaries; it's rude and nothing more. However, Yvette had an invitation to join you and it seems she came a long way at your behest. I am not going to pass any judgement here. I am just ordering you two to respect each other. Yvette, hunt responsibly, be it on the beach or at a dance club. Ken, there's no problem here besides your having a bruised ego and maybe a bruised heart. Treat Yvette like a friend and she'll treat you like a friend. Most of all, if you treat her like a friend, you won't mind her presence on the beach."

"Yes, Your Majesty," Yvette said.

"Not what I was hoping for," Ken said. "But you are absolutely right. I can't guarantee cordiality, but I'll back off the vitriol. I don't take relationships lightly. I didn't realize she was such a…"

Vance cut him off. "And this is where you go back to your seats. Respect goes both ways, Yvette. You should look for other hunting grounds when it's convenient for you. I won't intervene in this again unless the laws are violated. If it comes to that, I'll remember that I've already had to deal with the two of you once."

"We'll get on just fine, Your Majesty," Yvette said. "But I'm making new friends every night. One of those friendships might lead me to another interesting place. I love interesting places and new interesting people."

"Sheriff," the next vampire, a man in a grey suit and a white tie, said as he knelt. "I am not here to ask any favors. Out of my sense of duty to Queen Dai, I fear I must report a friend for making a new vampire in the city without seeking permission first."

"Dean!" a vampire from the front row called as he stood up. "I can't believe you'd do this. You didn't even give me a week to submit myself to the queen in a more private setting."

"Timothy," Dean said. "You procrastinate, and the longer you take, the more fear you'll have of a severe punishment. The more fear you have, the more you'll procrastinate. Trust me, I'm doing you and Gretchen a favor. Sheriff Vance will have a much less severe punishment than Queen Dai would dish out."

"I don't like that you're coming forward to me just because you see me as nicer than Dai," Vance said. "Dean, go sit. Timothy, come up here. Bring your bloodchild, Gretchen. Did I get that name right?"

"I didn't mean to," Timothy said as he climbed the stairs to the stage. He wore a t-shirt with the words 'Tim b. Tim' emblazoned across the front. A woman who'd been sitting beside him, wearing a different t-shirt with the same words, followed. "We were doing a show. I'm a deejay, pretty famous for my dance beats here and in Japan. Gretchen sang for my show and then did a pit dive into the crowd. Somehow, they missed. She got hurt pretty bad and I'm sure she would have died. I took her, saying I was taking her to the hospital, but I gave her blood and took her to a safehouse to make the change. She had a cracked skull. She wouldn't have lived. It's not something I could have planned ahead for."

"You say you're famous?" Vance asked. "You know your way around a mixing board?"

"I have a PhD in electronic composition," Timothy said. "I don't talk about it because, even in the club scene, they want their deejays to be trained by experience, but I know more about modern club music and how to compose it than anyone."

"I imagine you have an ongoing record deal?" Vance asked.

"Yeah," Timothy said. "If you're looking for business for Elaine Larson, sorry, I am contracted already and can't make music for her."

"Two hundred hours at minimum wage," Vance said. "Work for Lanie under a pseudonym. Nothing for yourself. She needs someone to help her get her bands recorded. You seem like the kind of guy who knows how to produce an album. Gretchen, you get fifty hours, same deal."

"Do I get to use my home studio?" Timothy asked.

"Work out the details with Lanie," Vance said. "Who's the third of my pre-court audiences?"

"J.J., Milord," the next vampire, a woman in a black and red gown, said. She had blonde hair and wore tiny sunglasses, just large enough to cover her eyes. She knelt and offered Vance a handful of eight-by-ten photographs.

Looking through the pictures, they were all of a couple, a man and woman, and a car with New Jersey license plates. "What's this?" Vance asked.

"Look closely at the picture with his arm out the window of his car," J.J. said. "Does that tattoo look familiar?"

Vance looked where J.J. indicated. He caught himself sighing, but only after he'd already done it and revealed the tattoo's familiarity.

"You do recognize the sigil of Henry the Inquisitor?" J.J. asked.

The tattoo didn't show well, but, by the red skin around the dark ink, the man had just gotten the tattoo that day or the day before. Even with the bad angle, once Vance knew what to look for, he had seen it. Henry hadn't used the symbol for over a decade before Vance met Henry. The symbol consisted of two swords and an arrow forming the letter 'H'. The words 'Undo the Undead' would be written in the scroll under the 'H'. Vance didn't know why anyone would have an outdated symbol of an east coast vampire hunter.

"You think these are vampire hunters?" Vance asked.

"I know they are," J.J. said. "They tried to kill me. Their tactics were weak. The woman tried to pretend to be prey while the man acted like a homeless man. Only, he had no beard and no stench. She couldn't stomach kissing a woman, though she pretended to lure me into an alley for, and I'll quote, 'the wildest sex of my life.' I'm twenty-two hundred years old and Roman. I can guarantee I've done things that are so degenerate, they're not only illegal, they're outside the realm of most people's ability to imagine."

Vance didn't even try. His experiences had been, according to Lanie, vanilla with only a slight amount of sprinkles. "So, you didn't kill the hunters when they tried to trap you?"

"I was about to; I'd already drank from each of them. I had the man pinned to the wall by his throat. He had perhaps ten, maybe fifteen seconds before brain damage would set in. Then the woman swears that Vance Silver will avenge them." She laughed. "Their seriousness amused me so thoroughly, I had to let them go. Do you know them? Would you have avenged them?"

"I don't know them, but I'm curious about them," Vance said. "No one is to kill these two until I get a chance to speak with them. Information leading to me finding them will be rewarded."

"I told them you could be found at Hallows," J.J. said.

"That's outdated advice," Vance said.

J.J. shrugged. "I hadn't seen you in months. I wanted to give them something. They'd each given me a pint of blood."

"If you see them again, call me," Vance said. He pulled one of his sheriff business cards out and handed it to J.J. "If you text, include your name."

"Yes, Your Majesty, I mean Sheriff Vance," J.J. stood and returned to the audience.

When no one else came forward, Vance gave a short speech thanking everyone for coming. He didn't have any vampire business to announce. He reminded people of J.J.'s warning about the hunters. He then promised to be more involved than he'd been and assured everyone that if they had any problem and needed help, they could call him. He took what business cards he had left and used his mind to float them to the edge of the stage and leave them in a pile. They didn't land as gracefully as he'd have liked, but they all stayed on the stage.

Katina showed up in the wings with Petra and Julian. Vance shook his head. He'd thought of how to handle her, and it involved not letting the other vampires know she'd spoken with him. Vance had to assume Dougal had more than one vampire in his employ.

Vance dismissed the crowd and, once the vampires had all left, he walked off to join Katina, Julian, and Petra backstage.

"No public execution?" Petra asked.

"I worried that Dougal might have others out there that would report you as compromised," Vance said. "I didn't want to risk your family."

"Dougal doesn't work like that," Petra said. "There's a five-thousand-dollar reward for giving Dougal the name of any of his other henchmen. He's that paranoid. We're not even allowed to know the names of the people we're working with. We just go by code numbers, usually one through five. Number one is in charge. Number five is usually a new guy. The standard rules are: Don't bring I.D., bring only the burner phones we were given with the job and don't tell anyone your real name. Only Dougal gets to know that. He doesn't even have captains or any other kind of leadership in his organization. It's just him and the peons. He sends people who've never worked together to go do a task, usually paying someone with a suitcase of cash or escorting a delivery. I don't know if there are other vampires in his employ. I know most of the vampires in Los Angeles. I've never seen one while working for Dougal."

"How does he contact you?" Vance asked.

"Random fast-food delivery, usually pizza," Petra said. "There will be a time and place and your assigned number. When you get to the place, you'll find a burner phone and Dougal calls at the assigned time. His voice is scrambled. He sounds just like Stephen Hawking."

"I want you to keep working for him," Vance said.

"Excuse me?" Petra said. "How will that help? I just explained how he's insulated from his henchmen."

"Julian found ways to contact me," Vance said.

"But Julian is dead," Petra said. "At least, to Dougal he's dead."

"He just got wounded and fell in the water," Vance said. "Cynthia had Dai's cleaner crew clean that scene before any law enforcement made an official report."

"It's true, I could heal," Julian said. "Dougal knows we heal. He's given both of us very risky jobs, knowing we'd survive getting shot. I've been shot at twice doing simple money runs for him."

"If Dougal sends someone to investigate us, they're going to see Julian isn't scarred. A pet takes days, sometimes up to a week, to fully heal a gunshot," Petra said.

"I know," Vance said. "I've been shot when I was a pet. I'll have to shoot Julian in the leg." He drew his gun.

Julian winced but stuck his leg out, away from his body. "You know where not to shoot, right? There's a nasty artery in there that can bleed out fast."

The thought of human blood made Vance hesitate. He'd drank from Marisol earlier that day. He should be fine. There would be a risk, though. Petra would not be strong enough to stop Vance should he lose control.

Katina grabbed the gun from Vance. "You should go to the back of the house," she said.

Vance jogged away. Just as he reached the top row of seats, he heard two gunshots.

"What the fuck!" Petra yelled. "You fucking killed him!" She lunged toward Katina with her hands bent into claws but stopped and stepped back when the blonde vampire snapped her gaze toward her.

"He's not dead," Katina said, staring Petra in the eye. "I'm glad you thought better of that. You can't take me."

Vance inched closer. He could smell live blood. It didn't trigger him, so he dared climb up on the stage. Petra knelt over Julian, holding her hands over wounds to his chest and stomach.

"I was going to shoot him in the leg," Vance said.

"The abdomen shot was through and through, just outside where any organs would be," Katina said. "The right lung won't kill him, either. As long as he doesn't laugh too hard, he'll be fine in a few days. This way he has real, believable wounds."

"I don't have any way of contacting Dougal to let him know I'm alive," Julian whispered, his voice cracking in pain.

"He'll contact us," Petra said. "He'll want to know what went wrong. He'll send another team to meet us and question us. Two will sit with us at a restaurant and two will be across the street with rifles ready to blow our brains out. I've been on that kind of team. No one died. Dougal doesn't kill henchmen. Like I said, if we're disloyal, he'll kill our families but leave us alive."

"Now, when you get questioned, you'll have scars," Katina said. "Does this mean he'll send someone who knows what a vampire is and what a pet is. How else will he understand why Julian isn't dead?"

"I don't know," Petra said. "This hasn't come up before. I just know he's always clear that failure is forgivable. Loyalty is what matters to him. How do you plan to keep in touch with us? I'm sure Dougal will be watching our phones."

"Which are still in the apartment since we left them there when we went on the assignment," Julian said. "I expect it will be up to me to keep the communications going. Dougal always uses the same low-end throwaway phone. I just buy one of the same model for myself at the drug store and, when I'm fiddling with it on the job, no one gets suspicious."

"Don't text me for drug deals," Vance said. "If the stakes are lives, I want to know. I only want to know about the truly important things to Dougal. Big deals and people. If you think you're actually meeting Dougal, let me know and I can track whatever phone you call me from. If you move something, I want to know the start and end locations. Eventually we will triangulate a base of operations, I'm sure. Once we get a location, my FBI contact can start tracking the money associated with that location."

"Meanwhile, you'll work on a plan to relocate my whole family if things go south?" Petra asked.

"We'll get some people we trust involved to move everyone at the same time," Vance said. "Are you wealthy enough to finance such a move, or will we need to find other resources?"

"I'm okay financially for myself," Petra said. "We're talking sixteen people in eight homes. And I guess we need the six spouses of the ones with families. All of them will need new identities, new jobs, new homes."

"That sounds like millions of dollars," Vance said.

"I can get IDs, with impenetrable provenance, even better than the Russian girls have, for six grand each." Katina said. "Karina had a side business. It's still running. They set up a hundred false births each year and have been doing so for nearly two hundred years. These are not stillborns or anything traceable. These people who don't exist are descended from people who never existed. But they had jobs and paid taxes, so the documentation of these people is perfect. The usual price for these IDs is a hundred and twenty grand, but it's my company now. I get a discount."

"Do those fake people vote?" Vance asked.

"They're registered but, no, it's too much work to find someone to go into the polling places and pretend to be each person," Katina said. "It got tricky back in the wars when fake people would get drafted. Then they had to quickly find some gung-ho kid who wanted to serve but didn't qualify because of some criminal record or immigrant status. Karina would sell them fake identities for cheap."

"Dai would have liked your sister," Vance said. "She seems to know how to see a problem and turn it into a profit."

"Dai has worked for my sister for over a century," Katina said. "I just figured it out a couple months ago, but Dai is one of thousands of investment advisors Karina worked with. Karina invested Elsa's money with Dai. Quite a lot of money, really. We're not Dai's only clients, but I bet we're her biggest."

"So, you have money to cover the costs of relocating my family?" Petra asked.

"I don't have any money," Katina said. "I spend Elsa's money. Azure spends Shauna's. I'll talk to Elsa. She doesn't like to talk about money, but she's typically happy to throw money at a problem if it makes it go away."

"Suddenly, I'm a problem?" Petra asked.

Vance nodded, but Petra nodded first.

"Never mind," Petra said. "I know I'm a problem right now."

Vance hadn't asked how Petra got involved with Dougal to begin with. It didn't matter. He had made the deal to disentangle her from Dougal. Still, his curiosity drove him to ask, "How did you get in…"

His phone rang, interrupting him. If it had been his personal phone, he'd have let it go, but the ring told him it was his work line. "This is Assistant Sheriff Vance Silver," he answered.

"Vance, this is Hannah Dwyer. I have a strong lead on Dougal. I'm in D.C. for a meeting and can't do anything personally. As much as it pains me to trust you to do it right, it's more important to save these women than to handle the protocols properly."

"What women?" Vance asked. "What kind of danger are they in?"

"The worst kind of forced prostitution," Dwyer said. "I'm texting you an address. Expect to find women stoned to hell on heroin and being used in ways you don't want to think about."

"I'll get a team headed there momentarily," Vance said.

"Do you need me to have some of my guys meet you there?" Hannah asked. Before Vance could answer, she continued. "I know you're going to go all lone-star cowboy, but I had to offer. I don't care how you deal with this. Rescue the women. I don't expect you to leave a pimp or henchman alive for questioning. I still need to ask you what happened to the henchmen at the docks. By the time my CSI team got there, the ground was two inches deep in bleach water. If you handle this one cleanly, and leave a crime scene

I can use, call me back. If not, I don't want to hear about it. We'll attribute any violence to a rival crime boss."

"I feel you're insulting me," Vance said.

"You're a crappy law man, Vance," Dwyer said. "You're a pretty decent hero, and right now these women I'm telling you about need a hero."

"Ok, I'm heading that way," Vance said.

"Dwyer out." The line went dead.

Vance put his phone away and said, "I'm going to have to get Cynthia from downstairs and go. Katina, could you hold the fort here until Dai or I return?"

"Do I let Petra and Julian go?" Katina asked.

"They should go home," Vance said. "They should stay away from here except on nights we have court."

"Okay, then," Katina said. "Go be a hero."

VI

"I'm going to cover the back," Cynthia said.

They'd driven by, careful not to slow down, to get a look at the location. Then Cynthia drove three blocks away and parked in front of a drug store. Sitting in the SUV, they finalized their plans.

The building had been small, an old four-unit apartment building south of downtown. Dim light shone through the front windows, but otherwise the building didn't look particularly nefarious. They'd seen a man walk in the front door so casually, Vance wondered if the address had been incorrect.

"I'm going to try to go in as a prospective customer," Vance said. He undid his belt and started unbuttoning his uniform shirt.

"Brave man," Cynthia said.

Vance didn't worry about leaving his gun belt in Cynthia's SUV, he'd have his derringer if he needed a weapon. He pulled it from his pocket and showed it to Cynthia. "I always keep this."

"I meant, going out in public with khaki pants and a white V-neck t-shirt," Cynthia said.

"I don't expect to find fashion police in there," Vance said.

"Good luck with your subterfuge," Cynthia said. "I'll keep my gun cocked so I can rush right in to rescue you when you get tongue-tied while trying to lie."

"How much conversation do you expect goes into this?" Vance asked.

"This kind of place?" Cynthia asked. "You can probably go in and hand the pimp forty bucks and he'll point you to a guest room."

"You know how this works?" Vance asked.

Cynthia shrugged. "I don't sleep much. I watch a lot of TV."

"I've never been to a whorehouse," Vance said. "I always imagined, if I did find one, I'd likely kill everyone but the prostitutes. I know I wouldn't. I'm totally against summary judgement and execution."

"Except where the five vamp laws demand it," Cynthia said.

"I'm against it there, too," Vance said. "I don't want to kill anyone. Even if we find a human who knows about vampires, we don't have to kill them if we can't coerce them to forget about us. We can, like we did to Randal, coerce them to never communicate that they even believe in vamps, let alone know of them."

"Dai chewed me out about killing those guys at the docks," Cynthia said. "I'm only allowed to kill in an active gunfight. Once the shooting stops, I'm supposed to arrest them and, if they need coercion, take them to you or Dai. If they don't, they go to jail and the proper legal system."

Vance chuckled. "Now that we've decided not to kill, I'm probably going to go all bloodeyes and kill everyone in there."

"Probably," Cynthia said. "I'll punch you in the nose again if that happens."

"Let's do this," Vance said. "Go around back. Join me inside in five minutes if no one bolts out the back. Come sooner if you hear gunshots or me losing it."

Not wanting to waste time, Vance walked in the front door.

"Do you have an appointment?" a man sitting at an old steel office desk asked. He barely glanced up from his laptop. He had several tattoos, some Vance recognized as prison style. A large handgun lay on the desk by the laptop. Two other men sat at a small table down the hall. They seemed engaged with an ice hockey game on a tablet computer on the table. Again, two pistols also lay on the table.

"I heard about this place from a friend and wanted to check it out," Vance said. Anyone who knew what to listen for would know he lied. Though the words were technically true, because he meant to deceive, all the tells of a lie, the slightly high voice, the strained gaps between words, and the lilt at the start, were present.

"Twenty bucks per ten minutes. An extra twenty for a black balloon. White balloons are forty," the man said.

"Just the time," Vance said. He set a hundred-dollar bill on the desk.

"Second floor, first door on the right." He tossed Vance a condom. "That's not optional. It's for your own protection, not hers. At least one of them has syphilis and we can't tell which."

"I'll, uh, definitely use this, then," Vance said. He went up the stairs. The door on the right stood open. By the sounds coming from the hall, other customers were present in the building. Inside the room, a woman wearing a tank top and underwear lay on a mattress on the floor. She barely moved her head to look at Vance, then reached down and slid her panties off. She hardly opened her eyes. Vance had seen people stoned on heroin, so he knew what he beheld in that room. He didn't need to see more.

Vance walked downstairs, taking each step with care and concentrating on keeping himself calm. As he passed the two men playing on the tablet computer, Vance leaned in and said, "This job isn't worth it. Go home!"

The two grabbed their guns and each tucked theirs into their belt. Vance followed as the two headed towards the front door. The guy at the desk stood and pointed his gun at the first of the two large men. "Where do you think you're going?"

"This job ain't worth it," both large men said in unison.

"No one quits," the man at the desk said. "Pete, Dan, you two aren't going anywhere." He shot both men, hitting each in the gut.

The smell of blood pushed Vance to the edge, but he controlled his bloodeyes. He had his derringer out in a heartbeat, but it was a heartbeat too late. A bullet tore into Vance's stomach.

"What kind of asshole are you?" the man at the desk asked. He then added, "I guess it doesn't matter, because you're about to be a dead…"

Vance never knew if the man finished. With the pain of the bullet wound, his willpower shattered, and he gave in to the bloodeyes. When he came to, he slumped against the door. Cynthia sat at the desk, filing her nails.

"That was one hell of a show," Cynthia said. "I was going to stop you, but one of the customers shot me in the chest. My armor protected me, but it pissed me off so, instead of breaking your nose, I gave you a push his way."

"The women?" Vance asked. There were several bodies and a lot of blood in the hallway. He couldn't see any women's bodies.

"Yeah, it was careless of me," Cynthia said. "You didn't try to get past me to the closest person, a woman tied to a bed. I wasn't sure if you had just a bit of control or what, but you left the woman alone, so I left you alone. After you killed the guy that shot me, you went room to room, killing the johns, but you left the women. I guess heroin suppresses Venae or something. Once I realized the women were safe from you, I let you wreak havoc on the people the women weren't safe from."

"So, no one lived for us to question about Dougal?" Vance asked.

"None of the women are lucid enough to talk to," Cynthia said. "Dai's out front, keeping the cops from coming in while we wait for Lanie to get here with a bus to transport the women to a hospital. Dai's telling the cops that this is a week-old crime scene. She was pretty upset at how much this was going to cost her to have her crime scene cleanup crew sanitize. Then we found like three hundred grand in a drawer here. It's far more than the cleaning crew needs, so Dai is less upset."

"I'm going to go talk to Dai," Vance said.

"You're head to toe blood, Vance." Cynthia said. "Go find a working shower. That room is the pimp's apartment. I can tell because it's the address on his driver's license."

The whole operation here seemed too clumsy for a Dougal operation. Hadn't the pimp called the two large men by name? "Hannah was wrong," Vance said. "I don't think this place is run by Dougal."

"Shower, Vance!" Cynthia said. "Lanie won't be here to help and that's not Dai's thing, so you're going to have to wash your own back. Dai will be in in a few minutes, I think, but you'll still be in the shower if you want to get all the blood out of your hair. She has the psycho killer bag."

"What's that?" Vance asked.

"Your spare clothes in a duffle bag," Cynthia said. "Don't look at me, I didn't name it."

"I'm glad everyone else thinks this is funny," Vance said. "If I'd killed any women, I would be done with this whole vampire life."

"I'm your friend, but not your counselor," Cynthia said. "This isn't the first time I've seen you lose it. You can't drink my blood, so you steer clear of me as long as I don't stand between you and someone whose blood smells tasty. I was standing between you and those women. I promise, I'd have stopped you."

"How many was it tonight?"

"Nine," Cynthia said. "Stop being so introspective and work on cleaning up the exterior. I know Lanie thinks it's hot when you're covered in blood, but it's really kind of disgusting."

"Lanie…"

"Stop talking, start washing." Cynthia pulled a pair of headphones from her shoulder and stuck them in her ears. "Noise cancelling!" she yelled, pointing at the ear buds. "If you're talking, I can't hear you."

Vance rolled his eyes and went through the door to the pimp's apartment. The door had one hinge torn free of the wall. Two bodies, a man and a woman, never made it off the couch. They'd been playing some video game. The television had a spray of blood across it. When Vance noticed some of the limbs were across the room from the bodies, he had to work hard to suppress the need to vomit. He ran for the shower. He turned the water on and didn't undress or wait for the water to get hot before stepping under the spray. Vance felt tempted to bless the shower head, to see if holy water would hurt. Then he realized if God ever had empowered him to create holy water, Vance would have lost that blessing long before he killed a pimp, two people who were in his apartment, two large henchmen and four random johns. Vance didn't feel terribly guilty about the killing. He worried about how little guilt he felt. He suppressed a feeling of righteousness, reminding himself that he didn't have God's authority to pass judgement. Every one of the people he'd killed knew the conditions of the women and what they were forced to do. Since these weren't the least deserving of the people Vance had killed, he just considered them a number to add to his tally—he just didn't know what his tally counted toward.

VII

Vance woke to find Lanie sleeping on his chest. Vampires didn't usually need sleep, physically, but Vance still liked to rest his mind. He'd spent the day filling out paperwork. He couldn't get away from explaining the raid on the whorehouse the night before. City police had created a report pointing to Vance as the officer in charge. Vance had to create a report corroborating and explaining how the pimp and other men had escaped since Vance saw the rescue of the women as paramount.

The women had spent time with Dai, ensuring they forgot the bloodbath and just remembered Cynthia freeing them. The cleaning crew wouldn't finish in one day, but Vance assigned the case to Cynthia, so she'd be the one to determine when to revisit the scene looking for clues on where to find the pimp. As Vance understood it, the pimp and all the men were transported to a boat where a school of tiger sharks were known to frequent. The boat would have been capsized there. The sharks would obfuscate any evidence of Vance's slaughtering the pimp and the others from the whorehouse.

"Did the johns' families deserve to be abandoned?" Vance asked, not meaning to say it aloud.

"No," Lanie answered groggily. "You didn't cause that. Those men knew what kind of place they patronized. They knew the women weren't willing participants. Perhaps they rationalized that the women deserved it for trading sex for drugs, but somewhere they knew it was a lie. Those women weren't using heroin, they were poisoned with heroin. There are bodies buried in the basement. Cynthia is waiting to dig those up for when she officially investigates the crime scene. We don't know how many. So, everyone you killed was involved in not only forced prostitution, but murder."

"I'm supposed to be a vampire hunter, not a creepy human hunter," Vance said.

"They shot first," Lanie said. "Think of it as self-defense with collateral benefits."

"I'm trying not to dwell on the negative," Vance said. "Apparently, moping is unattractive. So, if I have issues with what I've done, I'm trying not to talk about it. It's done. It's in the past. I need to live in the now and plan for the future."

"You know better," Lanie said. "You've taken psychology in college, right?"

"Several classes," Vance said. "Preachers are the only counselors many people will talk to. Talking to a shrink makes them crazy but talking about the same stuff to a preacher makes them pious."

"Oh my God, so many directions to go with that!" Lanie covered her mouth for a moment. She then said, "Text Padre Guillermo and tell him you'll be in after midnight to see him."

"It's my day off," Vance said. "I could just go, now."

"You have an audition at Eight-thirty," Lanie said. "It's on your calendar."

"If it is, it's the only thing there," Vance said. He reached for his phone and, after digging around for his calendar app, opened it. It had several things noted on it. His nights with Dai were planned out. Dai's court had been blocked out as well. For that night, he had an appointment with IrisDavid Productions. "What's the gig? I don't want to do another underwear commercial. The commercial that aired never even showed my face, which, come to think of it, was probably a good thing. My mom would have called and told me I was going to hell."

"No, she wouldn't," Lanie said. "Your parents are not terribly religious or terribly conservative. I talk to your mom every couple weeks, mostly because you don't. You know they're much happier with you as an actor than they were with you as a preacher. I haven't told them you're a cop, too."

"I haven't told them much since I left New York," Vance said. "The less I say to them, the less chance I'll have to lie."

"They're planning a visit next summer," Lanie said. "For some reason they want to see Disneyland. And you. Mostly you, but they kept mentioning Disneyland."

"Disneyland isn't open for the hours I can be outside," Vance said.

"We'll worry about that next summer," Lanie said "Go shower. Dress in nice jeans and clean sneakers. Either wear a really tight t-shirt or a button-up shirt with a collar. The gig is a western TV show. This one is cable, not streaming, I think."

"And they know I don't quit my day job to act?" Vance asked.

"They were happy to accommodate your schedule," Lanie said. "They specifically designed the lead role for you. I didn't understand what the show was about when they explained it, but I was sure that you wouldn't be playing a lawman. We don't want you pigeonholed into a type-cast."

VIII

Lanie pulled into the parking lot of a hotel. It wasn't as nice as the one where he and Lanie stayed. There weren't valets. The valets didn't park motorcycles anyway. The one question Vance had been dying to ask, but couldn't ask while riding, he finally got to voice when Lanie turned off the bike.

"Why would I want a full-time job as an actor?" Vance asked. "I make a living as a sheriff, and I still have the magic debit card."

"Several reasons, really," Lanie said. "You're a sheriff because it helps with your duties as the vampire sheriff. It's supposed to be a badge and gun with little to no actual time spent on that job. I know you feel a need to earn that paycheck, so you work more than you need to."

"I have a work ethic," Vance said. As they entered the hotel, Vance opened the door for Lanie. He tried to tell himself he wasn't being chauvinistic, he just got to the door first. He knew he'd had to try to get to the door first, though. Lanie never slowed down. She maintained a very brisk walking pace. As a vampire's pet, she could move faster than a person, but she seemed cognizant of her potential and kept herself to a quick walking step. Vampires and pets could run far faster than any human, but the speed of walking had a limit based on the balance of the body. Lanie walked close to that limit. Any faster and she'd have to lean into a run.

"Exactly," Lanie said. "You don't like money given to you. You hate every time we have to swipe the debit card you have from the vamp hunter trust. You have two valid professions where you have experience or training. Law enforcement isn't one of them."

"So my FBI partner keeps telling me," Vance said. "As the sheriff of local vamps, I'm mostly Dai's muscle. I have little or no detective work to do and people's rights aren't really a consideration. I don't even know what I'm doing as a human law enforcer. Everything I know, I learned from television. And I haven't spent a lot of time watching TV."

"And since you don't think yourself pious or righteous enough to preach," Lanie said, "I look for work for you in the one remaining field you have experience: acting."

"Well, then," Vance said. "Let's get me a new TV show."

The conference room doors were open. Two people, a man and a woman, sat behind a desk with what looked more like a scrapbook than a script. The man wore a suit that had been tailored for someone else. The shoulders sagged too much. He wore a tie, which made him the first person Vance did any kind of business with in Los Angeles that wasn't wearing a uniform and yet still wore a tie. The woman wore a formal dress, too fancy for what Vance would consider business attire.

"Mr. Silver!" the woman greeted him. "It's an honor to finally meet you. I'm Iris, this is my partner, David."

The man stood and offered Vance his hand. Vance warmed his hand before giving a quick handshake. "First, let me apologize for luring you here under false pretense."

"We should go," Lanie said. "There are far more couth ways to arrange an autograph. My time isn't worth this crap."

Vance started to turn away, then noticed the cover of the scrapbook: "Henry Olsen's journal. Personal. Do Not Open."

"Wait," Vance said. "This is something we need to deal with. Or I do, anyway. David and Iris here have a book that used to belong to Henry the Inquisitor."

"I don't want to stay for this," Lanie said. She kissed Vance on the cheek and then whispered, "If this goes the way it should, I don't want to see it."

Vance watched her leave and close the door behind her. He wasn't sure what she expected to happen, but Vance only planned to talk.

"You said the book used to belong to Henry," David said. "We came here hoping to return it."

"I'm his heir," Vance said. "You can give the book to me."

"He's dead?" David asked. "That explains why we didn't find him. We gave up on finding him and decided to find you, hoping you'd lead us to him."

Iris added, "I recognized you from a photo on the wall of the headquarters in New York."

"That building is locked," Vance said. "The superintendent is the only person in New York with a key, and he wouldn't be in the room with the team picture."

"We're creative," Iris said. "The roof hatch was locked from the inside, but the hinges were outside. A few turns with a socket wrench and we got inside. Henry covers basic breaking and entering methods in section five."

"You're hoping I'd be impressed by that?" Vance asked.

"We've studied this book for years," David said. "We've been tracking down leads on Henry since I found this book while cleaning out some apartment in New Jersey. This was under the bed and our instructions were to toss anything inelegant into the trash. This seemed interesting, so I threw it in my truck instead."

"We knew right away that the guy who threw this together had been on to something real," Iris said. "Vampires are not just a myth, but you, Vance Silver, Vampire Hunter, know that, right?"

"The scoreboard on the wall had two tick marks under Bloodsuckers Dusted by your name," David said. "You killed two vampires. Yours was the only name on the wall with any tick marks."

"That's all very interesting," Vance said.

"So, were we right?" Iris asked. "Was Henry right?"

Vance started to say it was all a myth, but his head nodded slightly. Rather than lie, he opted for a frightening truth. "You'll die if you pursue this truth," Vance said.

"We've been hardcore training," David said. "Both of us are black belts and Fairbairn-Sykes masters."

"Fairbairn-Sykes?" Vance asked.

"Knife fighting," Iris said. Once Iris mentioned it, Vance remembered something about where Henry derived his close combat techniques from. Henry didn't dwell long on knife fighting when Vance trained. Knife based martial arts focused on defense against other, similarly armed, foes. Vampires wouldn't fight with knives. Henry spent a lot of time training pistols and judo when Vance underwent his training.

"And we studied Henry's book," David said.

"Can I see the book?" Vance asked.

David flipped the book around and slid it towards Vance.

Inside, it still resembled a scrapbook. Pages of novels were taped in with highlighted paragraphs dealing with the powers and vulnerabilities of vampires. Drawings of vampires covered other pages, and the book had the occasional newspaper clipping of animal attacks or missing people. A few pages had handwritten notes or instructions, such as the most common documented traits and how to build a vampire hunting kit.

Vance looked at Iris and David more closely. They both seemed very fit, very muscular. David wore a gun under his arm. Iris had one in her coat, which she'd draped over her chair. October in Los Angeles didn't warrant a jacket from even the most cold sensitive people. At least the jackets were for a sports team, the Philadelphia Flyers, so they would explain being off season simply as being a sports team. They had a plan and had taken that plan as far as making it into a lifestyle. Vance didn't ponder the ideas of coercing them to forget about vampire hunting for long.

"Let me get this straight," Vance said. "You find a book while cleaning out an apartment and take it as gospel. You then break into my office and then, in order to meet me, you set up a false audition?"

"To be fair, if you'd been at Hallows, we wouldn't have needed to set up the false audition," Iris said.

"You're months too late for Hallows," Vance said. "How did you know to find me there?"

"Your log entry from the New York office. It said you were headed to Los Angeles, looking for a vampire hunter named The Black Dragon, and you were starting your search at a bar named Hallows."

"So, that was a dead end," Vance said. "Then you called Lanie to set up the meeting."

"Lanie was at Hallows," Iris said. "When we said we were looking for you, she asked why. I came up with the whole audition idea on the fly once she identified herself as your agent."

Vance felt confused. Why had Lanie been at Hallows recently? Hallows hadn't been there for months. With Dai's theatre down the block, it didn't seem too farfetched that she'd be nearby. The parking lot at Hallows was the only off-street parking on the block. Maybe Lanie parked there when she wasn't with Vance.

"And what do you want from me?" Vance asked.

"I thought it was obvious," David said. "We want to join your team."

"Oh?" Vance sat back. He didn't know what he'd been expecting, but he didn't ever consider he'd have a vampire hunting team.

"We know everyone in the New York office died in Romania," Iris said. "We did read the logs in New York. We know what we're getting into."

"We were hoping to find Henry. Your logs only refer to him as missing," David said. "You know he's dead?"

Vance nodded. He didn't explain that Henry didn't leave a body because he died as a vampire.

"And The Black Dragon?" Iris asked.

"I found her," Vance said. "We're very close."

"The Black Dragon is a woman?" Iris asked. She smacked her partner's shoulder. "See, David, I'm not the first woman to be a vampire hunter."

"Can we join you?" David asked.

Vance didn't have an answer. He couldn't think of a way to let such dedicated people down.

"We brought you in for an audition," Iris said. "At least let us audition for you. We can rent a larger conference room and show you our skills."

"How many vampires have you killed?" Vance asked.

"None," David admitted. "We haven't found a vampire, yet."

Vance turned to Iris, not wanting David to somehow see by Vance's glare that he knew the two had found a vampire and simply proven inadequate. Maybe David didn't lie. Perhaps J.J. had coerced them to forget her.

"Henry's advice on finding vampires among the homeless and prostitutes didn't pan out," Iris said. "How many vampires have you killed?"

"More than two," Vance said. 'Thirty' seemed like it might be bragging or, worse, encouraging.

"And has The Black Dragon killed more than two?" Iris asked. "How many do you know about?"

Hundreds, Vance knew. "Way more than two," he said. At the mention of Dai, Vance realized he didn't have to deal with these two on his own. Dai would have a better idea than kill them, he hoped. She'd likely just want to kill them, but even the chance of a better idea was worth taking them to Dai. "I'll introduce you and let you show us your stuff. Meet me at the Nocturne.

It's a theatre near where you met Lanie. Nine o'clock tomorrow?"

"We could go earlier," David said, eagerly.

"I have a day job," Vance said. "Vampire hunting doesn't pay the bills and neither does acting, most days."

"Nine p.m.," Iris said. "The Nocturne. Hah, I like the name. It's ironic, really, vampire hunters meeting in a place that sounds more like a vampire's hangout. We'll see you there."

Vance gave a polite laugh, as much of a chuckle as he could muster. After forcing the chuckle to die slowly, long enough for him to warm his skin, he stood and offered his hand to Iris. "It was good to meet you. I'll see you tomorrow."

"Until then," Iris said. David echoed her.

IX

Vance texted Dai the appointment. He got out of the elevator on the top floor of the hotel and took the stairs up to the roof. Like many of the fire alarms on roof access doors, this one had been disabled. Vance assumed he found so many roof doors unlocked and with their alarms disarmed so employees could take smoke breaks on the roofs. No one seemed to take seriously the risks of a break-in from above. Vance didn't mind; it made his getting around easier.

On the roof, Vance glanced around. Seeing no one, he took to the air. He flew east, over the highway. It didn't take him long to fly the thirty miles to the Chino Hills. The chapel still stood out as the only building in sight. Neither the dirt road nor the wrought iron gate were wide enough for a modern car. Sta. Isabella's didn't cater to a regular congregation. Vance had rarely seen anyone besides Padre Guillermo and the caretaker in the chapel.

"Vance!" Padre Guillermo called when Vance walked through the doors. He started towards Vance, arms outspread for an embrace, then he paused and asked, "Wait, are we friends?"

"I don't hold grudges," Vance said. "Well, I'm holding one, but I'm not blaming you for it. If I'd let you have your way, I wouldn't be holding any grudges."

Months earlier, when Vance had stopped him from killing Zylpha, Guillermo had reacted coldly. Ever since, Vance regretted it. Zylpha had killed so many of his friends and colleagues, yet Dai couldn't kill her once she had reached the territory of the King of Las Vegas. Since Dai couldn't, Vance, as Dai's proxy, couldn't. To Vance, that meant he had to stop Guillermo from killing her, lest anyone think Dai had ordered it, blemishing her reputation. Dai had a very dark past and didn't need anything else tipping her scales towards selfish and evil. Vampires like Zylpha epitomized why Vance became a vampire hunter. Then again, so were vampires like Dai. His standards changed over time, more before he became a vampire than after. Vampires like Padre Guillermo and Vance's fallen mentor, Dirk, convinced him that vamps were not, by default, evil.

"I could be holding a grudge, but I understand why you stopped me," Guillermo said. "For a few days after, I wanted to punch you. I even bought a Vance Starr action figure with intent to burn it in effigy."

"I didn't know I had action figures," Vance said. "I guess that I'm happy you didn't burn it."

"I shot it instead," Guillermo said. "Turns out, birdshot reduces action figures to dust. That made me happy until I forgave you."

"When was that?" Vance asked.

"When you came through the door, just now," Guillermo said. "I was pretty upset at losing a friend. I don't have many. You and Dai are the only vampires I know locally. Elsa has gone back to France or Philadelphia. I'm not sure which. I get included in her group texts to Katina and Azure. There's a bunch of vampires I don't know in that list too: Milady, James, Reilla, and Laura. She never contacts me directly."

"Katina is still in town," Vance said. "She's your bloodsister, surely you could get to know her."

"I didn't know she was in town," Guillermo said. "I assumed she stayed close to Elsa. But you didn't fly all this way to tell me about Katina. Did you come just to forgive me or to seek forgiveness?"

"I'm killing again," Vance said. "I killed nine men the other night."

"Humans, not vampires?" Guillermo asked. "We expect you to kill rogue vampires. That's your job. Humans are another story. Did they deserve to die? Were they trying to kill you?"

"Some were trying to kill me," Vance said. "I slaughtered all the men in a whorehouse. Bloodeyes took control."

"Was this a gay whorehouse?" Guillermo said. "You didn't kill women?"

"One," Vance said. "Not one of the prostitutes, though. It turns out, heroin in blood won't smell like food while I'm under the control of the bloodeyes. At least, that's my theory."

"I can tell you, from experience, heroin does not reduce the Venae of blood," Padre Guillermo said. "It's a perception your beast has. Perhaps it's smell. I don't think this is the kind of thing we should experiment with to see who throws you into a bloodlust rage and who doesn't. Do you want confession for the murders?"

"I'm still not Catholic," Vance said.

"That's better for you. I can't give you penance," Guillermo said. "Still, a formal setting often helps people forgive themselves."

"That's just it," Vance said. "I don't feel guilty. It's twice in a week I've lost it. The first time, Cynthia stopped it instantly. This last time, nine men, all using women in a most horrid way. I killed humans, hot-blooded murder, slaughtered them like throwing a cat into a cage full of canaries."

"And you're worried you're becoming a monster all the time, not just when you lose control?" Guillermo asked.

"I don't even rationalize it," Vance said. "I am stopping short of feeling righteous, at least."

"You've already rationalized it," Guillermo said. "You killed the dregs of humankind, and you know it. I'm not one to talk about this, I've been one of the dregs in my past. It's why I ended up a vampire, because I deserved to die, and someone saw that I did. Those men you killed may not have deserved to die, but they certainly didn't deserve to live. Maybe not righteousness in terms of holy, but on a balance scale, I'd weigh your actions as a positive. Unfair legally, but a positive outcome."

"You have a bleaker perspective of the world than I do," Vance said.

"I don't think I do," Guillermo said. "I'm just willing to say it. We're not hanging out when we're having good days. You only come to see me when things are bad. So, you only see me commenting on things that are bad. There are a lot of wonderful things in the world. You don't come to me about your sex life, which I understand to be phenomenal, if the rumors are true."

"Who told you?" Vance asked. "Does Dai tell you everything? Did Lanie mention something when she texted you earlier?"

"No one texted me today," Guillermo said. "Almost all of my interactions are with people I see face-to-face. There aren't any rumors, at least, none that I've heard. I bluffed. You, however, just told me everything. You actually blushed as you spoke both Dai and Lanie's names."

"I don't blush," Vance said.

"I don't know if you do or not, but you're terrible at being interrogated," Guillermo said. "You answer the questions I ask with the kinds of questions which give away the answers."

"I'm not good at deception," Vance said. "I'm working on deflection techniques."

"They need more work," Guillermo said. "What if you meet someone who asks if you're a vampire?"

"Actually, that's another thing I need to talk about." Vance described his meeting with David and Iris. "I know Dai will kill them, and she'll be disappointed in me for not doing it myself. I do feel guilty for luring them to Dai. I think I should tell them that Cuba is in dire need of vampire hunters."

"Except you can't," Guillermo said. "You won't lie."

"I can't," Vance said.

"Everyone can lie," Guillermo said. "You do it every time you're in front of a camera."

"Acting is not meant to deceive," Vance said.

"Then maybe you need a different perspective," Guillermo said. "For instance, when you're playing the part of Los Angeles Sheriff, whether or not the badge and job are real, you're still just playing the part."

"That's true," Vance said. "But I try to be a good sheriff. I try to do the best job I can, given the circumstances. It is a real job, I'm a real sheriff. I just don't deserve to be."

"But thousands of vampires are relying on you," Guillermo said. "For you, duty trumps honesty."

"It seems like a dichotomy." Vance pulled his badge out. "To fulfill my duty, I must sacrifice integrity."

"Integrity is more than truthfulness," Guillermo said. "Integrity is being someone we can all count on to do the right thing, which isn't always obvious.

How did you lure two vampire hunters to a vampire's lair without lying?"

"I am a vampire hunter," Vance said. "I'm just very judicious in choosing which vampires to hunt. I can't kill them all, so I focus on killing the ones who do the most evil. I could kill the evilest vampire in the city every year, and it would be a century before I got to Dai."

"Probably not true, if you look at the whole of her life," Guillermo said. "You base your judgments on the now, not the entire history of a person."

"I base my judgments on what I know," Vance said. "Stories of the past cannot avoid being tainted by time and perspective. I live in a world where video evidence is everywhere. I'm shocked vampires are still myths. How did no one catch one of us feeding on a surveillance camera and put it on the internet?"

"I'm sure they have," Guillermo said. "People believe what they want, but rarely stray from what their parents taught them. They want to believe in themselves more than anything, so they trust what they've always known more than absolute evidence to the contrary."

Vance wondered how true the priest's words were. "And this explains two people stumbling on a notebook written by Henry the Inquisitor long before he became a vampire hunter. Henry had a trainer, but from what is in that book, he hadn't met them yet at the time he wrote it. These two are taking something they just found, something ridiculous, and dedicating their lives to it."

"Just based on the book?" Guillermo asked.

"The book started it," Vance said. "I guess they found enough corroboration when they started tracking Henry that it made it all believable. Because Henry turned out to really exist, everything Henry made up in his book became reality to these two hunters. The book shouldn't have seemed real. I saw not a single bit of evidence of any kind in the book. It was typical conspiracy theorist stuff, linking works of fiction. Statistical occurrences of fiction where stakes kill vampires, where silver is a weapon against vampires and where the Christian cross is a deterrent. All of which the book concluded were true, by the way. Now, because of that stupid book, two people, who probably aren't bad people, are going to die."

"I'm sorry, Vance," Guillermo said. "I'm siding with the five laws. These two are human, not vampires, and they know about us. Therefore, they must die."

"I know," Vance said. "But we let mages live. Why?"

"I can only speculate," Guillermo said. "I don't know much about vampire history, and my only experience with magic is talking with Azure once or twice, and we didn't talk about mage society. My guess is that most vampires don't believe in magi, and most magi don't believe in vampires. The few that do have the wisdom to know they share the same secret. If one of us gets exposed to the public, the other won't stay hidden for long."

"Concerning David and Iris, you don't think it's a sin for me to kill them?" Vance asked.

"Vance, you're in a position where you must sin," Guillermo said. "Every action you take with them will be a sin, and not a light one. You have the trust of thousands of vampires in the city who rely on you to keep them safe from vampire hunters. That is your primary duty. Well, your primary duty is probably to God, but as we've discussed in the past, his rules on vampires are nonexistent. You will save more than two lives by killing two hunters. There are two scenarios that could happen when those two manage to track down a vampire. They might kill the vampire, in which case this scenario resets. Eventually, a vampire will get the best of them. The question is, how many vampires and pets will they kill before that happens?"

"I keep coming to that same conclusion," Vance said. In his mind, the idea had been vague, not yet formed into words, but Guillermo clarified it into logic he could follow. "Since I'm here and my problems aren't changing and I'm barely feeling better about them, how about we get a beer and talk about something that isn't religion or magic?"

"Like sex with Dai and Lanie?" Guillermo asked.

"No."

§

The cantina Guillermo took them to wasn't more than a camper trailer with two kegs and a few bottles of tequila and one of bourbon and another of vodka. Guillermo wore his robes, but no one paid him any special attention. Most were focused on drinking. Some talked about the football discussion on the sports channel playing on two large televisions.

Guillermo and Vance discussed movies. Lanie usually picked the movies they watched during the days when she wasn't running around town, working. The priest had seen everything that had come out on DVD, so he'd seen everything Vance had and far more. According to Guillermo, Vance hadn't seen much of what was out there and available. Lanie didn't always adhere to Vance's desire to avoid movies that were rated R, but she usually did, so Vance hadn't seen any of Guillermo's favorite movies.

"Vance," Guillermo said. "I know you don't think the harsh language, violence and nudity will taint you."

"I find myself cringing at unnecessary language or hiding my eyes from unnecessary nudity," Vance said.

"Just try to enjoy it for what it is," Guillermo said. "You're using movies to pass time because we have so bloody much of it. Movies are about escapism, and if anyone needs to step out of reality for a couple of hours, it's Vance Silver. You need to let yourself get pulled in, experience the unreal, so that your surreal life feels normal. Most people like movies to experience the adventure; you may need them so real life doesn't always seem so wild."

"That's something to think on," Vance said. "I'm not sure I agree."

"It's a thought," Guillermo said. "You might also try nature documentaries, but not the ones that highlight carnivores on the hunt. Maybe the ones about pretty fish and coral reefs."

"Lanie keeps recommending yoga," Vance said. His phone started vibrating and ringing. His screen identified the caller as Randall, a police detective who thought of Vance as a friend. Vance kept his distance because Dai had messed with Randall's mind so many times through coercion. She'd even had Randall as a pet, briefly. Somehow, Randall kept thinking Vance was a friend. Vance liked Randall, and could watch a football game with him, but he felt like he'd used Randall. Vance answered the phone. "Hey, Randall, how are things going?"

"This is semi-official business, Sheriff," Randall said. "I'm texting you the address of a crime scene. Be there as soon as you can. Can you be there in less than an hour?"

Vance didn't wait for the text. "I can be there." Wherever the address was, if it were in Randall's jurisdiction, Vance could get there.

"Okay, buddy. See you soon." Randall hung up.

Vance looked at the address and forwarded it to Cynthia. "Pick me up two blocks east, I'm coming in from Chino Hills." He put a twenty-dollar bill on the table and laid his hand on Guillermo's shoulder. "Gotta fly."

"Don't be a stranger," Guillermo said. "I'll make a point to come by Hallows sometime soon."

Vance didn't have time to remind Guillermo that Hallows had burned. He walked quickly from the tiny bar and, once beyond the light, he flew back to the city.

X

Cynthia met Vance inside the stairwell on the third floor of the building. She gave him a tiny squirt bottle of water and a comb and told him to fix his hair. Flying at any significant speed tangled any hair, even as short as Vance's. He wore his blonde hair scruffy, just a little longer and wilder than clean-cut. Lanie would cut it for him once or twice a month to maintain his image. Vance preferred a military cut, but his preacher training taught him such haircuts made men too respectable. Most people trust soldiers, but don't look to them to lead them. Preachers should look like a well-groomed everyman.

As a vampire hunter, he'd kept it closer to a soldier cut. But when Henry disappeared, Vance let himself go. He never developed a beard as a human. What he had started had stopped when he became a vampire. Vance, like most vampires, couldn't grow facial hair.

When Cynthia nodded, he stopped combing water into his hair and handed her the comb and water bottle. She tucked them into one of her belt pouches. She handed Vance his badge and shoulder holster. "You keep a spare of these with you?" Vance asked. "This isn't mine." He took it anyway and strapped it on. He affixed the badge to the shoulder strap. He'd been wrong, the badge number was his.

"Yes, it's a spare," Cynthia said. "It's technically counterfeit, but since the badge number is your badge number, does it matter who made it?"

"No," Vance said.

"Apartment 38," Cynthia said.

Vance led them out of the stairwell. Randall leaned against the wall outside the open door. Crime scene tape hung from one side of the door. "You fly here?" Randall asked.

"Um, I was local," Vance said. "Just a bit east of the city. Not too far to drive in an hour."

"Your hair is wet," Randall said. "You just combed it in the stairwell. You think I don't know what you are, don't you?"

"An actor?" Vance guessed, unsure what Randall meant. He shouldn't remember the truth. By the five laws, Vance couldn't offer it. "A sheriff?"

"Dai told me this would be hard," Randall said. "I have to pretend I don't know about your kind, what you and Dai are. I can't even say the fricking word. She told me I shouldn't try to talk about it, and for over a year, I just sit and hope you'll bring it up sometime so I could tell you that I know. But you don't."

"You called me here because I'm a vampire?" Vance asked. After one in the morning, Vance didn't expect many people to be paying attention. The excitement of a crime scene would have worn off much earlier.

"Yes," Randall said. "Exactly. This is the kind of crime scene I need the input from one of you."

"Dai was supposed to make you forget," Vance said.

Randall sighed. "That would've been nice. Coercion only works if the memories haven't written to long-term memory, or something like that, right? I knew for far too long, spent too many days as Dai's pet, to be able to have my memories wiped again."

"Of course." Vance should have known. "So, she just makes you unable to communicate about vampires to anyone but her, or, it seems, me?"

"And her," Randall said, nodding to Cynthia. "I don't even remember what she is, but it's close enough to what you are that I couldn't say it either. This is all worth it to be rid of the Nine Princes, but it gets frustrating when I can't even talk about something."

"What's special here?" Cynthia asked. "Fang marks?"

"I can say 'fangs'," Randall said. "No, it's weird. I can't really explain. It's a show-and-tell thing. Come on." He went into the room. A man lay sprawled in the middle of the room, arms and legs outspread. A sheet covered him. Randall pulled away the sheet.

Vance had seen a lot of dead people. He'd seen people torn apart. This man was completely intact: no wounds, no missing blood, and no visible blood. His body hadn't decayed at all, it still looked warm. But no body Vance had seen had ever looked more dead. Something about it was missing, but it wasn't a visible part.

"That's insane," Cynthia said. "My eyes tell me he looks normal, like a guy went to sleep spread-eagle on his carpet. Only everything about him is screaming death. I'd cover my ears, but it's not that sense that's detecting the scream."

"It's like when blood loses that last hint of Venae," Vance said. "Only this isn't Venae we're talking about, it's something else. Cynthia is right. Venae is like another sense of smell. This is like another sense of sound, only a violent silence."

"That's what I'm talking about," Randall said. "No one else who'd been here could see it. So, I thought it might be a v…" he paused. "You know what I'm trying to say."

Vance knelt by the man and put his hand on the man's chest. The body still felt warmer than the room. "The medical examiner has already searched for marks?" Vance asked.

"Crime scene has," Randall said. "The M.E. is sending someone by three. They've had a rough night. Something like six partial bodies washed up by Zuma Beach."

"Tiger Sharks?" Vance asked.

"That's not a guess someone should be able to make," Randall said.

Cynthia punched Vance in the back, hard. "Idiot," she said.

"Dai's business?" Randall asked.

"It's a very long story," Vance said. "Could we leave it at saying I lost control and several customers and owners of a heroin den whorehouse got on my bad side? I could lie to you, but you wouldn't believe me. So, you get to know the truth. No innocents died."

"I'm happier when I don't know," Randall said. "Thanks for the honesty. You know I can't do anything about it one way or another. I was going to say that their party boat capsized in a very unlucky place off the shore of Anacapa Island. Realizing that they know so much, so fast, I should be able to guess it's all planted evidence to hide something darker."

"This guy have a name?" Cynthia asked. "Does he live here?"

"Dr. Alexander Barrilleaux," Randall said. "He's an archeologist at the university. Nothing's missing here, as far as we can tell, but his laptop is neither here nor at his office. We're treating this like a murder for intellectual property."

Vance looked closer at the dead man's face. He had seen it just a day or two earlier. It didn't look familiar so dead, but with effort he was sure it was Alexander from the coven of fake witches. He had a hunch why the guy looked so dead. "Necromancer," he said. "This man was killed by a necromancer."

"What?" Randall asked. "You know I can't put that in a report."

"Vampires drain life," Vance said. "Life is a replenishing energy constantly renewed by the human body and soul. It's a wild guess—I don't even know anyone who would know for sure—but this guy had his soul drained. Cause of death is absence of soul."

"You can't talk anymore," Randall said. "These are the kinds of things I don't want to know about. The M.E. is going to either call this cardiac or sudden brain death. Either works for me. If this is murder, my laws can't handle it."

"I'm pretty sure mine can't either," Vance said. "I do know whose laws would, but vampires don't interact with mages on any official level. I'll have Azure put you in touch with some local mage elders."

"Don't," Randall said. "I know better than to take on weird cases. This is not a case. This guy was not murdered. You have forty minutes to gather evidence if you want to have a case in your world, but in the human world, this is just some fool who had an aneurism."

"We don't need to collect evidence," Vance said. "I can't use a crime lab for forensics. If you find security footage of the people who came and went, please send me a copy, but I know who did this and why."

"Why? You already know why? You've been here five minutes and you've solved this. It was the necromancer with the cauldron in the living room?" Randall sighed. He clenched his fists and turned to the door. "Whatever you do, don't tell me a single further detail. There is footage of the lobby, and the lobby's the only way in or out that isn't locked. We're not going to need the footage, because we're going to find this man wasn't murdered. I'll send it to your office."

"Thanks, Randall. I'll be sure to not tell you how this turns out," Vance said.

Randall chuckled. "How about you just tell me if you get the guy, but don't tell me how."

"If it comes up, he lent his laptop to a grad student. It's not missing," Cynthia said.

"I like it. Aneurism and kindness killed this guy," Randall said.

"We'll get out of your hair," Vance said.

"Funny," Randall said. He kept his head shaved. "I plan on coming down to see you next week. Save a stool for me."

As Vance and Cynthia got into her car a few minutes later, he said, "That's like the third person who's forgotten that Hallows is gone. I don't know how to deal with this. I can't keep reminding people, I'd be an ass."

"Yeah, I have no idea what's going on," Cynthia said, fumbling with her belt loop to unhook her keys. When she finally got the car started, she asked, "You want to go see Azure, I take it?"

"Yeah," Vance said. "Let's go to Long Beach."

XI

Vance felt the chill as they pulled into the driveway at Azure and Katina's house. At the first scream, Vance rushed to the house. Finding the door smashed in, Vance drew his pistol and ran in, but stopped when another scream echoed through the house. That had been a male voice, but not like any human or vampire he'd ever heard. It was too guttural and sounded eerie. Something moved on the ground in the hall. Someone crawled on the floor, bleeding from where one leg and one arm had been severed.

It turned to look at Vance a second then turned to crawl towards him.

"Is that a fucking zombie?" Cynthia asked. She shot the crawler in the head, and it collapsed. "Looks like it's not the only one. I count eleven bodies."

Vance looked around. Blood covered the room. Venae flowed weakly in the man Cynthia shot in the head. It wasn't even enough to trigger Vance. Other bodies in the room were like the man, missing limbs or had crushed skulls or bullet wounds. Then Vance noticed the puddles and piles of wet dust. "There's more than eleven," he said. Azure could draw all the moisture from a body, leaving nothing but dust. When she dropped the water, it would make some large puddles.

"We can take these as a good sign, they're alive here, somewhere," Vance said. He stepped over some bodies and tried not to look down at the body parts as he made his way to the main hall.

"Aren't there other liquids in bodies besides water?" Cynthia asked. "I've seen her do that to a lime, but where did the citrus oils go? When she's done, it's just dust and water."

"Magic doesn't make sense to the world as I know it," Vance said. The trail of bodies, dust and puddles led to the back door. The bodies seemed to be piled higher the closer they got to the door, as if Katina and Azure had tried to use it as a bottleneck to make a stand. "Perhaps it's a series of forced chemical reactions to change the oils to water?"

"In high school chemistry, that's called 'burning'," Cynthia said. "Hydrocarbon plus oxygen in the presence of heat becomes water plus carbon dioxide or monoxide. I didn't see flames when Azure dehydrated that lime."

"If we could explain magic with science, it wouldn't be magic," Vance said. The back door had a body holding it open. It led to a sunroom with a hot tub. The windows overlooking the beach were all shattered, several bodies leaned over the broken glass.

Another eerie wail came from outside.

"Azure!" Cynthia called. "Katina!"

"Out here!" Azure called from the beach behind the house.

Vance ran after her voice. He found her holding her arms out. Four zombies struggled to approach her. Water sprayed forcefully out of their backs. Azure seemed to be pushing the water of the bodies away so forcefully, it flew from every cell of the zombie's bodies.

Katina knelt over a man's body. The man held a sword. When Katina looked up, Vance saw the dead man was Karlo, Katina's pet.

"If he's not dead," Cynthia said, "you need to drain him."

"He's dead," Vance said.

"His death is pulling at me," Katina said. "Save Azure."

Around them there were only a few zombies moving, and they moved very slowly towards them. Cynthia started shooting. Vance knelt at Katina's side. "Be strong," Vance said. "Don't let it pull you with him. Hold on to my hand. Use my hand to hold you here."

"The grip on me is stronger than that," Katina said. She took Vance's hand and held very tight. "Stronger than you. It's every bit as strong as me and nowhere near as tired. It's pulling so hard, it's nearly tangible."

"Phase!" Azure shouted. "Drop into the Venae until you don't feel it's pull."

Katina shifted out of the physical world. Dai had phased with Vance in tow before, but Katina did it differently that time. Vance felt the pull as he went with her into the Venae. The world looked different while phased, as if overlain with a subtle swirling purple and red haze.

"Let go, Vance," Katina said. "Its grip is looser but still pulling. I need to dive deeper, and I don't know that I'll find my way out. You have to phase back." She let go of Vance's hand and pushed him away.

Gravity took hold once Vance was on his own. He had to fly to keep from sinking through the sand. He was stuck phased out. He knew he should have the ability to control his phasing, but unable to perceive Venae, he couldn't see how others did it. Until that time, he'd never seen the red and violet haze. Realizing he had to do something, or he'd eventually fall through the earth, he moved in the direction of the world he knew, away from the haze. He could see Cynthia and Azure and moved towards them. Though he'd been less than a few yards away in traditional distance, it seemed much further as he pulled towards them. The direction wasn't one he'd perceived before. Once solid, he dropped to the sand and looked for Katina. A phased vampire would still be visible, though possibly somewhat translucent.

"Where is she?" Vance asked.

"She disappeared with you," Azure said. "You went completely invisible to me. Then you came back, alone."

"Katina had to go deeper," Vance said.

"Deeper?" Azure asked. "I didn't think you'd make it back. You're not supposed to phase all the way out, all the way invisible. There is no deeper than that. I've heard Elsa warn Shauna and Katina dozens of times: never phase more than you need to pass through a wall."

"You told her to phase out and she did," Vance said. "I think it was working. The grip of death seemed to weaken in the Venae, so Katina said."

"You were gone," Azure said. "I heard nothing."

"If she doesn't make it back, it gave her a chance," Vance said. "She was dying anyway, wasn't she?"

"No," Azure said. "I can't lose her. Shauna would kill me. Okay, she wouldn't kill me, but she'd hate me, which is probably worse. Take my hand, phase me into the Venae so I can call to her."

"I don't know how," Vance said. He took her hand anyway. "Maybe I can try doing whatever I just did to get back, only backwards."

Vance closed his eyes and tried to imagine the direction he'd moved to get back, and then tried to pull himself the opposite way. Nothing seemed to change. He concentrated, trying slight shifts in direction and he tried pushing and pulling with more force. None of which seemed to do anything. Then he saw Katina's light coming from an unnatural direction and leaned towards that. Azure's hand fell through his. As he followed Katina's light, he heard a voice he didn't know.

"I love you. I miss you," the voice said.

"I'll find a way. I love you, too," Katina's voice said. Her light faded as Vance followed her toward the physical world. Azure ran up and hugged Katina as soon as Vance felt the sand under his shoes.

"Shauna?" Vance asked. "Is that Shauna?"

"You heard that?" Katina asked.

"Heard what?" Azure asked. "Vance phased and left me here."

"Karina," Katina said. "She guided me back."

"From the Venae?" Azure asked.

"I fell all the way in," Katina said. "It's not impossible to get back, but it's far harder to get back than it is to get there. There are currents, and it's mostly just finding the currents that flow this way. Karina found me and showed me how to get back."

"Is that who I heard?" Vance asked. "She said, 'I miss you. I love you.'"

"Yes," Katina said. "She would only tell me she loved me and missed me and that she was forbidden from answering my questions. I asked a lot of questions. She then hurried me back here."

"The metaphysical ramifications of what you're saying are beyond measure," Vance said. "There has never been proof of life after death. It has always been taught that proof is not part of the plan. We need faith. Proof would adversely affect faith."

"Now you have proof," Katina said. "You heard Karina. You heard the voice of a woman who's been dead almost three years. Is that going to fuck with your faith?"

"No more than being a vampire has," Vance said. "What's more surprising is that Karina's been dead three years but died a vampire. It means she's not in Hell. I'd assume someone in eternal punishment couldn't interact with the person she loved, anyway. It is going to be odd, knowing there's something more, something beyond, without having to rely purely on faith."

"Mages are taught that necromancers can speak with passed souls," Azure said. "According to our teachings, no soul has ever spoken of what existence is after death. This isn't the first time I've heard that passed souls will claim speaking about it is forbidden. They never even say who forbids them. Did you see her?"

"She held my hand," Katina said as she nodded and then smiled. "She still looks like me. It was very hazy when I could see her, but she didn't look different than I remember her. I couldn't see her when I could see the physical world. She could hold my hand right up until she said what Vance heard."

"So, you can go see her again?" Azure asked.

"Not unless I'm willing to risk dying," Katina said. "I now know she's with me, just out of reach, all the time. We're going to find that asshole of a necromancer and force him to do that spell. At gunpoint, if necessary."

"These are zombies?" Vance asked. "These were sent by the necromancer?"

"These are actual zombies," Azure said. "I'd never known anyone who'd seen one, but I've been learning everything anyone would tell me about necromancers since we decided to bring Karina back. We were on the brink of giving up when we found that archeologist's notebook. I suppose now that Katina's spoken with Karina directly, there's zero chance of letting something like a zombie horde stop us."

"I know that spell will do it," Katina said.

"The archeologist's ritual book?" Vance asked.

"That's not the spell, the spell is different, but it takes a full coven to invoke it," Katina said. "We found the spell in The Temple of Blood. It didn't include instructions of the full coven like the archeologist's find did."

"The correct term is Coven of the Stars and Moon," Azure said. "No one knows what that is because that hasn't been possible for over thirty thousand years."

Two zombies climbed from the rocks behind Katina. Vance drew his pistol and shot both in the head. "Head shots work on these, right?"

"They're just people," Azure said. "Anything that kills a person will kill a zombie. Only, the wounds that don't kill won't stop them. They don't feel pain. Until they bleed out, they'll keep fighting."

"You said they were zombies, not people," Vance said. "Tell me I didn't just murder two people."

"They were mostly dead," Azure said. "The necromancer sucked away most of their soul energy, but not all. The mind requires soul to function properly. Without a mind, there's no brain, without a brain, there's no life. So, zombie."

"You're saying that I did just kill two people," Vance said.

"No, I said you didn't," Azure said. "Soul energy doesn't grow back like Venae. Once it's gone, it's gone. Zombies will follow instructions and are capable of thought up to about a third grader's comprehension. They can't talk and have little motivation to do anything but are very compliant. They'll go kill for the necromancer, but not with any haste or enthusiasm. Killing a zombie is a mercy on the little bit of soul that remains."

Katina said, "You didn't know this much yesterday."

"I'm talking with the necromancer at the Pentacle," Azure said. "She's a good kid, new to the political side of the mage world. We don't usually have a necromancer at the Pentacle. She literally took her oaths yesterday and my mom had her call me. How my mom knew I was looking for a necromancer, I have no idea. I guess all the secrets I thought I'd been keeping from her are not secrets at all. Then again, I shouldn't have thought I could keep a secret from a mage with a lot of friends who are adept seers. The new necro girl is nice, but she's green as can be. Necromancers are trained by—get this—dead necromancers."

"But this girl is too green for the spell we need?" Katina said.

"I wouldn't want anyone under thirty in the coven we're putting together," Azure said. "There may be things to do where there won't be time to think. The people we need must all have the reflexes to reign in random sprites."

"Sprites?" Vance asked. "Like fairies?"

"Nothing sentient," Azure said. "When magic is being harnessed, sometimes unsteady control lets bits slip through that can have random and sometimes disastrous effects. Imagine spilling a gallon of pure elemental flame and having it splash over everyone in the coven."

"Pure elemental flame is bad?" Vance asked.

"Think the heat of a star," Azure said. "Hotter than molten steel. At that temperature, people flash boil."

"Okay, so experienced mages only," Katina said.

"And, keep in mind, the last time the world saw a Coven of the Stars and Moon formed, they all died," Azure said.

"Yes, and you've seen the book. You said it's not supposed to kill everyone," Katina said. "They did something wrong or the spell they tried was too powerful. We have to be careful, sure, but we're going to get that necromancer and we're forming a Coven of the Stars and Moon and bringing my sister back."

"I like this less and less, the more I hear of it," Vance said. "Since I now know Karina is out there, for real, I can't be the guy who says you can't do this. Maybe consider doing this far from a population center, though? There's a lot of big empty desert just a couple hours away."

"We already know where the coven would have to meet," Azure said. "There's really only two super nodes on the west coast. Since one is on a jet fighter training range, we're probably going to the mountains east of Bakersfield. Do I need to explain what a super node is?"

"It's probably a place where the veil between us and magic is weaker?" Vance guessed.

"Yes," Azure said. "Well, I can't explain it better without giving a long lesson on how magic works, but that's all you really need to know."

"I'm beyond believing all magic to be the Devil's work," Vance said. "I haven't really reconciled it with my faith. I don't know if getting more details will help or hurt that. For now, I'll stick to just knowing what I need to know. For example, if you go missing, I know where the necromancer will take you."

"These zombies imply that the necromancer doesn't want us alive," Katina said.

"He just now got his hands on Alexander's notebook," Vance said. "He might not have known how much he needs you."

"Tell me you're joking," Azure said. "Damn, I know you wouldn't joke or lie about this, but his is the kind of knowledge the mages can't know. Especially not a necromancer."

"I came here from Professor Alexander whatever-his-last-name-is' apartment," Vance said. "We're pretty sure we found a body drained by a necromancer. Alex is dead and his computer is missing. My friend Randall caught that case and thought something was odd, so he called me. Odd is the best word to describe it."

"We can trust Randall to keep our secret?" Azure asked.

"He's coerced to not speak of vampires," Vance said. "He used to be a pet, so we can't make him forget everything he knows."

"I'm talking about mages," Azure said.

"Randall's not going to risk his career by talking about hocus-pocus," Vance said. "Don't the mages have a local in charge of enforcement? A mage sheriff?"

"The mages have the Pentacle, but no local royals or anything. Mages over 55 years old are considered elders, but they're just advisors. The Pentacle has archons, mages, usually the few potent fire mages that survive until adulthood, they'll call on to deal with problems."

"Assassin mages?" Katina asked.

"No one knows," Azure said. "For all I know, it's all scare tactics and mage mythology. We have a lot of bogeymen we push on our kids. We're pretty much trained from birth to live scared of doing anything to draw attention."

"I don't know what to do about all the zombies," Vance said. "I don't think our usual crime scene crew would be able to do something with so many bodies."

"I'll get it," Azure said. She held out her hands towards a corpse and pulled the water out, forming a sphere two feet in diameter. Without coming into contact with the water, she flung the sphere towards the ocean and then held out her hands to her sides. "I'm too tired to take them on four at a time, but I can dehydrate one at a time all night. We'll still need a clean-up crew, but we can skip the body disposal."

"Karlo?" Vance asked.

"We'll be more careful with his dust," Katina said. "I'll call his mom and explain something. We know the right people to document it as a medical death. Are we getting to the details you'd rather not know?"

"I'm just not the guy to call to back up your deception," Vance said. "I'll help however I can. I won't bear false witness, but if this isn't investigated, it won't come up. Your home is so secluded, it's not going to come up."

XII

The building standing where Hallows had once stood had only a single window lit. It was more than he wanted to see. He kept his gaze from looking that direction again as he approached Dai's theatre. Vance landed on the roof of Nocturne and took the ladder down to backstage.

Dai spoke from her chair. "Your hunter friends are out front. I wasn't going to let them in and be forced into small talk with them. They're your problem to deal with."

"I was hoping for some help," Vance said.

"I know," Dai said. "It's why I am here. You don't want to kill them and you're hoping I have another plan."

"I'll do what needs to be done," Vance said. "Guillermo gave me some math I couldn't argue with. These two have their hearts and minds set on the idea of being killers. Coercing them won't change that. Every scenario ends with these two dead. The variable is how many people and vampires they kill before they die. If they are a danger to anyone, human or vampire, they have to be neutralized." The anger over the situation boiled inside Vance. It swelled when he used the non-emotion provoking word instead of saying what he knew had to happen. To alleviate the tension within himself, he had to speak the truth. "I'm aware that means killed."

"I swear I'm not happy about this either," Dai said. "Vampire hunters are never easy to deal with. We can't wait to catch them in the act, and we can't hope that they lose against their first target. If they win, we're guilty of neglecting our duties. That's the kind of guilt you'll never live down."

"I'm getting them," Vance said. He couldn't avoid guilt. His plan involved doing exactly what he'd promised he'd do. He'd train them, but when that training turned to combat, Vance would ensure no one held anything back against him, by working himself up to not hold anything back against them. He asked Dai, "Swords?"

"I brought up the chest you asked for." Dai pointed to an old steel-reinforced wooden chest. "We have twenty-three stage swords. There are also six dress swords that are combat ready and sharpened in that chest with the others. Your sword is at the side of your throne. Mine is by mine."

"Thanks," Vance said. He jogged up to the lobby where he found David and Iris sitting outside with their backs to the door. David browsed social media while Iris seemed to be playing a game on her phone.

Vance unlocked the door and invited them inside.

"This is cool," Iris said, gliding her hand across the brass fittings at the ticket taker's podium. "I like the vintage feel."

"Not me," David said. "It's quaint. I appreciate the aesthetics. I prefer the modern theatre with the recliners and full bars."

"This one has a wine bar," Iris said.

For a moment, Vance panicked. He worried the wine bar would give the theatre away as a vampire meeting hall. In truth, the theatre more often hosted human parties for companies and birthdays than it held vampire events like Dai's court. The wine bar shouldn't mean anything. Even if it did, neither David nor Iris were going to leave the theatre alive. Vance took a deep breath. The hunters chose their path. They had to know the risk involved.

"One night of training," Vance said. He heard the nerves in his voice. He knew David and Iris did, too. He hoped they were so eager to learn, they wouldn't be paying attention to Vance's nervousness. "We're focusing on sword combat. There is a chest on the stage. Go pick a dulled sword that feels right in your hands. You'll get to meet my partner, The Black Dragon."

Vance opened the door to the auditorium and let Iris and David go through first.

"Who's the girl on the throne?" David asked as they walked down the aisle.

"She's Daiyu Long," Vance said. "Call her Dai." Seeing her as David would, a college-age Chinese woman, Vance thought better of calling her The Black Dragon. Henry's book from decades earlier mentioned The Black Dragon. That infamous hunter wouldn't be the petite Asian girl who hadn't aged since halfway through her thirty-third year. He climbed the steps to the stage for the first time ever and stopped by the chest. He opened it and took out the top sword. It resembled his real sword in size and shape but had a rounded edge almost an eighth of an inch thick. "For now, let's see what you know of sword fighting."

"We thought swords would make us stand out," Iris said. "We have a hatchet in our hunt bag for removing a vampire's head after we shoot the vampire or stake it."

"Grab a sword," Vance said. "The first thing you want to do in any fight is establish that you have the power to win. Any vampire that's been shot before won't fear your gun. They'll hesitate when faced with a weapon that can actually kill them. If a vampire is aware of you, but not afraid of you, you cannot win in a one-on-one fight. The primary rule of using a sword in a fight is to keep it between you and your opponent. If your opponent has a weapon, keep the sword between you and the weapon."

"Even if it's a gun?" David asked.

"If you have a sword and your opponent has a gun, you are unprepared," Vance said. "You have two choices: get close enough so you can bat aside their gun with your sword before they think to pull the trigger or get far enough away that the bullets can't reach you."

"Vampires won't have guns," Iris said, then turned it to a question. "Will they?"

"Most vampires go about their nightly lives with little on their mind besides enjoying their existence," Vance said. "Like most people, vampires are rarely prepared for a fight. However, there are vampires that carry pistols, like this one." Vance reached into his pocket and pulled out his derringer. He'd had the two-shot pistol in his pocket for years and he always kept it loaded with gold bullets. "Now, don't go hunting vampires in Texas or Wyoming. Everyone, vampire or humans has the potential to be armed in those states. New York, Los Angeles, Chicago and other large cities won't have an armed population of vampires."

"Vampires won't have swords, though," Iris said. "No one will. They're too big to fit in a pocket."

"You won't hunt vampires on the open street," Vance said. "Where you hunt, you can have any weapon you can use. Choose your hunting grounds carefully. Killing a vampire will look like murder to an onlooker. You can't be seen doing it and no one will believe you if you say you killed a vampire. There won't be evidence. Vampires turn to dust and leave nothing behind."

"The book suggests that," David said. "It also says vampires will use their political influence to make sure arrested hunters never survive a night in jail. Is it true? Have vampires infiltrated law enforcement so as to be able to kill hunters?"

"There are certainly vampires who serve in law enforcement," Vance said. "You will need to plan so well that there won't be a witness, won't be a crime."

"Show me swordplay," Dai said. "Vance, you promised this wouldn't be boring."

Vance glared at Dai. She rushed him towards the inevitable murder of David and Iris. He couldn't argue with her. She was right that they shouldn't delay. He gestured towards the center of the stage. "Why don't the two of you spar for a minute, let me see where your mechanics need work."

Dai sidled up to Vance as Iris and Dave fought with the stage swords. They fought like actors, not really swinging at each other so much as swinging near each other or at each other's swords. Dai asked, "What are you doing? I admit, it's educational to see how hunters think, but you're toying with them like a cat toys with a mouse. I didn't expect such sadism from you."

"I'm going to let them fight me," Vance said. "In fifteen minutes, I'm going to get real steel out and let them try to fight for their lives."

"Will you tie your shoelaces together to make it more fair?" Dai asked. "Perhaps you'll go with the sporting challenge of wielding your sword in your teeth. If this is going to take that long, I'm going to make a phone call. I'll be back before your finale."

Vance took up a practice blade and stepped in and sparred with each of them, showing them how to control their blades with their whole arm instead of their wrists. David fought like a movie warrior, going for the glory shots. Vance slapped him in the back with the flat of his sword every time he exaggerated a move.

Iris fought conservatively, focusing on defense until Vance went a little off-center with his guard, then she'd strike.

Thirty minutes of sparring passed and neither Iris nor David tired. Vance exchanged their stage weapons for sharpened steel swords. He took his own sword from beside his chair and unsheathed it. The blade gleamed in the stage lights. The waves of the layered steel were barely visible, but he knew how to look for them, so he always saw them. Dai had the sword made for him when they'd met. The style had a heavy blade, heavier than a human would want to carry. Dai insisted medieval European swords were best for a sword fight. Vance hadn't tried many styles of swords to know if her preferences held true for him.

The swords he'd given David and Iris were American Cavalry weapons. They were replicas, but quality replicas. Vance had killed the prior owners of those swords.

"Now, we're raising the stakes," Vance said. "If one of you draws first blood, I'll give you another lesson."

David approached first. He didn't do anything surprising. He didn't do anything right, either. He kept trying to set up feints, but Vance knew to watch balance and gracefully had his sword in place to parry every time David tried to hit him. Vance swung back just enough to keep David trying.

A few minutes passed, and David's gambits got more grandiose with each pass. Every trick Vance had seen on television shows or in the movies, David tried. Vance didn't fall for any of it. Then David tried something utterly stupid. He dropped his sword onto his foot and kicked it at Vance. So surprised was he by the complete foolishness of throwing his sword, Vance barely managed to grab it out of the air by the hilt.

"Holy shit!" David said. "How the hell did you do that?"

"He's a vampire," Iris said so casually, Vance wondered how long she'd known.

"That's true," Vance said.

David stepped close, looking Vance in the eye, then sidestepping, as if from a flank, Vance's vampireness would be more obvious. Vance lifted his upper lip. "Vampires, in real life, can't retract their fangs."

"That is so cool!" David said. "It makes total sense. No one can hunt a vampire better than another vampire."

"Let me show you how true that is." Vance flipped David's sword and holding it by the tip of the blade, handed it to David. "Now come at me and I'll show you how fast a vampire can be."

David didn't try anything tricky that time. He just inched forward, swinging from just out of range to try to get Vance off his guard. Vance stepped in before David could pull his sword between them and slapped David's hand hard enough with his own hand to make David drop his weapon.

"You can't take a vampire on one-on-one," Vance said.

Iris said, from closer than Vance had noticed her move, "No, but if we distract you with one of us, we can surpr…"

The clang of steel rang close to Vance's ear. Half of a sword blade fell to the floor. Dai stood beside Iris, having just knocked her blade away from Vance so hard, Iris' cavalry blade broke. Dai checked her own blade for nicks. "Vance," Dai said. "You just showed them why vampire hunters sometimes succeed. You got cocky and distracted."

"You're…" Iris said.

Again, Dai interrupted her. "The Black Dragon? Yes."

"Does this mean you're going to make us into vampires?" Iris asked.

"No," Vance said.

"Yes," Dai said.

"Huh?" Vance asked.

"I talked to Artemis. She helped me find a way to not have to kill these two," Dai said. "You see, vampires just don't let anyone live with their secret."

"So, no one dies?" Vance asked.

"I didn't say that," Dai said.

"I'm confused," David said. "Should I be scared?"

"You're in a room with the vampire queen of Los Angeles," Dai said. "You're a vampire hunter. What do you think?"

"You said they'd live," Vance said. "What did Artemis say?"

"You're the last of the line," Dai said. "You can make a child. Artemis likes hunters."

"I can make only one of them into a vamp," Vance said. "Artemis vampires can only have one bloodchild."

"So, which one of us?" David asked. "Are you going to make us fight for the right to be a vampire? Can't you make one of us a vampire and then have that one make the other one of us a vampire?"

Vance couldn't look at David to answer him. Artemis' plan saved one of the hunters, but the choice wouldn't be left to chance.

"Having you fight for it sounds fun." Dai went to her throne and lifted the seat. She pulled out a pair of gold-plated revolvers with long barrels. She then handed one of the pistols to Iris. Walking towards David, Dai stopped and looked at Vance. She smiled, but her eyes were sad. She put on an act for Iris and David, but, like Vance, Dai didn't enjoy the game. She shook her head at David and went, instead, to stand at Vance's side.

"This might be the most evil thing you've done," Vance said.

"I haven't done it yet," Dai said. "I'm letting them make the choices."

"One of them," Vance said.

"Um, could I get the other gun?" David asked. He started inching backward, looking towards the door.

"Do you expect me to just shoot my unarmed boyfriend?" Iris asked.

Dai answered, "The thing is, Vance is an abomination, and one Artemis won't allow to happen again. All of Artemis' bloodline are women."

"Iris!" David yelled.

"Okay then." Iris raised her pistol toward David. The crack of a gunshot rang far closer to Vance than he expected. David collapsed, already dead by the time he hit the ground. Dai had shot him before Iris could.

"I wasn't going to let her live with that," Dai said. "No one should kill their lover."

Vance stared at David's corpse. The reality of killing the hunters seemed far less noble and entirely monstrous in the face of it. "Iris lives?" Vance asked.

"If she survives the change, she lives." Dai went to Iris, who stood still staring down the barrel of her gun at where David had been standing. After gently taking the pistol from Iris' hand, Dai led her back to Vance. "Since we're doing this without the best preparation and without years of precautions, we're going to do this the traditional way. Vance, you need to drink three pints of her blood."

"That'll kill her," Vance said.

"No, it will acclimate her blood to you," Dai said. "She'll get woozy. You'll then need to feed her your blood until she passes into unconsciousness. Then you drink her blood until she dies. This is the most likely way for her to survive this change. Artemis vamp blood almost always succeeds. Since they created their curse almost three thousand years ago, Artemis knows of two people who failed to make the change."

"I'm ready," Iris said. "If I die, at least I'll be with David."

"Dai, keep me coherent," Vance said.

"Cynthia told me about punching you in the nose," Dai said. "I find I'm surprisingly eager to see how that works."

"Of course you are," Vance replied and then looked at Iris, catching her gaze. "Pain is bliss," he said. He took her wrist and bit into her artery. She fell unconscious after a few seconds, but Vance drank until he estimated he'd taken in three pints. He then licked the wound on her wrist closed.

Dai took Iris' hand from Vance and pinched between the thumb and forefinger. Iris moaned a moment then woke with a start.

"I fell asleep?" Iris asked. "How much of that was a dream?"

"If it seemed like a nightmare," Vance said, "none of it was."

"What's next?"

"Half a cup of your blood, Vance," Dai said. She let go of Iris' arm and took Vance's. She bit Vance's wrist and handed his dripping arm to Iris. She drank thirstily, seemingly unperturbed by the taste. To Vance, blood tasted like honey. To a human, blood tasted like iron and sulfur. Iris pulled away once Vance's wound closed.

Iris looked up at Vance, then her eyes rolled back in her head, and she fell to the floor, spasming.

"I guess this is better than killing them both," Vance said.

"It lessens the guilt factor significantly," Dai said. "We're giving her a fighting chance."

"And David?" Vance asked.

Dai didn't respond. She stared at Iris. Vance understood. Dai didn't want to voice the fact that David died the moment he contacted Vance.

Iris fell still, her heart stopped.

"Is this right?" Vance asked.

"You didn't have a heartbeat for ten minutes," Dai said. "When I turned you, I was worried your heart would start again before the Nine Princes left Hallows. I don't know if that was normal or if we got lucky with you. Watching you turn is the sum of my experience. Artemis explained it all, but only insofar as to how to do this to maximize her chances of survival. Iris is strong-willed and healthy. She has about a ninety-five percent chance of survival, according to Artemis. If she were your pet, the odds would be even better. Artemis blood is the most reliable for making a vamp, but we have that limit of one vampire per generation."

Dai moved David to the back door and brought out a mop and bucket and cleaned the blood from the stage. Vance just stared at Iris, wondering when her heartbeat would return.

It never did.

XIII

"She was a sister we never knew," Thalia, Dai's bloodmother, said, setting a flower on the polished wood coffin at the front of the stage. David's coffin sat just offstage.

It surprised Vance when Dai insisted Iris be treated like a fallen sister of the Artemis bloodline. From the way she doted over the preparations, Vance didn't think her actions were just to appease him. A dozen sisters had arrived the night after Iris died. They talked through the night and most of the next day, telling tales of many other women who almost became sisters.

Vance sat in his chair on Dai's stage and listened while the women sat around a pile of large salt crystals illuminated from within by electric lightbulbs. Dai sat beside Thalia, though they didn't speak directly to one another at all that day. Before the massacre at Hallows, Thalia had directly contradicted Dai's wishes on how to treat a small group of newly made vampires earlier in the year. As far as Vance knew, they hadn't spoken since.

Callisto had more tales than anyone. She'd never made a blooddaughter, despite trying dozens of times. She knew stories about each fallen woman, all of them heroes of their time. Callisto predated the curse. She'd been part of the ceremonies and gained some effects such as losing her aura, but didn't count towards the one vampire per generation, and it seemed she couldn't procreate.

When the sun fell again, they carried the two coffins to the graveyard and buried them side by side, marking the graves with a pair of brass plaques. "David, love of Iris" and "Iris, sisters unto death and beyond."

Vance had spoken for David, using a sad, generic eulogy he knew to tailor to anyone he didn't know well. He mentioned David's eagerness to fight and his desire for righteous glory.

Thalia spoke for Iris. She didn't know anything about her but seemed to have endless fuel to talk about the heart of a hunter and the true spirit of a fury.

When they left, they each hugged Vance and Dai. Most called him brother, but a few insisted, despite his sex, he was a sister too. Vance had a dozen names and faces to remember. He'd never forget Callisto but wasn't sure he'd get the right names to match the faces for Hestia, Prima, Adrasteia, Natasa, Desma, Echo, Sophia, and a few names that never stuck in Vance's head.

"Are you okay?" Lanie asked as the last of the sisters to leave, Callisto and Thalia, kept talking with Dai by the gravesite.

"I honestly never thought I'd see anyone buried," Vance said. "Everyone

I care about turns to dust when they die. It seemed like, as I spoke over them, that I was speaking for everyone who'd died under my watch. Fiona, Nya, all my friends who died in the fire."

"You didn't come to that service," Lanie said.

"They held it at noon on a Wednesday," Vance said.

"We had a vigil at Hallows," Lanie said.

"I couldn't go there," Vance said. "As brave as I am, as strong as I am, I couldn't look at the blackened shell of bricks more than once. I saw it the night after the fire, and I never need to have such a sorrowful image burned into my mind."

"So much blood," Lanie said. "I understand."

"Dirk," Vance said. "Dirk loved that bar, even when he hated the modern era of music."

"Dirk loved the music," Lanie said. "He just had so little to complain about that he made stuff up, just so he could relate to people who actually had things in life to complain about."

"That doesn't help," Vance said. "He entrusted the bar to me, and I burned it down."

"You wouldn't tell me what it looked like inside after Zylpha murdered a hundred people," Lanie said. "But Dai did. It had to burn. We all know that nothing else would have concealed Zylpha's bite marks. We don't have the capability to hide that many bodies. Any story of so many people missing would have led to far too many investigations far too close to vampires. I would say I miss Hallows more than you, but it's the only bar you ever knew, and it was your bar."

"You know what's weird?" Vance asked. "At least three times, people have mentioned Hallows to me this week as if they don't know they're poking at scars that won't heal for years."

"Um," Lanie said. "That is weird."

"I know," Vance said. "It's nights like this I miss it more than ever. It's not the same drinking in a hotel room or even in the hotel bar. I think I need to see if I can actually get drunk. I keep doing the right thing and people keep dying around me. Don't even explain how Iris and David had to die. I know it. I've accepted it. I'm sick of the killing. Maybe I just want one night off. Can we get a six-pack of beer and just go back to the hotel and watch some movies? Maybe make it a case of beer and veg out for the next day?"

"You know, I know a place you'd like," Lanie said. "I've known about it for a while, but I wasn't sure you were ready. I'm still not sure this is a good idea, but we're going there tonight."

She walked quickly to her motorcycle and tossed Vance his helmet. "First stop is Nocturne," she said. "I need to get my wallet. Do we need to change clothes?"

"My experience with bars is a goth bar," Vance said. "You're wearing a black dress and a long black wig, and nothing but black make-up. I think you'll fit in. I'm in a black suit with a black shirt. I might look a bit overdressed, but I'll look good doing it."

"Okay, hold on tight," Lanie said.

She drove straight towards Nocturne, not taking the usual back roads to avoid passing where Hallows used to be. Vance stared at the building that stood on the old lot as they pulled into the parking lot.

A neon light across the front read, "Dirk Death's Hallows."

Vance had not meant to use his apportation power. Stunned, he had reached out and grabbed anything he could, which meant two cars they passed. The cars barely moved, but Vance, being of much less mass, stopped and fell off the bike as Lanie pulled into a parking spot by the building wall. He landed on the concrete and sat there. He stared at the sign and cried.

"Vance?" Lanie asked, squatting beside him. "Is this okay? Are you angry? Is this bringing back too much sadness? I'm confused. You're smiling. You're happy, right?"

"I think I'm happy," Vance said. "I have no idea how this is possible. How could I not know? It's like everyone's been telling me and I'm too dense to hear it."

"No one was supposed to tell you," Lanie said. "I didn't think you were ready. Dai wanted to tell you three months ago, when they started rebuilding the walls. I wouldn't let her. You'd find it when you were ready, I thought. I actually expected you to notice it before now."

"When did it reopen?" Vance asked.

"Grand opening is tonight," Lanie said. "You were coming here tonight, one way or another. We've been soft open for three days, auditioning bands and training staff. Callisto and Prima were already planning on being here in case we had to drag you inside kicking and screaming. If we'd shown up at Nocturne instead of here, well, let's just say they had a lot of gaffer tape ready. But you're here. I'm so glad you're taking this well. I'm happy that it makes you happy."

"I don't know how to talk," Vance mumbled. He couldn't think of the right words. "You did this?" he asked.

"I handled the planning," Lanie said. "Dai procured the loans. She wouldn't finance it herself, but she got some great rates and some hefty grants, too. It's a full restoration, which apparently means something if we rebuild it. There are a few changes, mostly to bring it to modern codes."

"I look like a fool sitting in a parking lot, crying," Vance said.

"Yeah," Lanie said. "But I love this fool."

"I love you," Vance said. "I still can't even begin to fathom how this is all here again."

"Yeah," Lanie said. "I understand there was quite a bit of graft involved to get it done so quickly. Wanna see inside?"

"I hope I can handle it," Vance said.

"Me, too," Lanie said. "I don't think I have enough bartenders on staff for this crowd. You'll probably have to help out back there."

"I can't wait," Vance said.

XIV

Hallows felt the same as Vance remembered. The dark corners didn't seem as dark, but the club wasn't really the lights or the walls. Hallows had always been about the people and the music they shared. It seemed like most of the faces were familiar. He even remembered the drinks for most of the people. When the band rested, people would congratulate Vance for reopening. A few would offer condolences for the loss of the old Hallows and for the many who died in the fire.

After closing, Vance went to talk with some of his old regulars who stuck around to catch up with each other. They spoke mostly of the differences. Vance hadn't noticed. The bar had a few minor positioning differences, but everything had been in basically the same place. The beer list had grown. Dirk wouldn't approve of so many microbrews represented, but he'd have succumbed to adding them because he would want to please his customers. Dirk came from an age where you got whatever the tavern brewed. Every beer in the seventeenth century would be a microbrew, but drinkers couldn't be picky in those days.

"The LED walls are incredible," one guy, a dentist who plays in a couple of Lanie's bands, said.

"Thanks," Vance said. "This is all Lanie's work." He looked at all the posters on the walls. They were still mostly the posters and flyers he remembered. The walls looked cleaner, but he hadn't noticed that a large swath of each of the side walls were paneled electronic screens. He had noticed the thick layer of plastic sheeting over the walls, but assumed it was there to protect the posters.

"It's color e-ink," Lanie said, coming up to Vance's side. She wrapped herself around his arm. "It's not lighted, we have to illuminate it. It makes it look more natural that way. I think the colors are limited, like classic poster printing. The pixels only come in four colors. Dai actually procured that from a start-up she'd investigated as an investment opportunity. Technically, it's a demo install, but it's permanent. Dai can be very coercive. She almost got them to pay to be able to use our club to demo their product. We had to pay for the half-inch acrylic overlay to protect the screens, though."

"Well, the club looks awesome," the dentist said.

"Thanks," Lanie said. "I'm going to take Vance. You guys can stick around for a while. No more drinks, though."

"I guess now I get the tour?" Vance asked.

"The walls were supposed to be the capstone of the tour," Lanie said. "They're not prototype; they're first run production, but the software still has some bugs to work out so we may have techies stopping by to update that every few days. Dai, a couple longtime customers, and I all worked hard to make everything look as much the same as we could. We have all the virtual posters and flyers the same as the ones we had before the fire. We replicated them from photographs, and Dirk had some in the basement that were ruined by water damage but still scanable. The building had to keep the same footprint, but we added some space to the club by eliminating the barbershop that had been closed for who-knows-how-many years. We found a company that runs a bunch of food trucks around the city to put in a tiny sandwich and burrito shop where there used to be a soup restaurant."

"I don't remember anything but Hallows on the ground floor of the building," Vance said.

"It's been a while since anything but Hallows was open," Lanie said. "The restaurant doesn't have seating. It's basically a food truck without wheels. Having food near means we don't lose customers who decide to leave to get a late-night snack. Now, they just run outside and grab a burrito and bring it back to our bar to eat. The downside is we have to take out the trash more."

"And this is good for business?" Vance asked.

"It means we'll get people in for dinner," Lanie said. "We might just be selling a soda and a beer, but it's normally a slow time for us, and a couple more beers and a handful of sodas would make a difference. Remember, our staff, you included, are not permitted to deliver food, even from the counter to a table or the bar. Seriously, we don't want to have to get that permit."

"What's upstairs?" Vance asked. "Did you restore the apartments, too? Even 3C?"

"Upstairs is all new," Lanie said and pointed up. "We don't have any themed apartments like 3C used to be. I looked into it, but specialty décor is like ten times the price of commercial elegant décor."

Vance looked up, instinctively. He couldn't see the apartments above. He did see something he hadn't noticed; the club now had a balcony level. From behind the bar, he didn't have a line of sight to it. He looked around and found the way up. Behind the bathrooms, a spiral stairway led up.

"VIP area," Lanie said. "See how it's over the hanging lights? It means our VIPs can do pretty much whatever they want without being seen."

Vance wasn't sure whether Lanie meant sex, drugs or vampires feeding. He didn't have time to ask as Lanie kept talking about the building. "Above the club, we have three levels of apartments. Eight studios on the third floor, six one-bedrooms on four, four two-bedrooms on five and our residence on the sixth, the top floor. The roof is thick enough to be vampire safe. The second floor is the club's high ceiling and the balcony. Above the sandwich and taco shop, the second floor holds our office and green-room."

"No more office downstairs?" Vance asked.

"Let me show you," Lanie said. She lifted the section of floor behind the bar that revealed the stairway down. The stairs were welded steel with grates for stairs instead of the wood and nails of the old Hallows' stairwell. Downstairs, the storeroom extended for the whole size of the building, though only a small section had shelves. Most of it was stark and empty. The unpainted poured-concrete walls and pillars gave the basement a less-than-homey feel. The old basement had been cozy and comforting. The new one just felt like a basement.

"There should be a bedroom down here," Vance said. "Maybe we can build one in all that empty space?"

With one finger, Lanie gestured for Vance to follow her. She went to one of three walk-in coolers and pressed the thermometer. It clicked like a button. Lanie opened the door to reveal another door, an elevator door. Those doors slid open to reveal a small elevator. Four, maybe five people could fit inside. Lanie got in, so Vance followed.

Lanie said, "There are eight floors including this one. We have an emergency shelter down fifteen feet under the basement. It was part of the old Hallows, we just built over it. I think it was a speakeasy at one time, then a fallout shelter. Now it's a survivalist cave. We added a tunnel to Nocturne. Neither of those show up on the plans we turned over to the city."

"I guess that means I don't get days off," Vance said. "The elevator doesn't go directly to the bar? I have to come down here to go up?"

"You can get to the elevator from the club. There's a concealed door on every floor, including the ground floor of the club and another on the balcony. Each leads to a little atrium for this elevator. The residents use elevators at the far end of the building."

"How many residents do we have?" Vance asked. "Dirk rented, usually at a financial loss, to friends and several members of the bands that played here."

"We're not changing that," Lanie said. "Dirk owned the building without any mortgages or loans, so he didn't rent for a loss, just not for a profit. We do have loans to pay for Hallows as a business, but not for the building. It was paid by grants and insurance, so the rent is staying the same for old residents. New renters will pay a little less than the going rate for a new apartment in this area. Dai protested. She wanted to charge luxury apartment rates since they're thoroughly modern and swanky. She doesn't have any financial stake or other reason to have a say in how we do things here. She considered having an apartment here, but we decided she's best having her place downtown and she can stay at our apartment should the need arise. Before you ask, she'll have her own bedroom."

"With the whole top floor being our apartment, I'd think we could have a couple spare bedrooms," Vance said.

"One for us, one for Dai, one for Marisol and a guest room," Lanie said.

"Marisol had her own apartment before," Vance said.

"She has a suite in ours," Lanie said. "There are fewer apartments now. Some of our old renters are back. Half the units are rented out now. Two are new tenants, both are vampires. They know there's a strict rule: no feeding on the clientele of Hallows."

"Is our apartment furnished?" Vance asked.

"We have some furniture," Lanie said. "The kitchen is done. We have dishes, pots, and pans. No table yet. The one I ordered will take a couple months, but we don't dine up there anyway, so no rush. I wasn't getting food until we had a move-in date."

Vance's phone buzzed. He'd gotten a text from Hannah. "They tell me you're here, but I don't see you."

"This is weird," Vance said. "She usually calls. We've barely met in person; once, actually." He texted back. "I'm in the stock room. Are you at Hallows?"

"Yes," Agent Dwyer replied. "Should I come down or are you coming up soon?"

"OMW up," Vance texted back. He told Lanie, "Even she knew about Hallows. Let's take the stairs. No sense revealing the hidden door."

"It's not supposed to be a secret," Lanie said. "It is biometrically locked, but that has a major drawback."

"Like Nocturne's fingerprint locks?" Vance asked. "How is there a drawback?"

"The fingerprint scanners at Nocturne use imaging, which is cheap and highly secure but old tech," Lanie said. "I invested in a more advanced system here. This one reads bioelectric signatures in your skin and vamps are too low voltage, or something. For what it matters, while we have carefully advertised the grand re-opening in our email groups and at the other goth clubs in town, none of it should have targeted Agent Dwyer, unless she's on our mailing list, and I thought I actually knew everyone on that list. I don't know how she knew to find you here."

"She's an FBI agent with a grudge," Vance said. "She's probably tracking my phone."

"Or, well, you know this is your address of record," Agent Dwyer said from the bottom of the stairs. "And I don't have a grudge. I've told you; I think you're a great guy. You just don't deserve your job and don't do it well."

"If you didn't come for me for my job, you're a bit late for social time. Last call was thirty minutes ago," Vance said.

"Right now, I'm looking for a bad lawman," Agent Dwyer said. "The thing is, we have a ton of evidence against Dougal and his closest lieutenants. The problem is that everything we have has been thrown out as inadmissible in court. Trust me, everything we presented had been acquired properly. We're very anal about our warrants in the FBI. We don't make mistakes. Somehow, Dougal turned one of our agents, and that agent testified that we used false statements and manufactured evidence to fraudulently file for the warrants. Everything else we had, every other warrant, every witness statement, had been driven from evidence collected from those three warrants. So, our whole investigation is tainted, and we'll have to start from scratch."

"You have to establish that you could reasonably have learned each fact without the evidence collected from the warrant," Lanie said. "But anytime you do that, you're still open to having it thrown out. You need Dougal to do something illegal and start a fresh investigation on the evidence of that illegal activity."

"You're Vance's lawyer girlfriend, not the banker, I take it?" Hannah said. "Yeah, it's frustrating, but it's not the first time we had to start a case over. The thing is, we have a situation where we learned of one of Dougal's operations and we can take it down tonight."

"It's four-thirty in the morning," Vance said.

"Which means the women we're going to rescue have been on shift for half an hour," Agent Dwyer said. "Don't worry we're only going a block to a clothing factory. We're just going to set the women free and be on our way. No paperwork. There will be two armed guards, but they're probably not paid enough to draw their guns. In case we do have to shoot, you'll need this." She pulled a black cylinder a few inches long and an inch wide from her pocket. "I hope that's a Glock 9mm in your shoulder holster." She handed Vance the cylinder.

"I'm not carrying my service weapon," Vance said. "You're giving me a suppressor?"

"You can call it a silencer," Dwyer said. "We do. If you need a pistol, I have a couple spares in my trunk."

"Your gun safe is in the office, upstairs," Lanie said.

"I guess I'll head up and grab that and meet you outside." Vance inspected the silencer, making sure the bullet pathway was unobstructed. "This is kind of cool. I hope I don't have to use it. I'm not in the mood to kill anyone," he said.

"You have a mood for killing?" Dwyer asked.

"Never," Vance said. "Today, I'm just particularly against the idea."

"If things get hot, I expect you'll shoot and aim for center mass," Dwyer said.

"I'm not going to get cold feet," Vance said. "I just won't escalate towards a fire-fight. If they even start to raise their guns, I'll shoot for the chest."

"That-a-boy!" Dwyer said. "Let's go. I wasn't exaggerating when I said it was only a block. We get to walk from here." She looked back towards Lanie. "Your security cams are the only recording devices in the area. Tonight would be a good time to upgrade your operating system or something to take the cameras offline for a couple hours. You're a lawyer. You understand how no one can subpoena evidence that doesn't exist."

"So, you can say you were never here?" Lanie asked.

"I was here," Dwyer said. "I just won't be leaving, should anyone ask, until after sunrise. Go, get your gun. Meet me at the bar when the cameras are off."

After Agent Dwyer went upstairs, Lanie led Vance to the elevator. She hit buttons for floors two and six. "I'll grab your gun and holster. You need to visit Marisol." She handed Vance a set of keys on a ring with a rubber 'Hallows' tag hanging from it. "Key marked with an 'A'. Her suite's key it he one marked with the 'M' and her door is the one closest to the back door. You should knock though, let her know her space is all hers."

XV

Vance could hear a couple dozen sewing machines. The cinderblock building had boarded windows and the doors were steel without windows. A pair of garage doors on a raised platform had a faded logo Vance didn't recognize over peeling paint and weathered wood. "A sweatshop?" he asked.

"The worst kind," Agent Dwyer said. "Inside there are sixty, maybe seventy people brought to the country with promises of jobs. Well, they got the job, just this one doesn't pay."

"What'll we do with them after we free them?" Vance asked.

"I lied when I said this was off the books," Agent Dwyer said. "This is a black-op, and we will have buses coming to take the victims somewhere safe. For now, we just need to go in and subdue two or three guards and maybe a floor manager. Get your silencer set. We can't go in there without our guns aimed at someone. Now, how do we get in?"

"This is your plan, isn't it?" Vance asked. "But if I had to come up with something on the fly, we'd go in through those garage doors. A crowbar would pop the panels of those doors apart."

"How about a two-hundred-pound man hitting them at a dead run?" Dwyer asked.

"I'd have to jump over a thirty-inch ledge," Vance said. The feat seemed within the range of a healthy, muscular human. He knew he could do it, but it had to seem like something a human of Vance's build could do. "I'm pretty sure I could do that."

"Give me your gun," Dwyer said. "I'll toss it to you when you're through, after I lay down some cover fire to make sure you don't get shot while you find your feet."

Vance handed her his service pistol and jogged back down the street from the door. He waited for Agent Dwyer to get in position beside the door and ran at it. He sprinted a bit faster than he could have when he was human, but not faster than an Olympic sprinter. He jumped at the door, angling his body sideways to impact only one panel. He knocked that panel askew and rolled to his feet. The loading area inside the building had pallets of boxes stacked to the ceiling, but no one else was in the room. His gun slid across the floor to him, and Hannah climbed through after. He picked up his gun and, noticing where the doors were, hid behind a stack of boxes. Two doors on the ground level and one up a flight of stairs led into the factory. Vance made sure his chosen cover protected him from all three doors.

"No," Agent Dwyer said. "If we go defensive, they come in shooting. Come on, we need to intercept them and let them know they're the ones under attack."

"Then we go in upstairs," Vance said. "High ground will give us a morale advantage. We want to intimidate; people are more inclined to feel threatened by people they have to crook their heads upward to see."

"You do get your tactical education from movies, don't you?" Agent Dwyer asked. "Upstairs has one door, it's a bottleneck that favors the few. We're the few here, so yes, we go up." She sprinted up the stairs. Vance stayed close. She put her hand on the doorknob and motioned Vance to take a position on the other side. Over the noise of the sewing machines, Vance didn't hear any footsteps or breathing on the far side of the door. He nodded to Dwyer, and she pulled the door open. It led to a short hallway and then to a balcony over a factory floor.

Vance advanced, his pistol aimed in front of him. He got a good view of what the factory was. Women and men on the factory floor below had chains padlocked to their necks and, at the other end, to cots at the sides of the tables. He couldn't spend too much time analyzing the horrid conditions below. He needed to find the threats. Two men with shotguns stood on the balcony overlooking the work floor. They hadn't seen him yet. He needed to get in front of them to coerce them to surrender.

He stepped silently, coming up between the two and tapping them both on their shoulders.

Three pops from behind him reminded him of Agent Dwyer's presence. The two men he'd approached dropped from bullets to the head. Instantly dead, the men's blood didn't have much power in its call to him.

"I thought we weren't killing," Vance said.

"You should have told the man with the machine gun." Dwyer pointed across the room to where a man lay crumpled on top of a large desk. An assault rifle hung from his hand and dropped onto the floor. Vance hadn't noticed him.

"Thanks," Vance said.

Screams filled the room and most of the workers dropped to the floor and hid under their tables or cots. Two men ran from an office room below, shooting pistols wildly in Vance's direction. Vance returned fire, shooting both in the chest. He ran for the stairs that led down to the factory floor, looking for more men with guns. He watched the workers faces to see if any were looking at anyone but him. Most just hid their heads and prayed in Spanish.

In Spanish, Vance asked, "Are there any more gunmen?"

One man pointed from under his cot towards the office. Agent Dwyer beat him there, firing three shots once she passed through the office door. "That's six," she said. "My intel says there's usually two, but never more than six."

Vance asked the man hiding if there were any more than six, ever. The man shook his head. Vance tried to assure the people they were safe. None seemed eager to believe him. He asked where the keys were. No one answered.

"I'm not good at Spanish," Dwyer said. "You either just asked where to wash your hands or asked for keys. I found these. She held up a large ring of what looked like a hundred keys, at least. She tossed them to Vance. "You get the honors. I'm calling in the buses."

Vance went to the nearest person hiding, the man who'd pointed at the office. It took him a while to sort through the keys, but he found where the locks were numbered, and each key had a number engraved on it and the keys were in order. Once he had that, going from worker to worker and unchaining them became easy. He had time to see what they'd been working on. "Movie costumes?" Vance asked.

"Haute Couture," Dwyer said. "That's a nine-hundred-dollar dress on that table. Open a warehouse for a couple hours with a runway show clearance sale and they can get three hundred for it. Unfortunately, its true value is now somewhat less than the fabric it had been cut from. These are knock-offs."

"I've heard of counterfeit fashion," Vance said. "They sell it at tables along many streets in New York. I haven't seen it as often in Los Angeles."

"You work nights," Dwyer said. "You'll see these guys selling from blankets along the beachfront shops or just off the shopping districts. It's not as bad as parts of New York, but it happens. More often you'll see someone pull up a truck to a closed gas station parking lot and set up a temporary shop for a few hours. Hey, there's something in the office you need to see."

Vance handed the keys to a woman after telling her how to match the numbers to the locks. He followed Dwyer into the office. He immediately knew the man she'd shot, who sat slumped in the chair, was still alive. By his breathing, he was conscious but trying to fake death or unconsciousness."

"I called the ambulance already," Dwyer said. "Two actually. I figured some of the people out there could use hydration, at least. Our file has you trained in interrogation. Think you can get him to give you the combination of the safe?"

The man's heartbeat accelerated at the mention of interrogation. Vance looked at the safe. It was an old safe, as tall as a man. It likely had been in the building since its construction. Three combination dials adorned the door by the wheel. It would be a complex combination. Vance hoped it was too complex to lock and unlock on a daily basis. He went to the safe and pulled on the door. It opened, revealing stacks of cash in both American and Mexican money. "Does this mean they sell their goods in Tijuana as well as L.A.?"

"It means they charge these people a lot of money to sneak them over the border then enslave them," Dwyer said. She tossed Vance an empty duffle bag. "This is all off the books, so no one's going to catalog that cash. Go ahead and grab a bagful for yourself."

Vance had to think about it. The money wasn't going to be returned to the traffickers or Dougal and it wasn't going to be taken in as evidence. Still, he couldn't get over the idea of stealing. "Take it and divvy it up among the workers," he said. "I won't judge you if you take a cut for yourself." Vance wasn't sure he hadn't already lost some respect for Dwyer, but she had a valid point that the money was free for the taking.

"You really are a fucking Boy Scout, aren't you?" she asked. Her phone buzzed. "My team is here with busses. If you don't want the spoils, you can go home; we've got this from here."

On the way out, Vance stopped to check the bodies of the gunmen. He specifically hoped to find one of the burner phones, but the only phones the men had with them were smart phones, and they were neither uniform nor cheap. He took the phones anyway. Maybe someone in his office could trace them back to Dougal.

Outside, Vance saw three yellow school buses parked by the door. Men in FBI jackets stood by the busses. Vance waved as he jogged away. He wasn't sure he had time to get mired in a conversation before dawn.

Vance made it back to Hallows with over half an hour to spare before sunrise. He had to call Lanie to figure out how to get into the apartment. The main elevators didn't go to the sixth floor without a key. The front door of Hallows was locked. Vance tried to phase, but after several minutes of not succeeding, Lanie arrived to let him into the bar.

"I guess I'm supposed to phase through the doors if I can't open them?" Vance asked.

"I gave you the key," Lanie said. "On the ring, the one marked with an 'F' for front door. But yeah, you should phase. Dai is quite sure you'll figure it out someday. From your story of what happened at Azure and Katina's, it seems she was right," Lanie said.

"I know I can," Vance said. "I just can't remember how I did it."

"You look like you could use a beer." Lanie pulled a beer from a cooler. It wasn't the brand Vance expected. He'd always drank the same beer at Hallows, an import from Pennsylvania. "I know, it's not Dirk's brand. We're still working with the company to arrange a monthly delivery. They want us to order more than you need and I'm not sure we'll sell what you don't drink."

"At least not for a profit?" Vance asked.

Lanie nodded. "It's my job to keep this place in the black, but you're the boss. If you insist on the nostalgia of it, we'll make it work."

"Order the beer," Vance said. "Sell whatever is more than I expect to drink as Dirk's special at cost, or whatever a good 'special' price is."

"That'll impact our profitable sales," Lanie said. "Someone who buys a cheap, at cost, beer won't buy one that keeps our doors open."

Vance felt stupid for not realizing how basic business should work. "Then charge a premium for it, way more than it's worth. Make it seem like something super rare and special. Are we the only ones who carry Dirk's beer in the city?"

"Actually, yes," Lanie said.

"Then charge twice what we charge for normal microbrews," Vance said. "Call it 'Dirk's Favorite Beer' and see if that doesn't sell a few bottles."

"I like your thinking," Lanie said. "So, how was the mission? I heard some gunshots. Did you rescue a bunch of people without killing half as many as you saved?"

"There were a lot more people to rescue, but between Dwyer and I, we shot six men with guns," he said. He went on to describe what happened in detail.

Lanie chuckled. "I love you, but I can't believe you turned down the chance at free money. No, I totally believe you did. Dougal's gonna be pissed."

"That's the thing," Vance said. "I didn't see anything there to link the shop to Dougal. I don't regret saving all those people, but I don't think Hannah had good information. I'm going back tonight to see what I can find. I do have two cell phones I'm going to take to the forensics tech guys at the sheriff's office. If Dougal is involved, someone had to write a memo regarding him or someone who will lead us to him somewhere in the sweatshop's office."

The floor shook followed by a rumble. "Earthquake?" Vance asked. It wouldn't be his first, but they weren't usually so abrupt.

"No, that was an explosion, and it was close," Lanie said. "It can't be a coincidence. I'm going to go up to the roof, since we don't have any windows to look out." She went through a door Vance hadn't explored. He hadn't yet been to many parts of the apartment beyond the living room and Marisol's suite. A moment later he got a message on his phone. It included a photo of a burning building. Vance recognized it as the same building he'd been in just an hour earlier.

"I guess I'm not going back," Vance sent. "Either Dwyer burned it to hide our presence or Dougal sent someone to burn it to hide his evidence. I guess that's a thing we do. We hide by burning."

"If we need to," Lanie replied. "Burning Hallows wasn't the tragedy that happened there. We could fix the building and Dai knew it when you two burned it. Dwyer burning a crime scene to mask an FBI black-op seems extreme. I'm favoring the Dougal theory. You didn't find evidence against him there and now you won't." She emerged from the same door she'd left through as Vance got the text.

"The people he had enslaved might know something," Vance said. "I doubt it, though. Dougal is too well-insulated from his operations. We did have one gunman who didn't die. Dwyer shot him, but not fatally. I'll see if she'll let me talk to him. For some reason, I think she won't. I'm not helpful to her official investigation. I'm only useful to her in her under-the-table work. She knows I don't deserve to be an Assistant Sheriff."

Lanie grabbed his shoulders and made him look her in the eyes. "She knows you don't have the experience someone would normally have for that position. You have the heart and mind of a good cop. If all cops had your morality, cops would never make the news."

XVI

Vance filled the beer cooler while Oscar, his daytime bartender, unloaded the dishwasher. Lanie sat at her table, sending emails and booking her bands. It all seemed so normal. The club's look during the day took some getting used to. Lanie changed walls to be more of a bar and grill feel before seven. At seven, the nostalgia pictures and art would fade out and the band flyers Vance had been used to would reappear. That wouldn't be for hours. The clock on the wall above the cash register read five minutes after four.

Dai walked in through the wall and sat at the bar across from Vance.

"Is that safe to do when we're open?" Vance asked. "You shouldn't do that when people are here. What if Oscar looked at you while you came through the wall?"

"He's been coerced to perceive anyone passing through the wall as walking through a concealed door," Dai said. "I've gone through orientation with all your employees, and it was hella boring."

"I know you don't have an apartment in this part of town," Vance said. "You've been at your theatre all day?"

"I finally got rid of the Russian women," Dai said. "With Karlo gone almost a week now and Petra avoiding our part of town, I had to work through a paid translator. I haven't been able to get Katina to answer her phone for two days."

"Did you find them jobs?" Vance asked.

"You know, I wish I could have," Dai said. "They went home to Russia. None of them were happy, but I wasn't going to be the one to set a woman up as a lifelong prostitute. I did set them each up with a trust fund. Nothing as fancy as yours, but it will keep them in food, clothing, and an apartment for ten years. It'll also pay for their college should they pursue a professional degree."

"And they weren't happy?" Vance asked.

"They really thought they'd be millionaires' wives and playthings," Dai said.

"And you paid for this?" Vance asked. "I never think of you as charitable."

"I give to charities," Dai said. "My father taught me to tithe either to the church or to other institutions that do good in the world, so I give ten percent. This didn't come out of that. This isn't my money. I'm spending Dougal's. When you catch that bitch, I get access to the financials and any cash Dougal has before it gets turned over as evidence."

"You know I can't make that call," Vance said.

"We'll see," Dai said. "You can at least point me to whomever can make that call and I'll handle the coercion. It's not stealing if it's taken to cover a valid debt, is it?"

"You should've been with me last night," Vance said.

"Lanie told me," Dai said. "Next time you have a safe full of money and no one to give it to, think of me and all the money I spent sending a bunch of lost Russian girls home."

"I'm wondering if I shouldn't drop off that case," Vance said. "I'm supposed to be a business card sheriff, a guy with the title but no real responsibilities."

"If you're expecting me to disagree, you'll be disappointed," Dai said. "I know you were brooding over the loss of Hallows and so many friends. I let you bury yourself in human sheriff work. But that's over. I want my vampire sheriff back. There are a thousand vampires in the metro area, three thousand in my kingdom. Every day, some vampire does something stupid, something a royal should be involved in preventing or repairing. I have been lax, intentionally, wanting to be anything but the draconian rulers the Nine Princes were. But the time has come for me to reign in the stupidity, and I can't do it alone."

"I should finish this one case," Vance said. "After that, I'll be one hundred percent yours."

"I just want your nights," Dai said. "Most of your daylight hours are still going to be Lanie's."

"That's what I meant," Vance said.

"And tonight, you're mine," Dai said. "Not for me, for the kingdom. Find Katina. If she's dead, I need to know. She's usually responsive to communication from me. After the zombies, I've been trying to contact her, but she isn't responding."

"How many sisters are still in Los Angeles?" Vance asked.

"Me," Dai said. "The rest went back to wherever they came from."

"Then I can find her," Vance said. Anyone with Artemis blood would show as a red light in his mind, which would give him a direction. He could use that to triangulate a location. The lights were always there, not visually, but in his mind. He'd mostly learned to ignore them. One had been moving rapidly for the last hour. That meant it was close. "She's close, then. She's either traveling in a plane or she's within a mile or so of us."

"Close enough to tell how far by leaning side to side?" Dai asked.

"You just want to see me move in silly ways," Vance said. He did it, though. He leaned to the left then to the right. "Actually, yes. Someone with the light is in our parking lot. Either they're packed deep in crates or it's Katina. She's the only one with our blood that could survive with just the protection of a thin layer of steel, like a car body."

"No, she's not," Dai said. "As Artemis sisters go, she's midrange in

109

purity."

"She's moving again, fast," Vance said.

The doors flew open, and Katina ran in giving off steam or smoke, but she looked fine. "You!" Katina shouted at the bartender. "You didn't notice anything odd about me. It's a good time for a long break. You have an errand you need to run. Vance'll say it's okay."

"Boss?" Oscar asked. "I need to go buy stamps. Do you mind if I run to the post office before we get busy?"

"Go ahead," Vance said.

Azure waked in as Oscar walked out. "I told her to use the back door. More shade."

"I'm fine," Katina said. "If I hadn't checked the theatre first, I wouldn't even be steaming. I didn't give myself enough time to fully heal in the car before coming in here. Three sprints through sunlight are not recommended."

"We were just looking for you," Dai said.

"Vance's not going to find us," Katina said. "We're using throwaway phones for one call then ditching them or borrowing stranger's phones for one call. You're not going to be able to use whatever tools the sheriff has to track phones."

"I can always see what direction you are from me," Vance said. "Figuring out how far is trickier, but possible."

"Can you find anyone? Or is it just me?" Katina asked.

"Any Artemis sister, which you are by blood, but not bloodline," Vance said. "I still don't understand how, but I know it's a sore spot with Callisto."

"I'm not explaining it," Katina said. "The reason we're here is that Stephanie emailed Azure pleading for help. Her shop didn't open yesterday or today. The necromancer is building a coven by force. He's going to perform that ritual from the book. Have we been clear on how dangerous that will be? It's not a specific spell beyond focusing six mages' power into one person. That one person can then do almost anything."

"None of your mage friends can figure it out?" Dai asked.

"I'm a vampire's pet," Azure said. "I don't know how, but the Pentacle found out about me. I'm now considered an outsider. I'm not banished, per se, just not allowed to discuss magic with anyone, mage or muggle."

"Or vampire," Vance surmised.

"The ruling didn't specify vampires," Azure said. "Then again, just talking with vampires is forbidden, so there's no need to specify what I cannot talk about."

"Did Stephanie use her own email account?" Vance asked.

"It has her store's signature block," Azure said.

"Then she might have used her phone to send it. I can track her phone," Vance said. "I'm going to have to open a missing person's case. The tool requires a case number, so I'll need an official case. Missing persons at least means I don't need a warrant."

"Do it," Dai said. "This case takes priority. It might seem like a mage problem, but if Katina is involved, it's a vamp problem."

"And the necromancer will need a vamp," Katina said. "Someone will have to stand in for the life mage and only vamps have the link to that magic."

"I want to know what spell he's planning," Dai said.

"We all do," Azure said.

"Then I'm ordering you to find out," Dai said.

"Ordering me?" Azure asked.

"She can," Katina said. "You're a vampire's pet and she's the vampire queen here. You're used to thinking we're outside the law, above it, but we're not. Shauna never was, nor did she act that way. When she was in Philly, she worked for Portia. In Europe, she worked for the Empress of the Northern Roman Empire."

"Elsa," Azure said.

"And Elsa is the one that acted against Zylpha by stealing slaves. When Shauna went back to usurp Zylpha, she did so with the blessing of the Elder's Council."

"And now, we're on our own secret mission," Azure said. "No one in their right mind would try to raise the dead."

"They warn you that you'll end up with a demon in a human body?" Vance asked.

"It's never worked," Azure said. "Turns out, since Cleopatra, there have been several tries to replicate it. Souls don't want to come back, or bodies rot and you cannot heal a dead body."

"I'm not optimistic," Dai said.

"I heard Karina," Vance said. "I actually am optimistic. I am in a state of cognitive dissonance, but there is a part of me that wants Katina to succeed."

"This necromancer that's gathering a coven by force is someone you want to force into your own coven to cast an uber powerful spell?" Dai asked.

"That's a good summary," Katina said.

"Tonight, we track Stephanie down by finding her phone," Dai said.

"Not all of us," Vance said. "If it's a trap for Katina and Azure, they should stay clear."

"I hadn't thought of it being a trap," Azure said.

"Vampire hunters typically know they are weak, so they set traps to give them the upper hand," Vance said. "Always make sure you're the spider and not the fly."

Katina said, "So Azure and I will do some research into the ritual, see if we can either predict what he's trying to do or what else he needs to do it."

"You're going to force me to call my mom," Azure said. "No one else will talk to me."

Katina shook her head. "I'm not going to make you do anything. Your mom is probably a good contact. She has archive access, right? She'll be a huge help—if she'll help. But I won't force you to call her." She pointed to Dai. "She will."

"Start dialing," Dai said.

Azure held up a cheap looking phone. "No contact list on this thing. It's not like I know her phone number."

"Vance?" Dai asked.

"On it." Vance pulled his own phone out. "Name and zip code are all I need."

"Patricia Mary Hamilton, 19146," Azure said.

Vance entered the information, and it returned a cellular phone number. "Does this look familiar?" He asked showing Azure the number.

"I wouldn't know," Azure said. "I'm totally reliant on tech for that stuff." She input the number to her phone then dialed. "I'm going out front for some privacy," she said as she turned and walked towards the door. "Hi, mom," she said when a woman answered. Vance tried to not hear, though it was futile with his vampiric senses. He couldn't help but hear the woman on the other end respond, "What's going on, baby?"

When the door closed behind Azure, Vance could no longer hear her conversation.

"That sounded remarkably friendly for someone who's been out of touch with her mom for years," Katina said.

"None of us will ever really be parents," Vance said. "We can be told about the boundless love and infinite forgiveness and acceptance, but we can't really understand."

"She'll be okay," Katina said. "She'd have a better response from her dad, but her mom has access to the information we need. We hope, anyway."

XVII

Hours passed. Vance had to call Marisol down to have her check on Azure after forty minutes passed. He had to be sure she hadn't been snatched by the necromancer. Azure came back inside as the sun was setting.

"Mom was pissed?" Katina asked.

"Most definitely," Azure said. "I guess she's been concocting stories to cover for me so I wouldn't be banished and truly be an outcast. We spent three hours making her lies into the truth."

"So, how did you redefine reality?" Dai asked.

"Vampires and mages are in a state of mutual denial with diplomatic acceptance," Azure said. "We defend each other's secrets while also avoiding each other, except in mutually agreed upon cases. The mages get a nonvoting membership on the Elders Council, an ambassador. The vampires get full representation in the Pentacle. The real key is that mages, in vampiric law, are now considered family."

"You did all this?" Dai asked.

"I conferenced in Shauna. She wanted to bring in James, but he made her bring in Artemis instead. Since the vampiric language is also the first language used to document magic, we're more alike than different," Azure said.

"You sold it well," Katina said.

"I'm not done, it seems," Azure said "They made me the ambassador to the vampires. The mages wanted Artemis to join the Pentacle, but Artemis didn't accept. She's sending her blood granddaughter, Callisto."

"I didn't think you went out to make some grand political alliances between vamps and mages," Dai said. "Will your mother help?"

"Yeah. A necromancer willing to basically kill a bus full of tourists, zombifying the lot of them, is very disturbing to the Pentacle. They're sending a fire team."

"Like a military strike team?" Vance asked.

"Like that, only a fire team is one fire magus and two mages whose job it is to limit the damage of the fire mage," Azure said. "I didn't know about them. Like vampires, they were a myth of my childhood. It's a water, an earth and a fire mage, specializing in threat removal."

"We still need the necromancer," Katina said. "Don't tell me you just fucked this up for me."

"Maybe no," Azure said. "If they take him alive, they will need a place to keep him for trial. They won't transport him, because necromancers can just turn anyone into a zombie if he's prepped for it and he manages to touch someone. So, when they…"

"If they," Katina corrected, her voice sharp with ire.

"So, if or when they capture this necromancer, they'll need a place to keep him. I heard about Dai's oubliettes, and they sounded perfect, so I offered them as a holding cell for the necromancer. We'll just have to borrow him while he's in custody."

"If the necromancer is able to zombify someone by touching them, why would I want one in my theatre?" Dai asked.

"Necromancers cannot do anything to a vampire," Azure said. "Their magic doesn't work on you guys."

"Our magic won't work on him?" Vance surmised.

"As far as we can tell, it still does. The necromancer on the Pentacle is a vampire's pet, I guess. She's an expert on these things. Her theory is that vampires are more like elementals than magi. An elemental is another of those myths that I didn't really believe in. Mages cast spells, use rituals to harness and control their magic. Elementals just do it. Mom's first thought was that this ritual is to empower a magus, turning them into an elemental of their chosen magic. Vampires are impure beings of Venae, the life magic energy. They're not quite pure elementals."

"Like, most mages have to prepare symbols and learn spells and make silly noises," Katina said. "Vampires just reach out, manipulate the Venae, and work with it to fly, whisper across rooms, and phase. Azure is almost like an elementalist. She hardly casts or makes silly noises when she does her water tricks."

"It's elemental, not elementalist," Azure said. "And that's another secret I learned today. Yes, I am apparently a natural elemental, which is, according to my mother, exceedingly rare. Like, I'm one of eleven."

"One of eleven living water elementals?" Katina asked.

"One of eleven naturally born elementals of any kind, ever," Azure said. "I always thought my parents were too protective of me. I guess I know why. The first two hours of our conversation were her trying to figure out how to extract me from the vampire world. Once I managed to convince her the vampires I hung with were the best bodyguards a woman could ask for, she went for the vampire and mage alliance. I had to have Shauna go to my parents' house and demonstrate how strong, how invulnerable she is."

"Shauna coerced her, didn't she?" Katina asked.

"No," Azure said. "Shauna promised not to, and my mom thinks she has wards against that set in our house. I don't know if that's true, but I take Shauna at her word."

"We're moving back to Philly, aren't we?" Katina asked.

"I couldn't talk my way out of that," Azure said. "Once I convinced my mom that Shauna was the best bodyguard in the world, my mom insisted I actually be where Shauna could guard me. So, I have a few days to get things in order here, then I have to go back. I figure you're coming too."

"I am," Katina said. "What I'm hearing is that we have three days to finish what we started here."

"The fire team will be on the next flight from wherever they're coming from," Azure said. "They could be here as early as noon tomorrow. I'm supposed to meet them at their hotel downtown and brief them as soon as they get here."

"That means that we have tonight or it's going to get tangled," Katina said. "Vance, find Stephanie."

Vance had her phone already pinged. He held up his phone, showing the blue dot on the map. "She's north of the city, past Bakersfield. It's a less than ideal ping. We only have it on one tower, but we know it was, at one point, three miles from the tower. We could fly up and follow the circle until we find her."

"Cynthia is driving us," Dai said. "She's got the Nocturne's van out in the alley. Katina, Azure, are you riding with us?"

"I can't go," Azure said. "Right now, the local mages are working their way through a phone tree to see if anyone besides Stephanie is missing. One of the locals is supposed to meet me at nine with that list and an amulet to protect against necromancy. Katina can go with you, though."

"I'm not leaving your side," Katina said. "We can fly up once they locate Stephanie and the necromancer."

"You have my permission to fly in my city," Dai said. "Fly low, just above the lights and below the radar, and fly fast."

"I was thinking helicopter," Katina said. "I have one on standby every night from dusk to dawn. Not mine. Not Elsa's either. It's just a service I'm paying to keep on standby."

"Using Elsa's money," Azure said. "Katina has a bottomless debit card."

"I have the same thing," Vance said.

"No," Dai said. "You don't. Your card covers normal per diem expenses. You can spend enough to get a few meals and a hotel each day. If Katina has a card linked to Elsa's money, she could buy a new hotel every day."

"Dai isn't exaggerating," Katina said. "My sister knows how wealthy Elsa is. I just know there are at least four commas involved."

"Now you're exaggerating," Dai said. "No single entity, outside of the US or Chinese Governments, controls over a trillion dollars."

Katina shrugged. "Like I said, Karina would know the exact amount. We're running low on time, so you guys start driving and Azure and I might not beat you there after we meet with the local mage representative."

§

Vance held Stephanie's phone in his hand. The battery alert flashed on the screen, but the phone wasn't locked. Vance found it in the middle of a wild growth area just outside of Bakersfield. He carefully didn't land when he grabbed the phone. Instead, he flew back to the roadside before letting his feet set down.

"Tell me your hunter training has some tracking skills in there somewhere," Dai said.

"No," Vance said. "Vampires don't run wild across fields and through forests. I know what signs to look for in a bar or club to indicate it's frequented by a vampire. Since vampires don't want to be noticed, it would be an inconspicuous, but barely visible, table or booth that is left vacant much of the time. When someone is there, it's always the same someone. Not a VIP booth, those are too conspicuous; just a regular booth or table treated like a VIP area."

"The Nine Princes were always conspicuous," Dai said.

"We weren't trained to deal with that kind of thing," Vance said. "Ironically, that kind of vampire is entirely the type that makes me feel righteous as a vampire hunter."

"Righteousness isn't going to find Azure's friend Stephanie," Dai said. "Do you want me to call Thalia?"

"Are you two talking again?" Vance said. "I know she's probably the best tracker in California, but we're still pissed about her killing those people she was supposed to make into dhampyres."

"All four survivors became vampires," Dai said. "None stayed in California."

"I just assumed Thalia killed them all," Vance said.

"So did I," Dai said. "I'm still very upset that they didn't respect your wishes. I spoke to Thalia briefly at Iris' service, but I made it clear we were not friends at the moment."

"I don't hold grudges," Vance said. "Hate is too much work for something that just brings yourself suffering."

"I wish I could be so existential," Dai said. "Sometimes it's nice to feel driven, to plot revenge, and there's satisfaction when hate can be resolved by grand means. I don't hate Thalia or any of my other sisters. I know why they did what they did. I just want you to be respected. I want me to be respected. Not feared like Asmodeus, but respected. I'm a bit unhappy that my will can be trumped by the will of Artemis within my borders."

"Artemis is, technically, part of the Elders Council, or Thalia is," Vance said.

"And they don't have jurisdiction, at all," Dai said. "I've asked Thalia to apologize to you. I told her, once she did that, we'd be like siblings again."

"And she hasn't spoken to me," Vance said.

"We're a prideful family," Dai said. "Unapologetically so. It might be centuries."

"I can't let that get in the way of saving Azure's friend," Vance said. He pulled out his phone and called Thalia.

"Is this actually Vance Silver?" Thalia answered.

"It is," Vance said.

"You've forgiven me?" Thalia asked. "Dai was adamant that you would take a long time to get over my turning those people to vampires instead of dhampyres."

"This isn't about that," Vance said. "Someday, long in the future, you can explain your reasoning, but for now, I need a tracker in Bakersfield."

"You'll have to explain," Thalia said. "I'm willing to help a sister in need, even my sole brother-sister, but I need to know what I'm helping with."

"I lost a mage," Vance said. "Azure's friend is missing and all we have to go on is a cell phone found in a field. We think she's been kidnapped to form a coven against her will for some ancient, powerful ritual. Azure mentioned a spell that could turn a mage into an elemental. I hope you know more about mages than I do, because I doubt I could explain."

"I've been doing research since meeting Azure," Thalia said. "I know enough to understand what's going on. If you're in Bakersfield, I don't need to come help you track. Up the hill from there, past Lake Isabelle, is a small crater atop a high mountain. I'll send a map. It's a place where the barriers between the physical world and several of the magical dimensions is thin. The pre-Mayan American Natives were big into magic. That's the site of many potent rituals that have nearly broken the barriers between the dimensions."

"What happens if they break?" Vance asked.

"When they break, disasters happen. Tsunamis, earthquakes, and for the most potent, volcanoes," Thalia said. "If there is a coven of six, they'll want to perform their rituals up there. There are only two such sites south of Oregon and west of the Rockies. One is up there by Lake Isabelle. The other is closer to me, just outside San Diego. Mages can't do a coven of six, though. They rarely get more than a coven of three."

Vance explained the necromancer, up to the zombie attack.

"I'll meet you at the crater. If you're driving, I'll probably beat you there," Thalia said. "I just sent the map location."

"Send it to Katina and Azure, too," Vance said. "They'll be heading this way soon, too."

"Gotcha," Thalia said, then the line went dead.

"She didn't apologize," Dai said.

"I'm not thinking about that," Vance said. "Once Stephanie is found, we can have our battle of pride with Thalia. I'm certain you'd win. Mothers care more for their children than children care about their parents. This is the kind of stuff we learn in counseling classes."

"Give the map to Cynthia and let's go," Dai said.

Vance forwarded the map to Cynthia as he and Dai got back in the car. They drove up into the mountains.

The roads stayed clear up the mountains. They parked at a scenic overlook and flew the rest of the way. Dai carried Cynthia since dhampyres cannot fly. Once they arrived there, they found a very cold crater with some ice at the bottom. A light layer of snow covered the entire crater.

Azure, Katina, and Thalia stood at the edge of the crater. Azure and Katina explained the entire story from the necromancer to Katina's plan to return her sister to life. Thalia, as a member of the council, already knew of Azure's treaties.

Vance waved toward the pristine layer of snow. "I'm not a tracker, as I've said, but no one's been here."

"My realization as well," Thalia said. She left Azure and Katina and walked towards Vance. She wore a golden breastplate and greaves with a leather skirt. A round shield hung across her back.

"You know, I have that same outfit," Vance said.

"I know," Thalia said. "Who do you think Lanie gets her antiquity reproductions from?"

"Seems a bit underdressed for the cold," Vance said. "At least we don't have to stick around up here."

"I'm sorry," Thalia said.

"You made a good, educated guess," Vance said. "No one can know for sure where a kidnapper takes their victim. All you had was my story and the location of her phone."

"Well, I wasn't apologizing for that, but I am sorry for that as well," Thalia said. "I'm sorry I let you believe we could do as you wanted with those poor souls Tyson left. I should have been straight with you. There was never a chance we would let them be dhampyres. Vampires have immense power with one severe limitation. Dhampyres might not have the mystical powers, but their strength, resilience and rapid healing are on-par with vampires. Every dhampyre in history has used their enhanced state to conquer men or hunt vampires. Cynthia is, honestly, the only one to use her strength solely unselfishly."

"Someone has to give them a chance," Vance said. "You cannot know how a transformation will affect someone."

"We learn from history," Thalia said. "And no one knows more about history than the Sisterhood of Artemis."

"Firsthand knowledge?" Vance asked.

"Don't be the guy to ask how old I am!" Her eyes scowled, but Vance thought there might be a hint of a smile on her lips. When Vance didn't ask, Thalia kept talking. "There have never been more than thirty-three sisters. That's not enough to have firsthand experience all of history. Yes, some of us are older than written history. I'm not one of them. Written history is our main source of knowledge, though. Immortality means plenty of time to read."

"So, you're apologizing, but saying I should heed your wisdom," Vance said. "It's difficult to put aside my nature and my desire to do the most good, but I should accept that you did not have evil in mind when you did what you did. I don't know. I can't condone making more vampires. That's not just four people saved, but four people they had to kill to survive as vampires. I know you guys don't value life the way I do, so I can't just throw away those four lives like you could."

"I can't defend that," Thalia said. "You're right. We murdered four people to save four people. We picked people that deserved to die by our standards, not yours. I won't tell you our methods of selection tonight. Someday we'll explain—when you've had time to understand the world as only ancient vampires do. For now, just trust that we have methods and standards."

"I still don't know how to respond to that," Vance said. "I'm grateful you are here, trying to make amends. I have to accept you for who you are; I know that. It's so hard to perceive vampires as anything but monsters. Even being one, I can only see myself as a monster."

"Hold on to that," Thalia said. "Once you lose sight of what you are, you stop acting to keep your monster in check. I called you a knight long ago, and I still see you as more of a champion than a monster. Because of that, and in hopes of rebuilding the bridge of family, I offer you this." She unstrapped the shield from her back and handed it to Vance.

Vance took the shield. The round, bronze shield bore the emblem of a falcon on the front. Vance had seen a shield like it in a movie, long ago. The inside, like the shield he'd seen in the movie, had a high polish, like a mirror. "I saw this in a movie about Perseus."

"Yes," Thalia said. "You may have. Perseus is a great legend. He's always been a fave of mine."

"Did you meet him?" Vance asked.

"Before my time," Thalia said. "I'm not yet three-thousand. Perseus is early Greek."

"But this is the shield?" Vance asked.

"The actual shield?" Thalia asked. "Yes, that's Perseus' shield."

"You're telling me I'm holding a three-thousand-year-old antique?" Vance asked.

"That's a thirty-year-old movie prop," Thalia said. "The real deal and quite the collector's item. They used that very shield in the movie. That's the pretty one, the actual bronzed steel one. The one he carried around most of the time was wood and not as pretty. This one had to have a very shiny mirror inside, so when I made it—and I make movie props, if you didn't know—I made it perfectly reflective. They scuffed it up for the fight with Medusa in the film, but I re-polished it. If you don't want to use it to fight, you can set it up over your bathroom sink. Of course, then you miss the intricately carved falcon on the other side."

"I feel like I'm being bribed," Vance said.

"You are," Thalia said. "It's a gift whether you forgive me or not, though, so it's not technically a bribe. It's a gesture of sisterhood. Only you can come to terms with who we all are. I apologized for letting you believe we would make dhampyres, that's the only apology I can make with sincerity. If I'd been honest with you before we did it, at least we would have convinced you ahead of time and there'd be far less ill will. But we would have still done the same thing."

"Consider there to be no wall between us," Vance said. "I don't have to like your standards or methods, but I'll treat you like family." Vance realized he hadn't had more than three or four conversations with his mother and father in the past eighteen months. He resolved to change that.

"Great!" Thalia said. "See you for Sunday dinner. Well, it's wine and gelatin."

"Gelatin?" Vance asked. "We can eat gelatin?"

"It's a liquid," Thalia said. "You just have to warm yourself to digest it. Be careful of the sugar rush, though. You probably haven't had sugar in a long time, and you won't be used to it." She slid past Vance's shield and hugged him. "I know we're not good by your standards. You have to trust that most of us are not evil, either."

"Artemis is on sixty-five of seventy-nine," Vance said. "At least the last I heard about it on the news."

"She's done," Thalia said. "You have to know, she's the most pure and good of us all, but she sees crimes of lust against women as unforgivable. That's her measure and standard for evil. No one's going to change that. She's politically aware, though, and won't start a hunt in another royal's territory without permission. She'll end a hunt wherever it leads, though. So as long as you or Dai don't let her, she won't be prowling strip clubs looking for men to kill."

"I can't see her as good," Vance said. "I can only see her as a force of nature, something I cannot control and…" His phone rang, interrupting what he tried to say. The number was Julian, his informant on Dougal. Since the phone rang as his sheriff's line, Vance answered, "This is Assistant Sheriff Vance Silver."

"Dude, help!" Julian called. "Dougal has Petra strapped to the roof. I can't undo the chains. I'm sending you our GPS location. I don't know where we are."

Dai peered over Vance's shoulder. "Don't wait for my permission. I'll take your shield back to Hallows."

Vance hadn't planned to ask permission. He said, "Wish me luck!" He handed Dai the shield then flew off as fast as he dared.

XVIII

Vance followed the GPS bleep on his phone, though he had to spend most of his attention keeping himself aloft and moving towards it. He recognized the part of town as local to his sheriff's office but couldn't zoom in on his phone while flying as fast as he needed to, so he didn't recognize exactly where Dougal had operations in relation to his office. It seemed closer than criminal organizations should be to law enforcement.

It took more than an hour to get to Los Angeles and find the building. Petra lay chained and shackled to the roof. Dougal hadn't taken any chances. He'd used chains with links made of steel thicker than Vance's fingers. Julian was also chained, but only by one ankle. "We need an angle grinder," Vance said.

"You're here!" Julian said.

"We don't have much time," Petra said. "Julian is willing to feed you if you need strength. Drain him dry if you must. He is prepared to die."

"I'm not," Julian said. "I'm not trying to be selfish. I swear! If we're both going to die and I might save her, yeah, I'd save her, I guess. I called because Dougal made me call you. We didn't really think you'd be able to help. I couldn't tell you to bring an angle grinder. I didn't think of it. But you don't have time to get one. They left the welding kit over there."

Vance saw the twin tanks of a portable acetylene torch system but saw the hose to the torch assembly had been cut through. "That won't help," Vance said. "Dougal's men cut the hoses. Lanie thinks I'm a superhero. Let's see if she's right."

Vance grabbed one of the chains with both hands and pulled. When the chains didn't give, he pulled with all his strength. His feet crushed through the roof of the building, but the chains didn't budge. He tried again with the chain holding Julian, but to no avail. "I think these are welded to the building frame. I can't break these."

"Well, do something," Petra pleaded. "Anything! The sky is pink. I have minutes to live here, and I am not ready to die."

"Fine," Julian called. "Eat me, save her."

"I have another plan," Vance said. He prayed that he'd figure out how to phase in the next few minutes. He lay on Petra, hugging her.

"This is awkward," Petra said. "If you're looking to let me feel loved when I die, I'd rather feel less awkward."

"Quiet, please," Vance said. "I need to concentrate."

He tried to remember which way to go, which shift in perception would take him into the Venae. He said, "Karina, if you can hear me, show me where you are!"

"Who's Karina?" Petra asked.

Vance tried to remember her voice, hoping the memory would trigger others from that moment. It must've worked. He fell through the roof of the building, holding tight to Petra.

A woman screamed. He realized that he floated above the desk in the middle of an office. By the looks of things, it was a law office of some kind. A woman ran to the corner by the window and crouched, still screaming. Vance pulled back into the physical world. He let go of Petra and rushed to quiet the woman. "No one is in here," Vance said, pulling her eyes to his and adding power to his words to coerce her. "You just dozed off a little and remembered a bad dream. Now would be a good time to go get caffeine. I'm not here. She's not here. You are alone in the room."

"Fuck!" the woman said, looking around the room, confused. Her gaze didn't stop at Vance or Petra. "I need more coffee." She grabbed a purse from a chair and left the room.

"Um, Vance?" Petra asked. "Thanks for saving my life, but we still have these shackles to deal with. They are much less comfortable now that I'm hanging by them."

Vance had phased not only Petra, but the chains and shackles as well. The chains merged with the ceiling above when Vance brought them back to solidity. Rather than try to move all of Petra back into the Venae, he grabbed one of the shackles around her ankle. It had been welded on and Petra's leg hadn't fully healed from the burns yet. She would heal, though. With focused thought, Vance phased just himself and the shackle, leaving Petra fully physical. He slipped the shackle away from Petra. He did the same with the other.

"You're supposed to be Dirk's bloodson," Petra said. "What you just did isn't something Dirk nor anyone else of his line could do. You're of Dracula's bloodline."

"No," Vance said. "It's more complicated than that, really. It's also best to keep my secret and let people believe I am Dirk's bloodson."

"You saved my life," Petra said. "You could be the devil himself and I'd tell the world you were an angel."

"I'm not the devil," Vance said.

"I'd still call you an angel," Petra said. "The world needs more angels like you."

"I wish I believed in that kind of angel," Vance said. "Angels are messengers, not warriors and not heroes."

"Dougal caught me moving my family," Petra said. "My family is safe, but she caught me."

"She?" Vance asked.

"Dougal is a woman," Petra said. "You thought she was a man?"

"Everyone thinks Dougal is a man," Vance said.

"I guess I used to, but the woman who stood over me in the moonlight while her henchmen welded shackles to me was definitely Dougal. Blonde woman, built like a six-foot-tall gymnast. She's stronger than my pet. I know she's just a human, but she's the super motivated type. I bet she runs marathons, probably double marathons, just to make sure she's better than the next girl over."

"I know the type," Vance said. His best friend among the hunters, Peter, had been a health nut. He'd convinced Vance to run a marathon more than once. When he beat Peter by twelve minutes in the first marathon, Peter wouldn't relent on getting better. The second marathon, Peter had beaten Vance by nine seconds. Peter didn't directly insult Vance, but the term 'nine seconds' came up over a hundred times in the following two days.

More recently, Agent Dwyer reminded Vance a lot of Peter, for her physical shape and for her demeanor and drive. That Agent Dwyer and Dougal had similar personalities seemed like the plot of a character driven crime drama movie.

Vance told Petra his story of Peter.

"Yeah, except Dougal would flat-out shoot you if you beat her," Petra said.

The sunlight through the windows became uncomfortable and, though they were on the shade side of the building, would soon become too bright to be survivable.

"We should find a room without windows," Vance said.

"The basement is the safest bet," Petra said. "I don't know where we are, but the top floor isn't the best place for us."

Vance looked around. With Petra hanging from chains and the screaming woman, he hadn't gotten a good look. He'd been in the office before. The woman hadn't been familiar, but it wasn't her office. She probably worked for the man who Vance knew. "We're in Los Angeles Sheriff's HQ. This is the sheriff's office. He wouldn't be in this early. On the brighter side, he's a vampire's pet, so I'll be able to explain the chains hanging through his ceiling to him. On the less bright side, for him anyway, he won't."

"We still need to find a darker room," Petra said.

"My office is one floor down, no windows," Vance said. "Used to be a file room, but we need far less space for files than we used to. So, they walled off a little section for my office. Funny thing, since I'm technically undercover, my name on the door is 'Classified.' Come on."

He walked out of the room with Petra in tow. They took the stairs down and made a beeline for his office. Before he started the Dougal case, he hadn't had an office, but the FBI might have wanted to meet there, so the Sheriff had one built for him.

"She's taunting you," Petra said. "This isn't just a building she picked at random. She wanted to get to you. This wasn't about me. I was going to be dead. She could kill me anywhere. She chose here to get to you."

"Was she hoping to demoralize me?" Vance said. "Neither Dai nor I are the type to be demoralized by a threat. It would seem maybe she's issuing a challenge, if she has any idea who she's dealing with. How does she know about me, anyway?"

"I might have mentioned the sheriff had a high-ranking vampire in his ranks," Petra said. "When she directly asked me if it was you, I probably said it was."

"This morning?" Vance asked.

"Four or five months ago," Petra said.

"Dai would have put you on her roof if she'd known," Vance said. "I can't promise she won't when she finds out."

"You have to tell her?" Petra asked.

"I'm not going to lie to her," Vance said. "She'll know if I do, and my honesty is something that's important to both me and her."

"I have to go away, far away," Petra said. "Will you at least let me get out of town before you tell her?"

"I can do better," Vance said. "I have Dai's authority to speak for her. Your crimes are as serious as any I've encountered as Dai's sheriff. Since our previous sentence can no longer be effective, I have no choice but to banish you. You have forty-eight hours to be out of Southern California. I strongly suggest you move to another continent. Don't come back to the Kingdom of Heaven or any bordering kingdom for at least a hundred years."

"Well, that's better than I expected," Petra said. "It certainly will make for a less awkward day since I think we're stuck here together for the next twelve hours. Speaking of stuck, what are you going to do about Julian?"

Vance texted Cynthia, "I need an angle grinder on the roof of Sheriff HQ. I'm not up there, but Julian is, and the chains are too thick to break."

"Petra?" Cynthia texted back.

"I got her off, safely," Vance replied. "But now she and I are stuck in my office for the day."

"Call Lanie," Cynthia replied. "Also, you should text Dai and keep her informed. I'm standing right next to her if you want me to show her the texts."

"I'll call," Vance said.

He did and explained what had happened since he'd found Petra.

"I'm glad you finally figured phasing out," Dai said. "I think you're being too kind to Petra. What she did is a capital offense, and she would have deserved her fate if she'd burned."

"I know you're right," Vance said. "I'm not going to sentence anyone to the roof."

"You will when you know it's the right thing to do," Dai said. "In this case, Petra's crime straddled the line between my values and yours. She's with you? She can hear me?"

"Yes," Vance said as Petra nodded.

"Petra, violating this banishment is a non-negotiable death sentence," Dai said. "If you see me or Vance again, expect us to kill you on the spot."

"If you're near our kingdom," Vance added.

Dai didn't respond to that. Instead, she just said, "Cynthia will take a couple hours to get to you. Lanie should be there sooner. She'll have Marisol with her. Someone is out to get you; you can't be running low on blood or control."

"I understand," Vance said.

"Lanie may have food for Petra with her as well," Dai said. "I want to make sure she has the strength to get out of my kingdom."

"Understood, Your Majesty," Petra said.

"Don't screw her," Dai said and hung up.

"What?" Vance asked. "I wouldn't."

"I would," Petra said. "You're the hottest guy in L.A. I know strong vampires, but not many look strong. They don't have muscles that flaunt their power. Vampires are so often androgynous or outright effeminate. Everyone in the city wants you, if only for a night or maybe just an hour. It's your body, Sheriff Silver." She purred his name and undid the top button of her blouse. "Dai cannot force you into monogamy. Every animal, especially vampires, needs a new conquest now and then. Dai will certainly appreciate the things I'd like to teach you." She started to unfasten another button.

Vance backed away. "I'm not that kind of animal. I've no doubt you have things to teach me, but I'll have to learn those another day—another way. I'm very flattered…"

Petra tore at her chest. She ripped her shirt away and fell to her knees. For a moment, Vance thought Petra had gotten too aggressive, but he'd seen vampires in cardiac arrest before. Something had happened to Julian, he'd died. Petra crumpled to the floor, unconscious and dying. Unable to think of anything else to do, Vance lay Petra on her back and started chest compressions. With a human, he knew to perform CPR until they resumed breathing. Vampires didn't breathe. He'd have to see if her heartbeat on its own, but her heart might only beat once a minute. That was enough time for her to die, so he just didn't stop.

For what seemed like hours, he knelt over her pushing her chest every other second. She hadn't regained consciousness when Lanie walked in the room.

"Vance, what the fuck!" she asked, almost screaming.

He realized she'd just walked into his office to find him with his hands on a topless woman's chest.

"CPR," he answered and demonstrated with a chest compression.

"That's not a vampire first aid method," Lanie said. Marisol stepped up behind Lanie and peered over her shoulder, glaring at Vance.

"How do you know?" Vance asked. "Has anyone ever tried?"

"I don't know, but you can't be the first to think of it," Lanie said. "Is she dead?"

"No," Petra said.

"Huh?" Vance asked, pulling away from Petra.

"You have nice hands and, though they're just resting there between compressions, barely touching where I'm sensitive, they're touching enough for me to be getting a little guilty pleasure from it. Thank you for saving my life. What happened to Julian?"

"I'll go look," Lanie said. "Do I need keys to get up to the roof?"

"The building key should work on that lock." Vance threw her his keys.

"Marisol, stay between Vance and this slut," Lanie said and grabbed Marisol by the shoulders and stood her in front of Vance. "I have a pair of fan club members waiting outside. I'll bring them in when I get back."

"Vance, why did Lanie leave you with a virgin?" Petra said. "She's of no use to either of us."

"I'm not really in the mood to have to explain everything," Vance said. "Right now, she's keeping you from taking advantage of my good nature. Please fasten your shirt."

Petra started to laugh, but her gaze went up to the ceiling. "It was so sudden," she said. "He was just there, fully alive in my senses, then with a snap, he was gone. Oh my God! It hurt."

"You were surprised, but how sad are you if were enjoying Vance's touch?" Marisol asked.

"Juli and I were lovers, once," Petra said. "We got over it and were barely friends lately. It's just easier to keep a pet than wean one. You can't make them forget; you know. A weaned pet always remembers. We pretend they don't so we can let them live, but they remember."

"I know," Vance said. "You coerce them to never discuss or admit to what they know of us."

"You'll see," Petra said. "Sometimes, they decide to talk or write about it and damage control falls to the royal or their enforcer, you. You'll kill former pets who can't hold their silence."

"I can only hope you're wrong," Vance said.

"I'm not," Petra said.

The door slammed open and Lanie rushed in. "I wasn't the first to find Julian on the roof," she said. "I couldn't get that close, but it looked like a gunshot to the head. 'High powered, long range,' I heard someone up there say. Everyone seemed very disturbed by the chains. Even the Sheriff of Los Angeles is up there. They're erecting a tent to keep helicopter news crews away, but I saw one traffic copter, so they were probably too late."

"At least they only found the one chain up top," Vance said. "The rest, I pulled through the roof."

"He is amazing," Petra said. "I wouldn't be here if he hadn't saved my life, twice in the past hour and a half."

"Yeah," Lanie said. "He's amazing and he's mine."

"Dai claims him," Petra said.

"I can't help that, but he lives with me," Lanie said. "Sometimes I share him with Dai. You're beautiful. If you weren't so underhanded, I might have been willing to share him with you."

"Um," Vance said. "I'm not a bicycle. You can't just lend me out for anyone to ride."

"Dai told him not to screw me," Petra said.

"Well," Lanie said. "Then it's just never going to happen, is it?"

"I am forced to beg of you," Petra said. "I need blood and if it's just from the normal humans you brought, I'll kill one."

"And an emotionally charged pet could give you enough?" Lanie asked.

"Yes," Petra said. "We can lock the door and collect bruises from the hard floor or clear Vance's desk."

"Vance," Lanie asked. "Would you mind if I helped?"

"Are you asking what…" Vance started to ask but Lanie interrupted him.

"Yes," Lanie said. "Like I said, she's beautiful and a damsel in distress. You saved her twice today. Maybe it's my turn."

"You know, I can't tell you what you can and cannot do," Vance said.

"Would it bother you?" Lanie asked.

Vance handed Marisol his derringer. "You know how to use a weapon?"

"I'm trained in pistols, archery and epee fencing," Marisol said. "I'm not a dead shot, but I won't be far enough to miss if you want me to make sure Petra doesn't drink too much."

"I still don't understand how a virgin fits in our world," Petra said. "But if you need her to keep Lanie safe so she and I can…well, maybe we'll take pictures."

"If we can take pictures, I'm totally taking pictures," Lanie said. She handed Marisol her phone. "You know how to use a camera?"

"I got top marks in erotic cinematography," Marisol said. Vance had to look away. He hated that Zylpha had trained Marisol as a kid to acclimate to sex. Even if Marisol had gotten out of Zylpha's slave pit as a virgin, she had been scarred, though Marisol didn't seem too disturbed. Vance found that most disturbing of all.

"I'm leaving," Vance said. "I'll be in the men's room. Text me or call me when you're done."

Vance slipped from his office and two young women hopped up to him. They had their phones out and, with remarkable quickness for a mortal, took several selfies with each of them kissing his cheeks. Vance even gave into their request to kiss their cheeks, but he rejected their requests to kiss his lips.

The location of the windows of the building didn't put him in direct sunlight while he stood in the hall, but it was bright enough to make him extremely uncomfortable after a minute. He excused himself and rushed to the bathroom. His fans followed him in.

"We were promised permanent ink signatures," one of them said.

"On my breast," one said, lifting her shirt.

"I want mine on my shoulder blade," the other said.

"We're getting them tattooed over, so they'll last forever," the topless girl said.

After everything Vance had just witnessed with Petra, signing a woman's skin seemed relatively tame. He did as the women wanted. They took selfies and pictures of each other as he signed. Once they had his signatures, they left. He knew Lanie had meant for him to feed from them, but without Marisol's blood first, it would have been too risky.

XIX

"Stop moping," Dai said. She walked behind the bar and grabbed a bottle of wine. With customers in the bar, she opened it with a corkscrew. "You've been barely here for days despite working every hour the bar's been open."

"Katina calls me every day to see if I found Stephanie. I have nothing on her. I set up cameras in both of the magic spots Thalia talked about. If the necromancer goes there, I'll know." Vance pulled a beer out and sat alongside Dai while she poured herself a glass of wine. He popped the cap off and drank from the bottle. "Katina really doesn't want that fire team finding the necromancer before either I do, or she does."

"Randall is working that case now, too, right?" Dai asked.

"I have him identifying every customer Stephanie's had in her shop by credit card receipts or special-order notes. He's calling everyone on the contact list on her phone. He's treating this like a missing person's case and he's supposedly working with the FBI on this one case, if his boss asks."

"Isn't the FBI involved?" Vance asked.

"We can't trust the FBI," Dai said. "Dwyer isn't reliable. Has she shared anything useful with you? And Dougal. You've never met the guy and he's got you so twisted around yourself in a time when we really need you standing tall and confident."

"She," Vance corrected Dai. "Dougal is a 'she', apparently. Petra is sure she was there when she got chained up."

"Well, then, she's got you twisted around. Find Dougal and stop her!"

"I can't do anything with that, either," Vance said. "Dwyer has been brushing me off since Julian was killed on the sheriff's roof. That made her look bad and she's not happy with me. We still check in once a day, but the calls are short and don't do more than a greeting and a goodbye these days."

"Wait, Dougal is a woman? Do you know where Dwyer is?" Dai said.

"I suppose I could track her phone," Vance said. "For some reason, you seem to be implying I shouldn't just ask her."

"I think you need to stop a moment and think. How many lies can that woman tell you before it gets through your over-trusting cranium?" Dai asked.

"What makes you think anything she's said has been a lie?" Vance asked.
"I know she uses me, much like you use me, to do dirty work."

"You take that back," Dai said. "I don't lie like she does. I let you know exactly what you are to me, but I'm not sure your cranium has that figured out yet, either."

"You trust me in the utmost," Vance said. "I have your complete authority and faith."

"Yeah," Dai said. "Let's not try with that yet. Let's focus on the massive web of lies Dougal's been tangling you in."

"I've never talked to Dougal," Vance said.

"Describe Dougal," Dai said. "Do you know what she looks like? Did Petra describe her?"

"She is tallish, blonde…"

Dai put two fingers over Vance's lips. Vance still had several words to describe her physique and attitude. Dai didn't let him speak those words. "Now, describe Hannah Dwyer."

Vance would have used the exact same words.

"Fuck!" he shouted.

"Finally!" Dai hugged him. "I'm so proud of you when you swear appropriately."

"Dwyer's been Dougal all along and using me," Vance said. "Why would she have me take out her own operations?"

"She wouldn't," Dai said.

"She did," Vance said. Then he stepped through the incidents. At the docks, Vance had chased a lead from a source other than Agent Dwyer. Her lead from that same night would have him never being on the docks to rescue the Russian women. "The whorehouse wasn't hers," Vance said. "No one there knew who she was. Same with the sweatshop."

"Where she literally had you help steal tens of thousands of dollars from her competitors safe," Dai said. "You were probably right when you guessed Dwyer burned it to hide the evidence of her raid. You were also right when you guessed it was Dougal hiding all the evidence. Ten grand says those workers weren't rescued so much as relocated to another sweatshop or worse."

"I'm not taking that bet," Vance said. "I don't think I have ten grand to bet, but I'd lose it if I did."

"You don't," Dai said. "Your magic debit card has a two thousand dollar a day limit. Your investment account is close, but not to ten grand yet. Give me two more months and it'll be self-feeding, but you still need to deposit a few months royalties to really seed it properly."

"Okay, let me ping her phone." Vance opened the app and put in the number. For the first time, he encountered a popup override box. It required the badge number of a senior ranking law enforcement official. Vance hoped his rank was sufficient. He tried his badge number and it worked.

Dwyer's phone pinged at a house south of Long Beach, close to the boundary with Thalia's kingdom.

"I know where that is," Dai said. "Cynthia is parked out front, waiting."

Vance called to his bartender, "I've got an errand. See you tomorrow."

"Whatever you say, boss," Ollie said.

XX

Dai pulled a black footlocker from the back of the SUV and opened it on the ground. Inside were blue jackets with 'FBI' written in big letters and half a dozen assault rifles.

"These are not current issue, but they'll do," Dai said. "Remember, we're raiding the home and headquarters of a crime lord and human trafficker. We are not here to arrest a rogue FBI agent."

"She knows our secret," Vance said. "We have to protect that secret at every cost."

"I know this isn't going to be easy on you," Dai said. "Sometimes it's my job to ask you to do unpleasant things."

"I think I'm okay with this," Vance said. "I'm not sure it's right, but it feels right."

"We're killing henchmen, too?" Cynthia asked.

"Only in self-defense," Vance said. "Or if they see us doing something undeniably vampire."

"So, henchmen, too," Cynthia said.

Dai handed Vance a sword. It wasn't his usual custom-made blade, just a samurai sword. "We don't know Petra was her only vampire. If she wasn't, any vampires in there are sentenced to die as of right now. If we let witnesses live, I don't want to be identified by my sword."

"I'm going to play it by ear," Vance said.

"Just be ready to step aside if I veto your good nature," Dai said. "There are times I want you to temper my wrath. This is one of those times you need me to stoke the flame of your wrath." Dai tapped her phone earpiece. "Lanie, we ready?"

"I got the filming permits," Lanie said. "That street is cordoned off and the police at the barricades are expecting to hear a lot of gunfire from that shoot. Oh, and it was damned expensive to get this done on an hour's notice, so don't blame me for three massive wire transfers from your graft account."

"Let's go," Dai said. "Even if you let someone live, make sure they're coerced to never discuss and, ideally, never remember what happened here. If they know what a vampire is and that we're real, I can't play it safe. They must die. Once we start shooting, we'll only have about three or four minutes to wrap this up. That doesn't leave us time to coerce the bad guys. Zip-tie the fuck out of anyone who surrenders, and we'll hope we can let them live after. Does that work for you Vance?"

"Can I be accepting without approving?" Vance asked.

"You can be whatever you need to be as long as you're by my side," Dai said. "Make sure your safety is off and let's go put an end to this whole Dougal distraction. Cynthia, set the mines and meet us at the back door."

"Mines?" Vance asked.

"Very important to know, actually. Cynthia is going to place a claymore mine at each side of the driveway heading to the gate so if anyone tries to drive out, well, you can imagine what happens to people on the wrong side of a claymore, right? She's also going to chain the gate shut. No one's getting out of here other than on foot. And we run faster than they do."

"Wow, you've been planning this," Vance said.

"Not really," Dai said. "I got two crates of old FBI munitions from when we confiscated Satan's stuff. I finally found a use for them. To be honest, I don't know that the claymores are still any good. The guns have been tested and the ammo is all stuff I got at the store this year. You have point." She pushed Vance ahead. "Fly up and let's just go in through a second story wall. No one plans for that."

"Dougal's pretty smart," Vance said.

"She's cocky, too," Dai said. "She's going to expect you to go in and ask questions."

"She's expecting me?" Vance asked. "You think so?"

"You tracked her phone. You don't think she knows we're coming?" Dai asked. "Let's go up, just above the tree line." She flew upward. Vance followed.

A gate at the street led to a long driveway that wound through walls of pine trees. A large house, not quite a mansion by local standards, glowed with light. A dozen cars parked in front of the front door and loud music came from around a pool in back. Dozens of men in dark suits stood around, almost looking like partygoers, but instead of drinks, they each held a small automatic weapon. Most had Uzi's, but a few had more modern, American issue firearms.

"The stakes sheathed to their thighs tell me this isn't going to go how you want it to go," Dai said.

Each of the men had two wooden stakes strapped to their right thighs. They were prepared to fight vampires.

Vance was about to say something about being hopeful coercion would still work when the sky exploded above the house. Bursts of orange and red light accompanied very loud pops. Dougal had added fireworks to her preparations. Not only would they help mask gunfire, but they would also make coming in by air very unappealing to vampires.

"Why is everyone better at combat tactics than me?" Vance asked.

"You're a white male with a bad case of honesty and almost no trust issues," Dai said. "You expect the world to be straightforward and think you can stride into a fight head-on and not get shot in the back. You don't usually need tactics because you're strong enough, fast enough, and smart enough that a simple trap won't be powerful enough to take you down, and you can take most people on face-to-face. I'm a five-foot-four foreign woman who's always been treated like I didn't belong there, wherever 'there' was. I didn't know I was strong enough to fight face-to-face, so I always made sure I had the advantage. We're going in through the wall on the second floor. That smaller window there. It's probably a bathroom, and that window won't be the type that opens. We're unlikely to find half a dozen men in the room ready to shoot anyone who comes through that window."

Vance dove, flying fast, just below roof level. He phased into the Venae and passed through the wall into the house. He landed in a bathtub and brought himself back to the physical world. As Dai predicted, no one waited for them in the bathroom.

"Time to test our Kevlar," Dai said. She pulled open the bathroom door and peeked into the hall. "Two guys watching the top of the stairs," she whispered. "I'll get the one on the left, you get the one on the right. On three. One, two…"

She didn't give Vance time to think about why not to do it. When Dai jumped into the hall, so did he. She shot one man; he shot the other. Men started shouting throughout the house. A man ran out of a room, looked at Vance and raised his gun.

Vance shot, dropping the gunman before he could level his gun.

"Room by room, then?" Dai asked. "Together or split up?"

"Together is safer," Vance said. "We're playing on her overconfidence; we shouldn't give her a play on ours."

"Together it is," Dai said. "On three, kick open the door and drop to the floor. When you kick the door, I'm going through the wall five feet to the side. Ready? One, two…"

Vance kicked the door and dropped. Bullets sprayed over his head for a moment before Dai took down anyone in that room. Vance counted two men dead or dying on the floor. The living man's blood called to him, but he fought against the draw.

"This is Dougal's office," Vance said, noticing the large desk and shelves of books and art.

"Where is she if she isn't here?" Dai asked.

A throng of men came through the door, firing wildly. It took a couple of minutes, but between Vance and Dai, they killed more than ten men before Dai stopped shooting back. Vance had been hit in the Kevlar three or four times. He glanced over to see Dai had been shot in the face. She grunted and knelt on her hands and knees. "I'll be okay," she said. "Don't look at me, please. I can't be pretty right now. I'll heal, but for now, find and kill Dougal."

Vance did as Dai asked and kept his gaze away from her. If she could talk, she'd be fine. Vance shot one more man coming through the door, but his gun ran dry as he tried to put a third bullet in the man's chest. He took a moment to gather some of the henchmen's weapons and a few spare magazines. He then ran into the hall, shooting everyone who even looked his way while holding a weapon. He managed to keep himself from killing a woman in a maid uniform and another dressed in a tuxedo. Neither were Dougal, but neither were armed. As he fought his way down the stairs, he came into a large dining room. He heard a sword being drawn from a scabbard behind him. He spun. A vampire woman he recognized from court, but couldn't put a name to, lunged at him. Vance raised his gun and shot the vampire in the head, emptying the magazine before the vampire fell to the floor. He'd removed most of her gray matter. Even a vampire wouldn't likely heal from that.

"I would have thought you were the 'bring a sword to a swordfight' type," Cynthia said from across the room.

"I'm better with a gun," Vance said. "This isn't a battle for my pride or my honor. Should I be trying to show off?"

"It would have been cool to see," Cynthia said. "But this isn't a movie, so the first rule is to stay alive and if that means shooting a swordsman, we shoot. You just put thirty bullets from a short-barreled weapon into a four-inch space. The kick from full-auto should have made that impossible."

"I knew where I wanted to shoot her," Vance said. "I didn't let my aim stray. That's a vampire. There might be more."

"Right now, you have a more important task," Cynthia said. "Dougal drove off. One of my claymores took out a car ahead of hers, but the other claymore didn't discharge. I was already in the front door, but by the time I got out to see how my mines had done, I saw a red Jeep with a blond driver speeding down the street. Where's Dai?"

"Upstairs recovering from a shot that missed her vest," Vance said.

"You go," Cynthia said. "Dai and I will clean up here."

Vance flew up, and saw the red Jeep heading south. He passed ahead of her and landed on the street. He stopped and waited. He looked behind him to see what the Jeep would hit if it lost control. There was nothing but beach and ocean unless she made a hard-left turn. Since she had a car and he hadn't even drawn a gun, he expected her to try to run him down. He planned to phase and grab her from the car as it passed through him. Then he'd cuff her and take her in. He hoped her home would provide all the evidence he'd need.

Dwyer hit her brakes, stopping her car a dozen feet from Vance. When she opened her door, Vance drew his derringer. She emerged with her hands up.

"Do you know where you're standing, Sheriff Silver?" Dwyer asked.

"I'm standing on the road, blocking the path of the biggest criminal in my county," Vance said.

"Welcome to the O.C., Mister Silver," Dwyer said. "You're not a sheriff here. We're in another county and, more importantly, another kingdom. I don't see a patrol car, so you can't claim hot pursuit. You have no jurisdiction here. You can't arrest me." She smiled and opened her coat, showing she wasn't wearing a shoulder holster. "I'm unarmed and no threat. What are you going to do with that pistol?"

"A friend reminded me recently that it's easier to ask forgiveness than permission," Vance said and shot her with both barrels of the derringer. She dropped and died before drawing another breath. He pulled his phone out and called Thalia.

"Vance?"

"We're even," Vance said. "I just killed an FBI agent in Orange County. I don't have the resources to clean this up."

"Send me the location," Thalia said. "I've got your back, Vance."

"You don't even question why?" Vance asked.

"You're Vance Silver," Thalia said. "Even if you weren't a sister, if you kill someone, there's an infallible reason. I don't need your story, but if you need to talk, and there's something in your voice that says you do, I'm here."

"I can't leave until this scene is clear," Vance said.

Thalia said, "I'll be there in five minutes. Clear the street of bodies and cars. We'll get the blood and dispose of the evidence before sunup."

Vance put Dwyer's body in the back of her car and pulled it off the road. He then sat on the curb and waited. He considered calling Dai but didn't want her going on and on about how he did the right thing and how proud she was of him. She'd try to rationalize why he did the right thing in a way he'd understand. Vance understood the need when he pulled the trigger. It had nothing to do with the crimes Dwyer committed against people in terms of human slavery or indenture by threat. He killed her because she knew about vampires, and he couldn't make her forget. Everything he'd tell himself in the days to come was that she was evil, and the world was far better without her.

Maybe, in the moment, he'd reacted to her taunt. How could he justify that? Even with all the logic and rationalization, was he the kind of person who could be goaded into committing evil on a dare?

A motorcycle drove up and stopped in front of Vance. A woman and a man sat on the seat. The man stepped off. "You're Vance?" he asked.

Vance stood and offered his hand. "Vance Silver," he said.

"I'm Walt," the biker said as he removed the helmet. "Thalia sent me. She'll be here soon. Leave this to me. Where's the body?"

"In the car," Vance said, nodding down the street to the red Jeep. He held out the car keys.

Walt waved to the woman on the motorcycle, and she rode off. "Any pools of blood?"

"Not really," Vance said. "I shot her twice in the skull: twenty-twos. They went in but didn't come out. There's a small spot over there."

The man pulled a bottle around the size of a hotel shampoo bottle from his coat pocket and poured it onto the blood spot. Vance could smell the vinegar.

"I'm done here," Walt said. "This is the easiest clean up I've done in years."

"What'll become of the body? The car?" Vance asked.

"The car's going to Tijuana," Walt said. "I know some guys who will paint, re-upholster, and then change the vehicle identification plates with a similar car that's been scrapped. The body? That's Hannah Dwyer, right? She's the local FBI liaison to the immigration department. Her body will show up in the desert where the Mexican Cartels are known to leave victims. Did you use a registered gun?"

"No," Vance said. "I used an antique derringer."

"Give me the gun," Walt said.

"It has sentimental value," Vance said.

"Sometimes they do. In that case, give the gun to Thalia," Walt said. "She's a weapon smith. She'll bore the barrel just enough to change the striations, so it won't match the ballistics of those bullets in Agent Dwyer's skull."

"I'm not that crass," Thalia said. "I'll take the materials of the barrel and melt them down, re-smelt the steel, re-mold the copper dressings. It'll be a whole new gun made of the same materials. I won't need to do anything with the stock or trigger mechanism. You didn't drop your casings, did you?"

"No," Vance said, handing Thalia his derringer. "They're still in there."

"I'm going to take off," Walt said. He climbed in the Jeep and drove away.

"She's human, right?" Thalia asked.

"Yeah," Vance said.

"And you don't like that you killed a person when you hoped to only kill monsters?" Thalia asked.

"She was a monster," Vance said.

"Maybe, but she was still human and not vampire. You didn't really sign up to kill people when Dai convinced you to stay alive as a vampire."

"First law," Vance said. "Protect the secret."

"Does it matter?" Thalia said. "You're going to kill people. It's part of this life. If you don't feel you did the right thing, if killing that FBI agent didn't feel heroic, you have to find your balance. What does make you feel heroic? What does make you feel like the man you envision yourself as?"

"For four years, I thought I'd be a preacher of God's Word," Vance said.

"No, you didn't," Thalia said. "You thought you'd be a leader of men. No one wants to be a shepherd of God as a twenty-year-old. They want to be a shepherd of men. Were you honestly in it to spread the word of God, or to bring men into God's grace? When you envision yourself speaking, which connection are you thinking of? The one between you and your god, or the one between you and your congregation?"

"I..." Vance was sure he'd meant to serve God. Thalia didn't have him as pegged as she thought she did.

"It doesn't matter," Thalia said. "You're a vampire. You're one of the hundred most powerful vampires in the world, probably top twenty-five. Dai thinks you're a hero. I know Dai is right. But you're not a white knight on a white steed. You're a war veteran who's done things they can't be proud of, even knowing they were the right thing to do. Your armor might once have been polished to a mirrored sheen and your horse might still be white, but both have blemishes, scars, and bloodstains. No matter whose body that blood started in, once it's on your armor, it's your blood. You have to own it."

"That's a new..."

"I'm not done," Thalia said. "You think you need to be more of a hero because you're more of a monster. You just have to be who you are. Be strong in yourself and the world will accept you."

"Just soldier on?" Vance asked, trying to summarize Thalia's words.

"No," Thalia said. "You're not a soldier. You're a champion. Be a champion, not a soldier. Soldiers can disassociate themselves from responsibility. A champion acts with determination and responsibility. You're a murderer Vance Silver, but you're a murderer the world needs. You're not a monster. You're a person who does monstrous things. You're also a person who acts primarily in the better interests of the world around him."

"Here's where Dai or Lanie would tell me to carry the guilt of killing a person to remind me to contemplate my actions, so if I do it again, I'll know I made the choice to do so," Vance said.

"Guilt?" Thalia said. "No, you don't need guilt for killing Dougal, or Dwyer, or whatever her name was. She deserved to die. Human society might be against the death penalty, more and more so each passing day. You don't live in that world. You live in the less refined, more primal world of vampires. Death in either world is a penalty for making poor choices. In our world, death is a penalty by necessity. We can't afford to have humans become aware of our world or both worlds suffer. There have, before modern times, been societies aware of us, and none have lasted in such awareness for more than a handful of years. This is why James built the temple and set the rules we all follow. This is what works best for everyone."

"I have to accept that it's okay to kill?" Vance said.

"No, you have to accept that death is part of life. You are not going to rid the world of vampires. Vampires are as much a part of this world as fire."

"Men can control fire," Vance said.

"Tell that to the people on the east side of the city who lose their homes," Thalia said. "Uncontrolled fire still kills more people every day than vampires."

"Dai and I killed about thirty men today," Vance said.

"And you're at the center of where deaths occur," Thalia said. "Because of who you are, you are at the darkest parts of the vampire world. You will see more death than most vampires. You will kill more humans than most vampires. Do you know how many humans I've killed?"

"Including pets of vampires you've executed?" Vance asked.

"That doesn't change the number," Thalia said.

"A couple thousand?" Vance asked.

"One," Thalia said. "Five if you blame me for the humans those new vampires had to kill last spring. I don't count it when death will claim one person and I have the opportunity to choose which of two will live. If two people are about to get shot but you can jump in front of only one bullet, did you kill the other person?"

"No," Vance said. "That's first year philosophy."

"Then, in almost three thousand years, I've killed one human," Thalia said. "I've executed twenty-six vampires, but I know how to keep a human alive through their vampire's death."

"CPR?" Vance asked.

"Actually, yes," Thalia said. "You just have to start forced heart pumps on the pet before the sun touches their vampire."

"It works the other way, too," Vance said. "You can save a vampire by keeping their heart beating after their pet dies."

"It's rare," Thalia said. "Worth trying, but only succeeds less than half the time. It's not a situation that comes up often. No one kills a pet without also wanting to kill the vampire. Vamp royals don't execute pets. Most of us put the blame of a pet's action on their maker."

"But I'm supposed to be okay with killing humans because I'm in the vampire world and death happens?" Vance asked.

"Yes, only I wouldn't say you need to be okay," Thalia said. "You need to be aware of the world and that the death in your world isn't your doing. Sometimes you are the hand of fate, sometimes you are the instrument of your own will. Killing thirty men pointing guns at you, that's you as an instrument of fate. You had the choice to either kill or be shot, and that's not a choice, that's a reflex. With the woman who bought and sold people, you chose to act as judge, jury, and executioner. I cannot judge you for that. I don't know what you knew about her. If you felt you knew enough to act as you did, you have to trust in yourself."

"She was unarmed and taunted me, dared me to shoot her," Vance said. "So, I did."

"You didn't act on impulse. I know that much about you, sister," Thalia said. "She'd done enough over time to guide your measure of her so when you had the opportunity to give her a just reward, you didn't need to hesitate."

"Yeah," Vance said. "I knew who she was and what she'd done, and there weren't any doubts in mind that she'd continue to do those things. I don't believe the human justice system would have punished her. She knew how to manipulate that."

"I'd have shot her," Thalia said. "If I knew what you knew, my kill count would be up to two."

"Human morality doesn't give me that leeway," Vance said. "The legal system certainly doesn't."

"You're not human," Thalia said.

"That's the one thing that everyone who's given me advice can agree on," Vance said. "Padre Guillermo tells me to be a good person, whoever I am, but I can't look to God to define what it means to be good or evil as a vampire. Dai tells me to accept that I am stronger than my monster, but I can't be the hero I thought I was meant to be. She can't define who I am meant to be; that's up to me. Now, you tell me to be a vampire, not a human."

"Dai is wrong," Thalia said. "You can be exactly the hero you always wanted to be. I just think you had the poster boy image in your head and not the dirt-and-blood-under-your-nails reality. You haven't really thought about what it means to be that hero. Like I said, you'll scratch your veneer now and then and you will get bloody. You're a medieval knight, not a comic book superhero. Your vision is a two-dimensional façade. That image, when you learn what it is in reality, is held up by many raw and scarred supports."

"And you like me just as I am, you don't see me for my flaws," Vance said.

"I see you exactly for your flaws," Thalia said. "Stop trying to be something. Be you. When faced with a decision, don't think what each choice will do to who you are, don't think about what Dai wants or what Lanie wants. Think about what's important to you. And I can't define that for you."

"Being noble and good are important to me," Vance said. "Doing the most I can do to help everyone around me is important to me. Making the world a better place is important to me."

"Which of those did you act against when you killed that FBI agent?" Thalia asked.

"I think there could have been a more noble solution," Vance said.

"Sometimes being noble means doing the ignoble thing, letting the action blemish your ego, to make the world better. Nothing good could have come from letting that woman live one minute longer, except it might have made you feel like you did the noble thing to take her to the human legal system."

"Life is sacred," Vance said.

Thalia punched his arm. "You're kidding right? You've already taken up the mantle of a warrior. You've long since accepted that you are ordained to kill to make the world a better place."

"I wonder sometimes," Vance said.

"My opinion is that if the only people who killed other people were people with your morality, no one would ever kill," Thalia said. "You kill killers. I know your victims under the bloodeyes aren't always so clearly evil, but that's like Artemis. It's an element of nature you can't fully control. You do it responsibly and control it when you can, but you save lives every day you are out in the world. Not just the ones you actively rescue, but vampires don't do bad things because they know you'll come after them if they do. Most vampires, like most people, are good, but there are always that tiny fraction that choose their own actions purely by the consequences."

"Dai is…"

Thalia continued, interrupting Vance. "Dai's reputation is less because she's a woman. It's stupid. I know she's far more dangerous than you, but you're daunting. With Dai, vamps would commit the crime and take their chances and lose, but there's still a victim, somewhere. With you around, no one takes that chance."

"At least not without a more immediate threat, like Dougal," Vance said.

"And that's why you put an end to her," Thalia said.

"So, I'm putting too much thought into this," Vance said. "Dai keeps telling me I overanalyze this whole good/evil thing.

"You do," Thalia said. "You are naturally good. But I would say it's good to keep thinking about it. Know who you want to be so you can make sure you're on the right path. But don't let it get in the way of your jobs. Trust yourself to make the right decisions quickly. If you make a mistake, learn from it. If you find yourself making a lot of mistakes, that's the time to stop making snap decisions. Slow down, relearn yourself and clarify your goals. Make careful decisions until you're sure you would make the same decisions if you had to decide in the blink of an eye."

"I like a lot of things about your philosophy," Vance said.

"Ultimately, we each figure out how to stay sane," Thalia said. "For most of us, that means accepting a little insanity and pretending it's normal."

"Bloodeyes." Vance didn't need to explain more.

"You might have to accept more insanity than most," Thalia said. "If the other sisters and I thought your bloodeyes would cause more harm than good, we'd kill you. You're still alive. That should tell you something."

"Artemis and the rest of the sisters sometimes have a very skewed definition of 'good'," Vance said.

"No one is perfect," Thalia said. "That includes you."

XXI

"You are perfect," Lanie said. She ran her fingertips over Vance's chest and stomach, tracing his muscles.

"We just showered to wash off the sweat from when you started caressing my skin an hour ago," Vance said.

"Yeah," Lanie said. "We shouldn't keep Azure and Katina waiting any longer. They've been in the bar since seven."

"You should have said something," Vance said.

"I had things I needed to do," Lanie said. "So, I'm telling you now."

"I'll get dressed quick and head down." Vance said. "I know you need time for makeup and hair."

"Don't wear your sheriff uniform," Lanie said.

"I haven't put it on since killing Dougal," Vance said. "I know Dai likes me in uniform, but I feel like it's a costume. It also feels out of place standing behind the bar. I could do it when I was just wearing a costume and playing a sheriff on TV, but now it seems weird."

"That's what I'm saying," Lanie said. "We sell fewer drinks with you in uniform."

"Yeah, that makes sense," Vance said. "I'm not really sure I have much use for the uniform. I guess Halloween is in a few days. I can dress as a sheriff then."

"Dai and I are working on a costume for you," Lanie said. "So that's one less thing for you to worry about."

"Should I bother trying to dress myself?" Vance asked. "Or will you be telling me not to wear black jeans and a black button-down shirt tonight?"

"Faded blue jeans," Lanie said. "The ones with the gothic cross I drew on the thigh. You can't see your shapely ass in black jeans in a dark bar. The black shirt is a good call, though."

Vance inhaled deeper than he needed to just so he could sigh with more noise and duration than would be natural. He finished dressing, putting on the blue jeans Lanie suggested and the black bowling shirt. His boots were combat boots—the modern kind with breathable fabric instead of the solid leather of the goth fashion combat boots. He took the elevator to the basement and climbed the stairs to emerge behind the bar. Azure and Katina sat at the end of the bar watching the band onstage. It would be too loud to talk at the bar, so Vance went and waved to get their attention, then gestured for them to follow him.

They brought their glasses of wine. Katina brought the bottle as well. Vance led them to the basement. When they got to the bottom of the stairs,

Vance noticed a woman with dark features, Middle Eastern perhaps, had followed them.

"That's Qamra," Azure said. "She's from the Pentacle. She's another necromancer and also a vampire's pet."

"Winnie won't let me stay involved in this," Qamra said. "It's too dangerous."

"Just tell him about the fire team," Katina said.

"I was getting there," Qamra said. "The four of us, the three fire team members and me, were walking on the beach when a dozen cops approached us with a woman who wasn't a cop. We realized too late that the woman was an air mage, and the cops were all seeing some mirage or illusion she created. This was a crowded beach, so when the cops charged us with billy clubs, we could not use magic to defend ourselves. I woke up with some Good Samaritan trying to give me water. Some of the cops were still there and they were more confused than me."

"And your friends were gone?" Vance asked.

"Two of them disappeared," Qamra said. "Howard is in the hospital with a broken arm and fractured skull. He was the water mage of the fire team. Witnesses saw them putting Norm and Halley into cop cars. Norm is the fire mage; Halley is the earth mage of our fire team. I guess they didn't take me because they don't need a necromancer."

"Or a water mage," Azure said. "The necromancer must be close to being ready for the ritual."

"Are there any powerful dates coming up?" Katina asked.

"Today is a black moon," Azure said.

"Not here," Qamra said. "In America, the black moon was last month."

"Black moon?" Vance asked.

"Like a blue moon," Azure said. "The second full moon in a month is a blue moon. The second new moon is a black moon. Because it's a different time of day here than on the International Date Line, sometimes it's a different month here for a few hours. This month, at the apex of the new moon, it was October in England but still September here. That was our black moon. European is on Sunday. I doubt the necromancer is going to Europe."

"So, it's Halloween," Qamra said.

"It's really a magically powerful day?" Vance asked. He'd learned enough that he knew as soon as he asked that he didn't need to.

"People give a day power," Qamra said. "Any holiday has power. People also choose the magic that is most potent on a given holiday. For Halloween, it is the magic of the soul: necromancy. Other magics gain power on that day as well, on every holiday, so for a necromancer to perform a ritual with a coven of six, the power could be unfathomable by modern understanding of magic."

"No one's thought to use a vampire to complete a coven in over ten thousand years?" Vance asked.

"No," Qamra said. "Every mage must participate and contribute to the ritual, and vampires cannot control their magic through ritual."

"Not in this one," Azure said. "This is a pure power focus."

"It's what?" Qamra asked.

"Six mages focus their power on a central being, giving them the power to do almost anything their element would allow," Azure said.

"You didn't share that with the Pentacle," Qamra said.

"I deemed the ritual too potent for anyone to know about," Azure said. "Right now, a vampire named James is taking a sledgehammer to a recently unearthed wall in Syria. I've burned my copy of the ritual. This isn't something anyone can know."

"But your necromancer does?" Qamra asked.

"Yes," Azure said. "And if he left you and a water mage, he has his coven complete, I'm sure. We are assuming he will be in one of two powerful locations. And now we have to assume that Stephanie isn't a prisoner, she's an ally to the necromancer."

"How do we stop it?" Vance asked.

"The mages will take care of it. But if you find yourself in need to stop something like it, you must prevent it from starting," Azure said. "Once this ritual starts, it will only end when the controller ends it. He can't do that if you break his concentration, and I don't think this guy is going to stop before he drains his coven dry. I'm not actually certain he can stop it once it starts."

"Show me what you know," Qamra said.

Azure looked at Vance. Vance nodded. How he ended up in charge, he didn't know, but if Qamra was going to help, they needed the help.

Azure went and grabbed a case of beer. She brought it over and set it down. She took six bottles out and set them in a circle. "There will be a pattern of lines connecting the six, probably made of blood, and probably cow blood. Another set of lines of vinegar or wine will connect each mage to the center where the necromancer will stand. Once the ritual starts, any disruption of those will kill them all."

"And that much power will render the earth," Qamra said. "A fissure or, more likely, a volcanic eruption."

"You're kidding?" Vance asked. Again, he shook his head at the question he shouldn't have asked.

"Power has to go somewhere. If it doesn't, it pretty much just explodes," Qamra said. "When I joined the Pentacle, I got to see a lot of images of sites where rituals were interrupted. That big eruption at Mount Saint Helens, that was a failed ritual with a coven of four. The necromancer is going to have something big planned to do with that power."

"I bet he's going to try to make himself into a spirit elemental," Azure said.

"A ghost?" Qamra guessed. She then said even louder, "A lich."

"That's bad?" Vance asked.

"There have been liches in history," Qamra said. "They make themselves into god-kings and they have the power to steal a man's soul with a glance. Killing them is nearly impossible. They don't procreate like vampires, but they must feed far more often, and they devour souls, and not partially."

"Aztecs?" Vance asked.

"I can't say for sure," Qamra said. "We know of several that had tiny demesnes. As far as 'god-king' liches go, we think the Mayans, maybe. We're almost certain there was one in China before written history there. No one really knew how they came to be, but this ritual could do it."

"What if another mage were the center?" Vance asked. "What if Stephanie is the center?"

"Stephanie is air," Azure said. "That's light and illusion, but at that much power, she could redefine perception, which is a simple way of saying she could change reality."

"Immortality is certain," Qamra said. "Elementals don't age."

"Not once we reach adulthood," Azure said. "Even made elementals—and there have been quite a few—don't age. But the ritual to make an elemental, even a lich, has never been done with six, has it?"

"Nope," Qamra said. "Only takes four and a focus. The four die and the focus becomes an elemental. We have a few documented willing sacrifices, but most are unwilling, and those elementals are hunted. Elementals are powerful and, if they know what they're doing, can kill with a thought."

"I've seen what Azure can do," Vance said.

"Imagine fire," Qamra said. "No one's ever done earth. Fire and Spirit are the most common."

"So, if it only takes four, what if he has six?" Vance asked.

"A more powerful lich," Qamra said. "There's never been a coven of six, so no one knows what it can do."

"Make vampires," Katina said. "The first vampire came from a coven of six. It created a volcano that buried the Middle East in volcanic ash several yards deep. It created Reilla, the first vampire and good friend of mine. If I need to say it, consider you all sworn to secrecy and, yes, you can tell Dai and Lanie."

"Well, that's good," Lanie said, stepping out of the cooler that housed the elevator. Dai followed behind but walked fast enough to be in front of Lanie when they got to Vance's side.

"We're Artemis line," Dai said. "We're allowed to know, anyway."

"Really?" Katina asked.

"Yes, really," Dai said. "You've met Artemis, right? You know she's just dying for any excuse to hunt someone. I guess that's a warning to your Iranian friend."

"You can tell that?" Qamra asked. "I can't even tell Iranians from some Turks or Iraqis. Never mind; you talked to Winnie, my vampire."

"She did the proper thing and came to introduce herself at sunset," Dai said. "She made it very clear that I wasn't to let Qamra accompany Vance anywhere. He is a focal point of danger, and she is very protective of Qamra."

"I'm just a Pentacle representative gathering information," Qamra said. "Now I have more to go on when I gather the next fire team. We weren't expecting an illusionist. Now we know better."

"Today is Sunday. Halloween is tomorrow, Monday," Vance said. "Can you have a fire team here by then?"

"I certainly hope so," Qamra said. "I'm not sticking around this time. It was their job to keep me safe, not my job to save them. I've called it in to the others of the Pentacle, and they're in an emergency meeting since three today. All I know is Azure is supposed to be on the next plane out. I'm supposed to escort her."

"They didn't take your water mage, they don't need Azure," Vance said.

"My logic precisely," Azure said. "With what we know, we can't use that ritual to bring Karina back. But Qamra thinks if she's close enough to talk to, she wouldn't require the ritual from the wall. It might require a human sacrifice, though."

"You're vampires," Qamra said. "Since when is killing against your morality, right?"

"Choose a victim that deserves it," Dai said.

"Qamra, you're okay with killing?" Vance asked.

"I have qualms, but it's not killing, it's trading one life for another," Qamra said.

"So you're all leaving town?" Dai asked.

"Plane is fueled and waiting for us," Katina said. "We just need to go back to our house and destroy a hard drive we scanned the pictures of the wall onto. We're leaving the necromancer to the mages to deal with."

"Since the necromancer has his coven, we should be safe enough to run in, hit the hard drive with an axe, drop it in a bucket of ferro liquid, and get on the plane by midnight." Azure said, gesturing the swinging of an axe as she did.

"Vance, you're still involved in this," Dai said. "We are both going to stop that necromancer. With or without Azure and Katina and any mage help, there's still a vampire involved, right? They need a being of Venae magic for the coven of six. That's a vampire, which means we have someone to rescue."

"I'll start the phone tree," Lanie said. "We'll find out who's missing." She pulled out her phone and typed in a quick text and sent it. "Phone trees are way easier with texts. Is it still a tree if I sent the text to all the vampires?"

"No," Qamra said. "That's just spam."

"Weren't you leaving?" Lanie asked.

"We'll come visit in a few months," Katina said. "I'm going to probably have some things I'll have to explain to Vance if he sees through my eyes during sex too often."

"What?" Qamra asked.

"That's a long story," Katina said. "I'll explain on the plane."

"I'm heading straight to the airport," Qamra said. "I'll meet you there."

"We're just destroying the hard drive and we'll be there by midnight," Katina said. "Tell the private plane gate guard you're on a Vela Azul plane. Your name is on their list. They'll tell you where to go. You won't have to go through security at all. It's the best part of private planes."

"Yeah, you can imagine why I hate airport security," Qamra said and framed her face with her hands. "Don't I look like I was born in Richmond, Virginia?"

"Before you go, does anyone know this evil necromancer's name?" Dai asked.

"Adrian," Qamra said. "Adrian Scheer. He's off the radar, so you won't find him on the internet or in the law enforcement databases. He's kept out of mage circles, too. The mages only know about him because they have me. Necromancers are so rare we don't get teachers, mentors, or such. There are a handful of us at any time. But since we speak with the dead, our ancestors mentor us. They also can share things, like the name of a particularly evil necromancer."

"You could talk to anyone who's dead?" Katina asked.

"No," Qamra said. "Karina, for example, I can't find her. Distances and spatial references don't mean anything where the dead are. They stay close to those they bond with. It's a remarkably simple ritual to see the spirits close to a person, and I see only someone named Karlo near you. There's no Karina. No one else you're close to is still in the place where the dead go. But people don't stay there forever."

"I still feel Karina," Katina said.

"I have other rituals to see dead that are harder to find," Qamra said. "We can try those on the plane. Don't worry; soul magic does not interfere with electronics."

"Yeah, we're going." Azure tugged at Katina's sleeve and pulled her towards the stairs.

Qamra hung back. "My dead mentors tell me this necromancer is three hundred years old. There are remarkably simple rituals we can cast to devour a soul, which can prolong our lives. It's considered an aberration among mages."

"But you've done it," Dai said.

"Excuse me?" Qamra asked.

"You had a lot of confidence in describing the ritual of soul devouring as 'remarkably simple,'" Dai said.

Qamra stared at Dai a moment before responding. "Necromancers see it as evil but accept that it's sometimes not abhorrent to remove a particularly dark soul from existence. Adrian Scheer does it several times a year and is not picky about his victims."

"But becoming a lich would let him do it with far greater ease?" Vance asked.

"He wouldn't need any ritual and wouldn't need to touch his victim," Qamra said. "Vampires are not immune to that ritual. He can't make you zombies, but he can devour your soul. If you go after him, don't let him touch you."

"Use my gun! Got it," Vance said.

"He's still just a man," Qamra said. "A gun will kill him as easily as it would kill any man." She handed Vance a business card. 'Qamra Shirazi, Pentacle Consulting.' It had a couple phone numbers and an email address as well as a couple social media accounts referenced. "Call me for advice. I doubt I'll be able to help in person. My vampire is borderline overprotective. You'd kick her ass, I'm sure, but we don't want it to come to that, 'cuz then I'd kick yours."

XXII

After spending most of the night and most of the morning in a fruitless search for anything relating to the necromancer, Vance lay in bed. Giving up on resting for an hour or two before getting up for the night, he climbed to his feet. On Lanie's side of the bed where she'd normally set out clothes for him, she'd left the suit of Classical Greek armor he'd worn for the photoshoot at the hotel. Of course, she'd planned his Halloween costume.

Next to the armor, she'd left the shield Thalia had given him and a sword. It looked like a Roman gladiator's style weapon: a gladius. He'd used the sword for the photoshoot as well. A note under the sword handle said, 'From Dai, with love.' It was written in Lanie's handwriting.

Vance started donning the armor, starting with the boots and bronze shin plates. Lanie had left a pair of black bicycle shorts to wear under a skirt made of thick leather strips. The breastplate was gold-painted embossed leather with bronze fittings and decorations. Once he had the breastplate and some bracers on, he grabbed his phone to call Lanie and find out if she'd gotten a matching helmet.

His phone rang as he unlocked it. This time, it was his personal number. So few people knew that number, but the caller just showed up as a number from a Virginia area code. Vance answered. "This is Vance," he said.

"This is Qamra. I've been forced to give up on waiting for Katina and Azure to show up."

Vance set his phone to speaker and sat on the edge of the bed to put a pair of boots that matched the armor on. "What do you mean? Did they call you?"

"They did," Qamra said. "Just a minute ago. All they said was that I was to fly without them and to call you. I'm taxiing now. They said they got caught and didn't know how much they could talk before the necromancer realized he hadn't taken Azure's phone. Don't call her. She'll call you when the necromancer isn't in earshot. She said you'd have a way to find them."

"I do," Vance said. "Call me if they call you back."

"Of course," Qamra said, then hung up.

Vance opened the app with his video feeds from the crater by Bakersfield and the lake close to San Diego. Neither showed any signs of anyone being nearby. He could see the sunset over the lake. The sun neared the horizon but wouldn't set for ten or fifteen minutes. Trying to locate Katina shouldn't be hard. She would be one of the lights in his mind. Vance could see several but couldn't make out which light was Katina's. Only one shifted in relative location as he moved across the room. Dai was at her downtown apartment.

Vance called her. After explaining in detail what he'd learned from Qamra, he said, "I don't see any lights north. I always see several far to the east, a few northeast and a couple south."

"I just texted Cynthia," Dai said. "She will have the theatre van behind the bar in three minutes. I'll meet you guys at the high school."

"What?" Vance asked, but Dai had already ended the call.

Vance grabbed his sword and shield and took the elevator to the bar. He cracked open the back door and the theatre van waited there with the side door open. Vance rushed in and pulled the door closed behind him. The shade of the building prevented more than a brief burning sensation on his skin. Inside the van, he felt fine. A thick curtain blocked his view of the front window and there weren't side or back windows.

"Are you dressed as a Gladiator??" Cynthia asked as the van started moving.

"Um, happy Halloween?" Vance offered.

"Yeah, Dai dressed me up as Alice from Alice in Wonderland," Cynthia said. "Do not pull that curtain between us aside. You don't get a good look at me until I get a good look at you."

"Deal," Vance said.

Cynthia arrived at a high school far to the south. They'd driven almost an hour. Dai waited by the football field entrance.

"You came in costume?" Dai asked. "Kevlar and guns would be better."

"I have my gun belt in the van," Cynthia said. "Too much cleavage with this costume for Kevlar."

Her costume seemed typical of adult women's costumes where they add the term 'sexy' to the title of the costume.

"I have a sword and shield," Vance said. "I'm armed and armored and didn't have time to change."

"Your derringer?" Dai asked.

"This costume has a tiny pouch," Vance said. "I do have my phone and I just got my derringer back from Thalia yesterday, so I have that, too."

"We know what we have to work with. Let's triangulate," she said as they walked together onto the field.

"That sounds like something you two should be doing with Lanie, not me," Cynthia said.

"That means...," Vance started to say, but Dai interrupted him with a hard slap to his shoulder.

"Don't mansplain. Cynthia was making a joke."

"Good one," Vance said. "So, how are we going to do this?"

"I have an app," Dai said. "How many lights do you see to the south?"

"Actually, eight right now," Vance said. "All south and a bit east. Thalia must be entertaining this weekend."

Dai tapped the screen of her phone as she replied, "Hopefully Katina will be one light separate from the others. Can you keep your perceptions on one light long enough to walk across a football field?"

"I can," Vance said. Each light had a distinct flicker or something to make it unique. Vance could only recognize Dai's easily. Most days, he could identify Thalia's.

"Okay, take my phone, walk to that corner of the end zone, look at a light, lay the phone flat, point the red arrow at the first point of light and tap the first box next to point one. Then walk down the field to the opposite end and tap the second box. Do that for each of the eight points."

Vance did as Dai instructed. When he finished, he handed the phone back to Dai. She pulled up a map with two points on it. "Thalia was point four?" Dai asked.

"I think so," Vance said. "Why only two points?"

"Six are in Mexico City, probably for Day of the Dead celebrations," Dai said. "Those are off the map. Let's assume the one at Thalia's home is Thalia."

"So, this one at Crater Lake is Katina," Vance said. "I checked the camera I had set there." He pulled the app up on his phone to check again, and still didn't see any signs of people. "No one's there."

"Let's go check," Dai said. "We know someone is there, just not showing up on your camera. Perhaps it's been hacked, or someone propped a still image in front of the lens. It's the closest vamp to your vamp-dar, so the first one to check. Get in the van."

"We could fly?"

"That's too close to Camp Pendleton," Dai said. "I've never been shot with an air-to-air missile, and I don't plan to find out what I'm missing. I flew here, but I won't fly there. Get in the van. I'm driving."

"Shotgun!" Cynthia said. "If I'd brought my SUV, I'd have my shotgun, too."

A few minutes down the road, Vance's phone rang. Azure called.

"Are you okay?" Vance asked.

"Fuck no," Azure said.

"We're in a cave, a big cave," Katina said, sounding distant from Azure's phone. "Somewhere south of Los Angeles."

"I pinged you," Vance said. "We're less than an hour out." Being in a cave would explain why his camera didn't see them.

"You're going to walk for a while, then hit a cave entrance, then it's an hour through the cave. You can't run here," Katina said.

"The ritual will start in an hour or so, but will culminate at solar midnight," Azure said.

"We're in fucking gilded cages," Katina said. "I can't phase through gold."

"Once the ritual starts, the necromancer will be at the center. Killing him will stop the ritual and kill everyone involved. If you have to kill us to stop the ritual, you must kill us," Azure said. "Do you understand what I'm saying?"

"Sometimes, to be a hero, we have to kill everyone?" Vance ventured.

"Yes, kill everyone if you must to stop the ritual," Azure said.

"Only, don't!" Katina said. "I'm counting on you to save us. I've been through too much crap in the last few years to die here in this cage."

"If you can, yes, save us. If you have to kill us, we're okay with dying to stop this evil."

"Only save me," Katina said. "If you can, and I mean if you must move heaven and hell to do it, save me. Save Azure too if you can."

"And don't get killed, Vance!" Azure said.

"That is important," Katina said. "You can't save me, I mean us, if you're dead. Don't die."

"Gotta drop," Azure said. "Hurry!"

The line went dead.

"You both heard that?" Vance asked.

"Save Katina," Cynthia said. "Otherwise, save the world and Katina?"

Dai laughed. She then said, in dead seriousness, "Vance, you are forbidden from dying. Save the world if you can, but don't even think of dying."

"We need to fly," Cynthia said. "We're still thirty minutes out by my GPS."

"Yeah," Dai said. "Ditch the van by the side of the road. I'll carry Cynthia. Vance, get on your phone and try to find cave entrances near Crater Lake. Any mention of a huge chamber underground would be great!"

"On it," Vance said. Internet searching while flying proved to be anything but simple. Flight required concentrating on keeping himself pushed off the ground and moving forward. He had to spend all his time keeping up with Dai who flew just above the ground on a straight line toward their destination.

Dai stopped thirty feet in the air just over the ridge alongside a tall row of trees. "What do you have?"

Vance was about to look at his phone when he caught the roving glow of flashlights down the slope behind them. They weren't moving anywhere and hadn't turned upward. They just meandered back and forth.

"There's an entrance behind us," Vance said. "It's guarded by at least four guys with assault rifles. Aim for the flashlights. As long as you're not a crack shot, you might hit the guy behind it."

"With a pistol at seventy yards?" Cynthia asked. "I'd be lucky to hit within a foot of the guy. Still, I'd rather shoot someone who isn't shooting back. Could one of you people who can't be killed by bullets go about twenty feet that way and make some noise?"

"Yeah, I'll try to do something," Vance said. He unstrapped the shield

Blue of Blood

from his back and wore it on his arm. He flew down to the ground and landed six or seven steps from Cynthia. He held out his shield to his left, his arm outstretched, to show the shiny, mirror-like side towards the men with guns. It might make him more visible if their light reflected better. Then he drew his derringer and shot into the middle of the group.

The lights all shone towards him, and a hail of bullets hit him. He'd never regretted any decision so much in his life. Only four bullets hit him, but it had seemed like more at the time. Cynthia dropped eight men in the time it took those four bullets to find Vance. He fell to the ground and lay on his back and tried extremely hard not to breath or do anything to cause any part of himself to move.

"Stupid heroics," Dai said, kneeling by him. "I'd have probably moved around a little and made myself harder to hit."

Vance crawled to his feet once the bleeding stopped.

"You're weakened," Dai said. "Those soldiers were bereft of Venae. Zombified, I'd guess."

"I'll be fine," Vance said. "I'll soldier through this."

"No," Dai said. "I'll be right back. There were homes just a few miles from here." She flew off only to return a few minutes later with two men, one under each arm. "You get one, I get one. They can survive losing three pints. I already coerced them to want to help, despite the pain. You need someone's arm to hold during the field surgery, understood."

Vance took one man's offered arm and bit. The world went blood-red, and he woke with Cynthia sitting on his chest. Dai climbed to her feet, picking her sword off the ground a few yards away.

"I had totally forgotten to be prepared for that," Dai said. "Let's just remember these as the two corpses I picked up at their meth lab."

"They were meth heads?" Vance asked.

"They made the drug," Dai said. "They weren't stoned, or they might not have had Venae. I don't know if meth works like heroin did. Either way, their sins are between them and Saint Peter now."

"I killed them both?" Vance asked. He hoped for a different answer than the obvious one.

"I killed one," Dai said. "Your stabbing him in the neck with a sword reduced his chances of living to about zero, so I took advantage of that. You still threw me across the clearing even after I ate his death."

"I can't even stop to ponder how evil this was for us," Vance said. "I'm just going with the ends justify the means in this case. These guys would be dead from the volcano if we fail to stop this ritual, right?"

"You don't wear pragmatism well," Dai said. "The only thing wrong with what you said is that you said it. I want you to be better than this. I'm fine with this, but I like you more when you're better than me."

"I hate this," Vance said. "I can't control myself at times like that and…"

"I like that better," Dai said. "It's a hundred percent true. You are not in control when the bloodlust takes over. We all had a chance to realize you shouldn't feed. None of us made the right call. It's a mistake, and a costly one, but it's a mistake."

"Let's finish this rescue," Vance said. He found the cave entrance the eight men had been guarding. It was the first time he got a good look at the men. They were all in military uniforms and two were women. Again, he had to remind himself that they didn't kill them. They were already gone thanks to the necromancer. Vance picked up an assault rifle and a spare magazine from a dead soldier.

Signs declaring the caves unsafe for spelunking and a steel gate blocked the cave. The padlock had been cut off. The gate opened to reveal darkness. Not just an absence of the light from the moonless sky, but some magic had to be in effect. The flashlight on the gun didn't illuminate his hand if he held the light and his hand just in front of his face. They had to feel their way through. The tunnels led downward, but not gently and not always offering a place to grab hold. Vance fell twice down straight drops. At the bottom of the second, he heard a gunshot, but rolled away, toward the gunfire. He tripped one gunman and managed to break the soulless man's neck, and then shoot another before Dai landed behind him.

Fourteen more men died in that chamber, though they'd put up more of a fight than the men on the surface. By the end of the fight, every bullet, even the last shot from Vance's derringer, had been fired. Cynthia killed the last zombified soldier with a two-by-four she scrounged off the floor.

Electric lanterns spread around the chamber with three on a desk made from sawhorses and two-by-fours. Pages from the Syrian ritual lay across the table, recreating the wall. Vance didn't stop to read the notations. He heard the loud chanting from down a tunnel. Vance rushed in, ready to shoot whoever stood at the center.

He stopped when the cave became the New York headquarters for Henry's vampire hunter organization. Vance found himself standing behind a desk. 'Vance Silver, Commander,' adorned a nameplate on the desk. A whiteboard had a tally sheet. Large letters at the top read, 'Blood Suckers Dusted.' Vance's name had at least twice as many tick marks as the name below his; Peter's.

Vance looked to the wall, expecting to see a picture of himself standing alongside Henry. A brass plaque on the picture would read 'Henry the Inquisitor with his first officer, Vance Silver, November 2011.' Instead, the picture showed Vance standing over a corpse, holding Henry's severed head. 'Henry the betrayer meets his end at Commander Vance Silver's hand, November 2014.'

Everything felt wrong, but it tried to feel right. Then Vance saw the framed picture of he and Lanie sitting on a porch swing. Lanie held a pair of babies, one in each arm. Both he and Lanie looked happy.

Vance sat down and examined the picture more closely. He could remember sitting in the hospital waiting room with Peter, joking about how his life would never be the same. Everything would be better now, they agreed.

Vance turned back to the tally board. He counted the tallies up to two hundred and nineteen. That's where everything was wrong. Vance hadn't killed two hundred and nineteen vampires. He attributed two hundred and nineteen deaths to himself. A handful were revenants; mindless vampires that had to die and he felt no guilt over. A few others he'd killed in line with his duties as either human sheriff or vampire sheriff, and usually both. He'd killed a few times while learning to control his bloodlust. And when the Civil War vampire biker gang showed up, he killed twelve vampires that day and four of their pets. He would always feel responsible for letting Fiona down. The others were humans killed by Zylpha. He should have stopped her sooner. He should have killed her afterward, but he didn't, so he blamed himself for their deaths. Even not counting the people Zylpha killed, Vance had killed thirty-two vampires and far more than thirty-two humans.

He couldn't let that false number represent even a facet of truth. The whole room, the whole world it existed in, was a lie. A woman screamed and the world fell apart, each surface falling to the floor and shattering. The floor shattered too.

As the world shattered, he found himself standing in a cave. A woman held her hand to his forehead. Vance recognized Stephanie from the factory in Long Beach. "You should have wanted that!" she said with a growl.

Vance grabbed her, pulling her other hand free of Cynthia's head as he did. Needing strength, he took a deep breath, and focused his mind on staving off the bloodeyes. He bit into Stephanie's neck. Blood filled his mouth, and he drank. She fell unconscious and limp. Vance couldn't drink as much as he wanted to. He had another mission to finish. He laid Stephanie on the floor. He knew, with the smell of fresh blood, he wouldn't be able to stand near her long. It surprised him that he managed no to succumb to the bloodeyes when he bit her.

"What the hell was that?" Cynthia said. "I was a movie star, everyone around me pandered to my whims. It was so wrong, though. I am so in love with being a dhampyre and a cop. I get your pride and your righteousness. I know I'm not as good as you, Vance, but I want to be. Sure, it was cool to be loved for my beauty and treated like a princess, but there's no sense of fulfilment in that life."

"Tackling a difficult role and making it believable?" Vance asked.

"I never even thought of acting in that light," Cynthia said. "I was just in it for the glamor."

"Where's Dai?" Vance asked.

Cynthia pointed down at Vance's feet. Dai lay on her back, a satisfied smile across her face. Her eyes were wide open, but not focusing or moving.

"I'll get Dai back," Cynthia said. "You go stop that chanting."

Vance picked up his shield.

"Wait, Vance," Cynthia said. "You should kiss her."

"Why?" Vance asked. "You think we're in Cinderella?"

"That would be Sleeping Beauty or Snow White," Cynthia said. "No, well, yes. Just do it."

Vance knelt and kissed Dai's lips. His kiss was gentle and chaste. He didn't let it linger for more than a second or two.

"Vance, my love," Dai said, her words slow and dreamy.

Vance watched her a second, but her eyes still didn't focus. Her smile might have gotten bigger.

"This is awkward," Cynthia said. "I'm going to stab her with her own boot knife. That'll wake her up. You need to go because after I do wake her up, Dai's going to finish off that chick that got in her brain."

"Off I go, then," Vance said, then jogged toward the chanting voice.

Six golden cages, the kind that barely held a standing man and didn't offer even enough room to turn around, stood around a large dome made of gold-coated steel bars. It looked like a climbing toy from a park for small children. Thin beams of light emerged from the chests of the people in the six cages and shot straight into a glass orb hanging above the central dome. Vance located Azure and Katina in the two nearest cages. He ran over.

"Kill him," Azure said. "Let us die to save the world."

Katina just said, her voice tired but calm, "Karina, my sister, my love, I am close."

"You're too late, Mister Silver," a man inside the central dome called. "I have completed my ritual. All I have left is to reap my rewards. Destroy me and you kill twenty million people."

The light beams from the six caged people stopped and another beam, a beam somehow brighter but of a darker light, shot downward from the crystal orb into the necromancer. Other than Katina and Azure, Vance recognized none of the other four mages. Two were from the Pentacle's fire team. Vance didn't know which two. A young boy, maybe old enough to be a teenager, slumped in one of the cages.

Vance realized he'd come too late, too unprepared. There he stood with an empty gun and a shield. His sword, even with added extension from his arm, wouldn't reach the necromancer inside his protective cage. Vance saw his heartbroken reflection in the mirror of the shield. He saw himself smile when he realized he'd brought exactly the right equipment. He flew to stand on the gold bars of the necromancer's dome and took off his shield. He thrust the shield between the crystal and the necromancer, reflecting the beam of light away. When the light hit the ground, it caused every grain of dirt to explode. It hadn't harmed the necromancer at all, though. Vance hoped it only took a person as the target to keep the beam harmless. He turned the light toward Azure, then thought better of it.

Katina glowed brightly when the light hit her. The cage around her exploded, vaporizing into bright energy. Dai and Cynthia ran to stand behind Vance. For several minutes, the light poured from the orb and Katina absorbed it all. Then the orb exploded, throwing Vance across the chamber. The explosion threw shards of glass throughout the chamber. Cynthia fell to the ground gasping for air and choking on blood. The necromancer, being as close as he was, became little more than a puddle of red goop.

Vance's shield had protected him from the glass, and Cynthia had protected Dai. The ground shook and stones as large as Vance fell from the ceiling.

Strands of light flew through the cave as if in a cyclone. When the light came in contact with anything, whatever object it hit exploded.

Flying as fast as he could, Vance reached the cage with Azure. He found the lock and briefly wondered what he had that could be used as a lockpick when he remembered his sword would work fine as prybar.

As the world collapsed around him, he struggled to bend steel. The blade of the sword broke, but Vance didn't give up. He used what little blade he had left to try again. Stone not only fell from the cave ceiling but leapt from the ground. As a boulder crushed the steel cage on the opposite side of Katina, Azure's cage sprang open.

"Vance! You can get her out," Katina yelled. "Save Azure! Drop into the Venae, all the way. Don't come out until you are in Los Angeles. Dai, take Cynthia and go."

"I hope you know what to do with that power!" Vance shouted. "I'll save Azure, but don't let that power kill you, or anyone." If Azure was alive, she didn't look it. Then she coughed, spraying blood all over Vance.

"Give me blood," she gasped. "It's been too long since I fed from Shauna."

Vance didn't think to hesitate. He bit his own arm and held it to Azure's lips. When another stone fell not a yard from him, he stopped. "I hope that's enough," he said as he pulled Azure free of the cage. He carried her over to Katina.

"I can't do anything with this," Katina said. "Why did you send me the power?"

"To save your sister," Vance said.

"Karina!" Katina said. "I don't think we did this right. If you can hear me, and I know you can, tell me what to do." Katina's body glowed red with Venae. From cracks in her flesh, jets of red and violet mist sprayed into the cave.

"Take it into the Venae," Vance said. "Maybe you can do something if you can touch her."

"That's all I have left to try, Vance," Katina said. "Take Azure and go!"

"Do what you told me to do," Vance said. "Phase all the way out. Let your sister find your way back. Use whatever frickin' power you just got to bring her back with you."

"Stop telling me what to do. I'm holding this because as soon as I release it, everything near me is going to explode. Get the fuck away from here, now!" Katina said. "If I go first, you'll probably die." A boulder crashing a few inches behind her cage cut her off. "I'm out." She disappeared.

The world became fire. Vance wrapped his arms around Azure and phased deep into the Venae.

XXIII

It took what seemed like hours for Vance to navigate the red mist. Direction didn't seem to matter. Vance had two beacons of light. One he knew to be Dai, but her light moved with him. She was using him as a beacon. Thalia's light remained recognizable. He couldn't use that to find Los Angeles, but he could find Thalia. He moved toward her. He emerged in a museum of ancient weaponry. Thalia sat on a raised throne before a hundred or so vampires.

"Clear my throne room," she said. Vance fell to his knees, "You don't need to kneel, sister."

"I'm exhausted," Vance said.

"We'll talk in a moment, when my vamps are gone," Thalia said. "Come back in an hour, my subjects. Vance will have the answers for me, which I'll pass on to you."

The audience of vampires took only a minute to clear the room. Vance started to ask, "What answ…"

Thalia interrupted him. "You do have answers, right? Your being here has something to do with why I had a hundred panicked vampires in my throne room?"

"Probably," Vance said.

Dai and Cynthia solidified beside Vance. Both she and Cynthia were naked.

"I had to just bring us, no foreign objects, to separate her from the glass shards," Dai said. She turned her back to Thalia. "Do you have something I could wear?"

"Gift shop is down that hall," Thalia said.

Dai sprinted away.

"I don't care if I am naked," Cynthia said. She ran over and hugged Vance. "You saved my life again."

"I hope you saved a lot of lives," Thalia said. "If that's you, a lot of people just died and millions more will die within hours." She held out her phone for Vance to see. A helicopter showed a video of a volcanic eruption. Unlike movies, the volcano seemed mostly flat to the ground. Smoke jetted to the sky, and where the bubbling lake of lava hit the ocean, steam joined the smoke.

"Millions?" Vance asked.

"That video is coming from Bakersfield. Look again, understanding the scale of it. That grass in the foreground is the skyline of Los Angeles. They say the lava pool is ten miles wide. Nothing downwind will survive for hundreds of miles."

"We stopped it from being worse," Dai said, jogging into the room wearing a full set of futuristic soldier armor with glowing lines running across black plastic armor. "At least, that is our hope." Dai carried another sword and shield exactly like the ones Vance had lost at the site of the magic ritual. "I like you in that outfit. I'll pay for the shield and sword. How much is this armor?"

"Unlike Vance's shield, that armor is a one-of-a-kind piece," Thalia said. "They didn't make the movie, so they never paid me for it, but it's one of my favorite works. You wear it well, Dai. I'd normally sell that for a hundred grand. It's fully functional Kevlar. But you're my blooddaughter, so I can give you half price."

"You're my bloodmother," Dai said. "I wouldn't ask you to suffer a loss for me. I'll pay your full price." She put her hand on Azure's shoulder. "Are you well? You don't look good."

Azure started to say something, but never managed to form a word. She coughed again, then fell to the ground. Vance reached for her, and she reached for his hand. As their hands wrapped around each other, before he could lean to comfort her, she splashed to the ground as a puddle of water. Vance felt a wave of nausea overcome him and he had to cover his mouth to prevent himself from vomiting.

"What the...?" Thalia asked.

Before she could finish the thought, Azure reformed. She climbed to her feet, confused, between them, then doubled over and started coughing again. She then splashed into a puddle again, only this time, instead of water, she became blood.

"Seriously, what in Heaven's name is happening to her?" Thalia asked.

Vance stumbled as he felt himself start to faint. Thalia caught him. "I gave her my blood," Vance managed to say. As he got used to the wooziness, he explained. "She requested it. I don't think she's fed from Shauna in several days, maybe more than a week."

"You can't turn an elemental into a vampire," Thalia said. "It's magic 101. No one can have two magics in their body. A mage can become a vampire, but it costs them their magic. Elementals cannot lose their magic; they are their magic. They cannot become vampires. It would take a very potent vampire to make Azure a pet. I know her vampire and I won't be the one to tell her what you did to her."

"She would have died," Vance said. "She did die."

"And she's still dying," Thalia said.

Azure formed into a human form again, looked up at Vance with a look of complete fear and then fell into a puddle again. This time, she looked like blood. Instead of red, it had the electric blue color of her hair.

Thalia kept Vance from falling again, holding him upright by his breastplate. "Welcome to the weirdest fucking day of a three-millennium life,

Vance. You are forbidden from dying before you can fix it, or at least explain it."

A bright light flashed in the room. Katina stood alongside a duplicate of herself. Both were also naked. The duplicate, Karina by Vance's guess, had a flow of white tendrils spraying from her back.

"Please tell me the blue puddle isn't Azure," Karina said.

"She's failing to transition to vampire," Vance said. "Something about not being able to be an elemental and a vampire."

"Can't be two magics," Karina said. "Let's hope I can do something with this." She stepped toward the puddle of blood Azure had become and raised her hand. Violet light emerged from her hand in the shape of a sword. "Before I save her, Jackie, I need your okay. I can save either her or you." Karina seemed to be calling Katina, 'Jackie'.

"I'm fine," Katina said.

"No, you could be better. You could be what I am. We could be the same," Katina said. "For what it matters: if Azure dies, Shauna won't die, too. I promise your love will be safe."

"Vance?" Katina asked. "I can't do it. I can't decide. This is your life; you will die if Azure dies."

"I don't care about me," Vance said. "Save Azure, whatever it takes."

"Yes, that's the decision I knew I had to make. It's the only decision here," Katina said. "Sister, save Azure!"

Karina plunged the blade into the pool of blood.

"If anyone can explain what the hell is going on," Thalia said, "please say something."

"It might be impossible to explain, but I'll try," Karina said as the blood boiled around her sword. "I don't know what coming here is going to cost me or what they'll let me remember, so I'm telling you fast. I died in battle, so I became a war angel or Valkyrie, or Amazon, depending on your cultural name for me. I am very much not supposed to be able to come back, but I have too strong of a bond with Jackie to be anywhere but where she is. Now, with the shatter of reality, I'm here and banished from where I was. No, banished isn't right. They're thinking of what is to become of me. It's not what…," she trailed off.

"I was still Jackie when she died," Katina said. "She doesn't know that because it was the man we were named after that killed her. Elsa started having me use my original name and only referred to Karina by hers."

"I don't know much of anything," Karina said. "I feel like I knew everything, every facet of existence just a moment ago. Now I can't remember how I got here. Who are you people?"

"I am…"

"Thalia," Karina said. "I recognize the voice. Where are we? This isn't Paris."

"I am the Queen of Hell," Thalia said.

"No," Karina said, but Thalia waved for her to wait.

"Hell is the counties from Orange County across the Mexican border, to include Tijuana. You're in San Diego."

"I don't remember anything other than Elsa promising to love John Bertellus," Karina said. She clasped her hands to her neck. "Did I die?"

"You still look like an angel," Vance said. "You have wings." He couldn't think of a better description of the light tendrils floating behind Karina's back.

Azure jumped from the floor, throwing the sword of purple light away. The blade disappeared into a sparkle of light. She had a body again; one that glowed very similarly to Karina, though with a pale blue light instead of white. She even had the tendrils of light that looked like wings. "I know what happened," Azure said.

"That makes one of us," Thalia said. "Care to share with the other six of us?"

"Magic doesn't work in pairs," Azure said. "I can't be a water elemental and a Venae elemental, though vampires are half-elemental at best. Still, that's two flavors of magic. Karina shared her magic with me, splitting it right down the middle. Now we're both celestial beings. She'll never go back to that afterlife. For all of eternity, she is bound to lesser existences. I don't know what that means, I'm hearing it explained to me. Karina gave me half of her magic. Now I'm a half-celestial, giving me three kinds of magic. There can be balance with three; two will tear each other apart. They can't take our wings, or our swords. They are part of our magic, which defines us. They're not happy. The ones talking to me are jealous and angry, but it's not my fault, so they are trying to be nice."

"Who?" Vance asked.

Azure said, "Just a bunch of celestials like Karina was. She's only half of one now. That's not right. Celestial magic either is or isn't. There is no half. They're filtering her memories and going to return most of them. She'll remember enough so that she'll know how to use her magic. Do no harm except in defense. That's the law of celestials. One guy is telling me he has a message for Katina. Next time you are given the chance to use near infinite power, use the other ten percent to end the Los Angeles drought or something."

"The leftover ten percent did that?" Thalia said, showing the massive pool of lava on her phone again.

"If the necromancer had stayed the focal point of the spell, he'd have become a lich," Azure said. "Which would take far less power than bringing a celestial into our world. The other celestials have reached a consensus. Karina and I are allowed to stay because the covenant that kept god-like beings off this world also forbade humans from trying to attain god-like power. Covens of the Sun and Moon were specifically forbidden. Man broke that arrangement, so we're changing it. Thalia, you are the oldest in the room, so the elder who will speak for humanity. In exchange for not having lots of god-like beings on this world, would you agree to renew the covenant and swear that humans will not try that ritual again? Two of us, Karina and I, will remain to enforce the treaty."

"I'm happy to limit the power of mages," Thalia said. "Azure, you'll be the one to pass on the changes to your arrangement to your people?"

"Yes, but hold on a second," Azure said. "The other celestials want to filter some of my memories out. I guess I saw something I shouldn't be able to talk about." She paused to take a deep breath. "Why am I standing here, naked, in Thalia's museum of movie props? Am I bluer?"

Vance had already turned his gaze away. With four naked women in the room and enough reflections off the many display cases to be reminded of that, he had to stare at the ceiling.

"Yeah," Katina said. "You're paler. Your lips are blue. Your nipples are blue. Open your mouth. That is so weird. Very cool. You're blue everywhere normal people are pink or red."

"Okay, I have it," Karina said. "Apparently my name is Karina again. That's going to take getting used to. I don't remember a few years, but I know how my magic works. Azure is getting fed the minimal details of what she needs to know, too. I'm what Azure would call an elemental of celestial magic. I guess there are a lot more flavors of magic than the six she was aware of. Most don't manifest in humans; just those six do. Azure was right, we're both full potency celestials. Our wings will show when we use large amounts of power, such as summoning our swords. Our swords are our gift and our tool. They do everything from slay demons to heal the sick and injured. They are part of us and cannot be taken or given."

"I'm an angel?" Azure asked. She reached forward and a violet blade of swirling light emerged as if she held a sword. "This, as cool as it is, is going to give my mom a conniption. I'm serious, I'll have to be there to heal her with my sword when I tell her."

"Someone, tell me they have a cell phone," Dai said. "Seeing that volcano is probably going be enough to cause Azure's mom to have a conniption. There's no way every mother in the country with a kid in Southern California isn't worried. Azure, you need to call home. You don't need to tell her that you're half water elemental and half angel."

"Full water elemental, full angel, full vampire," Azure said. "I'm, in the technical terms of the Pentacle, what we'd call a big fucking mess of magic. The good news is I can walk in the sunlight. The bad news is I'm going to need about twice the blood of a normal vampire and I can't make a pet. I'm not looking forward to my first kill. I can't fix that death with my sword, but it's pretty amazing the things my sword can do."

"I know, right?" Karina said.

"This is disturbing and amazing," Vance said. He tried not to contemplate the religious implications of seeing an angel. They weren't exactly as he'd pictured, but he couldn't deny what his senses told him. "You can't talk about God and Jesus, can you?"

"Mortal men must define their own religions," Karina said. "We won't discuss it again."

"I do need to call my mom," Azure said. "We're blaming the necromancer and not going to name the celestials, just mention that there are two on the planet now. Well, two more, but that's a whole slew of other stories. She'll be interested to know that, because of the necromancer's transgression, no mortal will ever again be born with necromantic power, either as a mage or an elemental."

Vance pulled his phone from behind his breastplate. The screen had a crack it hadn't had before but seemed to work. He unlocked it and handed it to Azure. "Say 'hi' for me," Vance said. "Maybe mention I saved your life so I can be on friendly terms with your mother."

Azure dialed the phone and held it to her ear. "All circuits busy," she said. "What a surprise with a sudden volcano where there shouldn't be one."

"I'm going to assume I'm sworn to secrecy," Thalia said.

"Vance?" Azure asked.

"Yes?" Vance asked.

"Do we keep secrets from our sisters?" Azure asked.

"Why ask me?" Vance asked.

"Think," Azure said. "Or should I say 'feel'? Who is my bloodfather? I'm not calling you sister or mother."

Vance felt her like he felt Lanie or Dai. She'd been another vampire's pet when he made her, which lashed her pet bond to him as well as the sire-child bond. That explained why Vance felt so woozy when Azure kept losing her form. Being emotionally tied to three women was going to be too interesting, he realized.

Thalia answered while Vance processed the layers of implications from what Azure meant. "No, sister, we don't keep secrets in our bloodline, but we keep all of our secrets from everyone not of our bloodline, which is no one here."

"If that volcano is causing havoc, I'm going to have a few thousand vampires with questions in Los Angeles," Dai said. "We need to head back."

"Wait, watch what my sword can do," Azure said. She produced her sword of purple light and cut through the air. A hole ripped in the middle of the air. Through the hole, Vance could see the stage of Dai's theatre. "Go on. The door won't close on you. It'll remain open until I pass through. Don't take too long, though. These things can implode in a very messy way if I don't pass through soon. Think of a vacuum that can suck in a whole building."

Vance didn't waste another second before stepping through. Lanie stood with two women at the center of Dai's stage. One woman had blood-red hair the other had jet-black hair but looked nothing like Dai.

XXIV

"Shauna, wait!" the black-haired woman said as the red-haired woman charged at Vance.

"Why can't I feel my pet?" Shauna screamed. "You were supposed to be this superhero of a sheriff, capable of protecting her from anything. She's gone! You were supposed to protect her!"

"Leave him alone!" Lanie screamed.

An unseen force threw Vance against the wall. The velvet curtain Vance hit did little to lessen the pain or the damage. Wood cracked and Vance wasn't sure a rib hadn't cracked as well.

Lanie slapped Shauna. Vance felt the additional pain of Lanie's broken fingers. Shauna didn't react at all to Lanie's strike. She flew toward Vance.

"Shauna!" Katina yelled. "Stop! Azure is fine!"

"I can't feel her!" Shauna glared at Vance, but then turned to Katina. The red-haired vampire flew over and embraced the pale-haired twin. "You're okay, my love?"

"I can't even answer that," Katina said. "You won't be able to answer either, once you see who's behind me."

"Karina?" the black-haired woman asked, whispering as if she didn't have the courage to ask aloud. "Karina?" she screamed and rushed across the stage as Karina stepped through. "How?" Karina looked normal, just like Katina. Both twins were still naked.

"You know that volcano that just tore open south of Los Angeles?" Dai asked. "Let's just say, that's how."

"Where's Azure?" Shauna asked.

Cynthia came next through the portal, but Azure followed quickly behind her. Her sword and light had also faded.

Shauna rushed over and hugged Azure. "I don't feel you," Shauna said.

"Can I tell her?" Azure asked Vance.

"Yes, please tell her before she hits me again," Vance said. "Artemis would let you tell her. And the other one, Elsa, if the light in my mind is right, Artemis likes her, too."

"Why are you asking permission?" Shauna asked.

"For starters, and probably the least important, Vance is my bloodfather," Azure said.

"You're a vampire now, and that's the least important?" Shauna asked.

Azure said, "I'm so much more than a vampire. My memories are hazy, though. Give me a minute and I'll get back what I need, I'm sure."

"I remember quite a bit," Vance said. "Let me tell you the story. It all started a few weeks ago when I was staking out a truck full of enslaved women.

ABOUT THE AUTHOR

Wil Ogden was destined to be a wastrel but thwarted fate. During his second junior year in high school, he discovered he had a muse and a talent for writing. Despite taking almost a decade to complete a bachelor's degree by changing majors eleven times, he managed to grow up. Along the way he worked as a blacksmith, a record store manager, a candy store manager, too many years in food service, a four-year stint in the USAF, and finally settled down into information technology, which he uses to pay the bills and support his family of himself, his wife, eight kids, some dogs, some cats, some ferrets, some chinchillas, some chickens, and a parakeet or two.

Made in the USA
Columbia, SC
17 November 2023